The Sapphire Sphere

Timestream Travelers
Book Two

Sher J. Stultz

This story is dedicated to the pack:

Juniper, Ruby, Blue, Remy, Thor, Murdock, & The Charlies.

Timestream Travelers Who's Who

Fall/Winter 2015, Spring 2016, and Summer 2019

Entwistle Family
Archie (Father)
Miranda (Mother)
Socrates (Older Brother)
Aeneas (Middle Son)
Persephone (Youngest & Daughter)

Willoughby Family 1
Charlie (Father)
Sakura (Mother)
C.J. (Son, Cousin to Tabitha, Sadie, and Seth)

Willoughby Family 2
George (Father)
Martha (Mother)
Tabitha (Daughter, Cousin to C.J. and Sadie)
Seth (Younger Brother, Cousin to C.J. and Sadie)

Willoughby Family 3

Catherine (Mother)

Sadie (Daughter, Cousin to C.J., Tabitha and Seth)

Carl Hoffsteder (Dad to Sadie, Ex-husband of Catherine)

Also Featuring:

Harold Torkelson (Housekeeper to Entwistles, Caregiver of Eleanor)

Eleanor Meachum (Widower)

Jesùs Catalina (Dance Instructor)

Everett Veltkamp (Teammate/Classmate of Aeneas and Tabitha)

Bethany Purvine (Classmate to Tabitha and Aeneas)

Bob North Sky (Time traveler, Shaman, Mentor to Aeneas)

Sheila North Sky (Daughter of Bob North Sky)

Gerry Archambeau (Time Traveler)

Reg and Russ Archambeau (Brothers to Gerry)

Timestream Travelers Who's Who Spring 2053

Cassie Entwistle (Daughter of Aeneas and Tabitha)

Lux Entwistle (Twin son of Aeneas and Tabitha)

Tor Entwistle (Twin son of Aeneas and Tabitha)

Missi Entwistle (Daughter of Socrates and Keniah)

Thena Entwistle (Daughter of Socrates and Keniah)

Keniah Collier Entwistle (Mother of Missi and Thena)

Caitlyn (Wife of Persephone)

Meg (Wife of Harold)

Lyla (Wife of C.J.)

Lana and Lanna (Twin sisters from Saskatoon, Canada)

Toshiro (Time Traveler)

Southern Alaska, Summer 2019

"WHY DO YOU CALL it the river of time?" Aeneas asked Bob North Sky shyly.

"It is the translation from my language, but you have traveled it. We flow through time in a stream of images."

"Oh, like a time stream?"

Bob shrugged. "Stream or river."

"Is there a beginning and end? What happens when someone dies?"

"There is a beginning and end to the time in a life. After I die, I'll let you know."

"But you'll be dead and can't tell me."

"How do you know? I have not died yet."

"I've seen my beginning. Can I also see my end?"

"Do you need to? Is that the real purpose of this gift?"

"I guess not," said Aeneas thoughtfully. "Will you teach me to how to use the river of time even though I'm not going to be a shaman?"

"You have not grown up yet and you may one day be a kind of shaman to your people, so I will teach you our laws."

"Why do time travelers need laws?"

"Shamanic law forbids us from using the gift for our own gain or interfering with the past or the future."

Aeneas nodded. "I get it. So, travelers don't get greedy and try to make things always go their way."

"Something like that," agreed Bob.

PROLOGUE

Swept Away

April 2016

SADIE HAD SPENT A few hours working on a set for a friend's sweet sixteen birthday party. She loved creating a musical background for parties and events, especially for her friends. Her head was filled with the songs from the birthday playlist, all covers she played from her classic rock collection. She called out to her mother, Catherine, who was busy weeding the daffodil bed.

"Hey, Mom. I want to take a walk to clear my head. Can we go out to the jetty for a little while?"

Normally, Catherine would jump at the chance to spend time with Sadie. More and more, Sadie was with her friends or practicing for her latest gig. But today, for no reason other than that she wanted to finish her task, Catherine declined, and suggested Sadie call her dad.

Carl had been in town for a few weeks recovering from the flu. Normally, Carl traveled for his job as a consulting engineer, but he decided to take a few weeks off to rest and recover. He'd been napping when Sadie called. Because he didn't often get to spend time with her, Carl felt he couldn't say no to Sadie and agreed to take her, despite his lingering fatigue.

Carl and Sadie headed to the South Jetty of the Columbia River at Fort Stevens State Park. Sadie loved the powerful confluence of the Columbia River and the Pacific Ocean. The freeing energy of these two great water movers was just the place to clear her head so she could tackle an original song she'd been composing.

Carl was breathless and cold as they headed toward the sandy path, swearing under his breath when he realized he'd forgotten his beanie. He told Sadie to carry on while he returned to the parking lot near the observation tower to grab it from the car.

As Sadie walked, the wind buffeted at her back, blowing her long blonde hair around her face. The sun moved in and out of the altocumulus clouds, tiny little puffs high above in the sky. Sadie smiled, pushing her hair out of the way, and turned her face to the sun. After another long, wet winter, a day of mostly sunshine was cheering.

Sadie arrived at the beach and decided to climb out onto the jetty. The South Jetty stretched along the mouth of the Columbia River as it met the waters of the Pacific. Sadie knew her dad was feeling weak and wouldn't want to climb out too far, so she stopped after about fifty feet and found a flat spot to sit. Sadie closed her eyes and turned her face to the sun as the wind rushed around her.

If Sadie felt the tremor, it might have seemed to her like the jetty shifting slightly against the surf.

The Clatsop County Search and Rescue and the U.S. Coast Guard actively searched for Sadie for two days by air and sea while a local group of volunteers combed the Washington and Oregon coastline north and south of the Columbia River. It was presumed she was washed out to sea after a large wave briefly engulfed the jetty. Carl, being five minutes behind Sadie, never saw what happened. No trace of her was ever found.

CHAPTER 1

Aeneas Comes Clean

November 2015

AENEAS FOLLOWED THE SMELL of Saturday morning breakfast and sat down at the kitchen table, his nose buried in a worn old paperback of *A Wrinkle in Time*. C.J. had suggested it to him ever since Aeneas confided that he was now certain his disappearances were indeed time travel episodes. Sput came in and nudged his thigh as if to say, "Surely it's time for another walk to see Tabitha?"

As Thanksgiving approached, the rainy season returned to the Pacific Northwest, piquing Harold's culinary creativity. He was busy making pumpkin pancakes for the Entwistles along with what smelled like a pot of his magic chicken soup—he added grated lemon, fresh rosemary, thyme, and red chili flakes. The soup would hold them for the weekend along with a few leftovers, and Harold knew how Aeneas *loved* leftovers.

Over at the Willoughby household, Tabitha was knitting a wool sweater for Sput while she snacked on a carrot-raisin muffin and hot tea. Sput occupied a special place in all their lives as he was a dog shared by two families. Given his unique situation, Tabitha wasn't sure who should receive the sweater at her mother's annual solstice celebration. Should it go to Aeneas? Or to C.J.? Tabitha stopped for a second and thought about it, letting her intuition guide the decision. She supposed the better question to ask was, *who would be least upset to not receive it?* The answer to that was obvious—Aeneas, of course. However, Aeneas was now her boyfriend and would need an equally thoughtful gift. Tabitha stopped her knitting and searched through the Ravelry database until she spied a pattern. The yoke neck sweater had squirrel and autumn motifs and the brown and orange colors would suit Aeneas perfectly. It would take her about a month of fiendish knitting to complete the sweater. The weather had turned cold, and Tabitha liked nothing better than to curl up on the couch in the evenings and knit by the gas fireplace while she watched reruns of *The X-Files*.

Martha had left Tabitha to herself with most things throughout her adolescence, but she was anxious now that Aeneas was more than just a friend. It wasn't that she had any concerns regarding Aeneas personally, it was because Martha had her own teenage heartbreak scars. She had no wish for Tabitha to feel the same unhappiness. So, when she asked about the sweater pattern that came through the printer in the office, her words came out differently than she'd intended.

"Tabby, have you ever wondered what might happen if you and Aeneas break up?" asked Martha earnestly.

Tabitha collected the pattern from the printer in her parents' shared office and looked at her mother in surprise. "Why would we break up?"

"Well," sighed Martha, "when people are young, they often change their minds, and find someone else they prefer. Sometimes people get hurt."

Martha's mothering mask betrayed a tiny crack and Tabitha realized she knew nothing about her mother's teenage love life. She turned to Martha to reassure her.

"Aeneas and I will always be friends, no matter what. Don't worry—it'll be okay, Mom."

Martha shook off her feelings of worry. Tabitha was honest, courageous, humble, and above all, exceedingly observant. She'd have to trust that all these qualities would give her daughter some resilience in her young love life.

The doorbell rang and Seth yelled from the kitchen, "Aeneas is here!"

Martha smiled. She liked that Aeneas rang the doorbell instead of texting Tabitha to let him in. It was proper and respectful. Aeneas and Sput came in with a cold, wet wind behind them. Aeneas took off his boots and hung up his bright orange three-in-one coat. Martha smiled at him and decided it was time to begin her Saturday chores. This thing with Aeneas would be whatever it would be and all she could do was trust that she and George had prepared Tabitha as best they could.

Aeneas and Tabitha sat on the couch chatting while Seth played with Sput.

"Aeneas," said Seth enthusiastically, "Tabby is making Sput his own sweater."

"That was a surprise, Seth!" hissed Tabitha.

Seth looked perplexed. "Sput can't understand me."

Aeneas laughed. "Hey, buddy, why don't you take Sput up to your room for some tug of war?" As soon as Seth could walk, Tabitha had figured out Seth was prone to suggestions. She'd used this to teach him about the finer points of housekeeping when she wanted to avoid her own chores. Now, Tabitha raised an eyebrow as Seth scampered off with Sput. Aeneas turned to Tabitha, his expression serious. "Sox and Harold want to train me." Socrates, affectionately known as Sox, was Aeneas's genius older brother who'd been enlisted to help Aeneas withstand the pull of the timestream by their quirky housekeeper/master programmer, Harold.

"Train you for what?" asked Tabitha, setting down her knitting needles, giving him her full attention.

Aeneas hesitated. "It's hard to explain."

"Try me," said Tabitha, activating the patience usually reserved for Seth.

Aeneas leaned in close and whispered, "Train me not to vanish."

Tabitha eyed her boyfriend, who was also her best friend. Something seemed to be missing from his explanation and she waited for him to continue instead of asking more questions. It was a strategy she'd been developing for her future counseling practice. The less she said, the more people talked.

Aeneas fidgeted, tapping his feet then finally asked if there were any snacks. The interrogation he'd anticipated seemed to have stalled. Tabitha went to the kitchen and returned with some leftover egg rolls from last night's takeout adventure. Somehow, her father had managed to order more egg rolls than main dishes.

"You are awfully quiet, Tab," said Aeneas with a mouthful of egg roll.

Tabitha shrugged. "Well, I was hoping you would finish telling me about your training."

Aeneas finished chewing and took a breath. "The thing is, Tabitha, I'm not sure how much I *can* tell you."

Tabitha set down her egg roll. One thing she'd noticed about human beings was their insistence of not being able to do things that were perfectly reasonable. "Then tell me what you can," said Tabitha diplomatically.

Aeneas remembered what Socrates and Harold had said about divulging too much to anyone, especially people close to him whose lives could be impacted by his time travels. Tabitha sat patiently as Aeneas shifted uncomfortably on the couch. He knew she could outwait him and what was the big deal anyway? He could tell Tabitha about the time travel hypothesis and steer clear of any specifics.

"My disappearances are linked to time travel," said Aeneas quickly, shoving another egg roll in his mouth to stop himself from saying anything else.

CHAPTER 2

Lux Makes a Leap

Spring 2053

LUX HAD SPENT THE better part of a day sorting through his Grandma Martha's old photo albums. He noticed they were bulky and crackled as he paged through them. He worried they had not been preserved, something he thought he should mention to his mother, Tabitha. One of the albums was filled with tiny black and white photos of his Italian ancestors, an assortment of musicians, singers, painters, and craftsmen. But he was in search of a particular image—his great grandfather's sister, who'd abandoned the notion of the traditional maternal role occupied by her own ancestors and made her way to the circus. Finding the yellow leaflet had been a treasure. Faded, but carefully preserved in an old manilla folder, it read *Mirabelle the Magnificent Flier*, and it had given Lux's budding hypothesis a leap toward a theory.

Grandma Martha had been delighted to share the contents of an old trunk with him a few days ago. "Lux is here," cried Martha. His grandmother always announced him like an important dignitary. Martha had been over the moon when Lux and Tor were born. Tabitha kept Cassie mostly to herself in the early years, but when the twins came along, Martha and George happily stepped in to assist.

"Hi, Grammie," said Lux, leaning down and planting a kiss on her cheek.

"Hey, fella, come help Gramps with this trunk," called George, struggling to shift a battered old steamer trunk into the living room.

Lux took several long strides and nudged his grandfather gently.

"I got it, Gramps."

George stepped out of the way and Lux ported the trunk next to the couch as Martha entered with a plate of biscotti and pine nut cookies. Lux smiled. His grandmother made the best cookies. They'd spent the afternoon reminiscing over relics of their family history.

Now back home, Lux sketched a branching tree, labeling names with small stars, attempting to trace the Willoughby time-travel genes. Then he compared the genes to the Entwistle tree, which drew his mind back to the most significant Entwistle genetic discovery he'd made so far. He'd met his father's Uncle William only once, when he was fourteen, on a trip to Iowa. William had spent a summer there, interning with an environmental engineering firm, and never moved back west. Glancing through his genome, Lux knew why. William had seventeen of the markers associated with time travel, enough to enter the timestream, but not enough to be as adept as Cassie or Aeneas.

Lux sighed. "That's one way to manage it, I guess."

"Manage what?" asked Tabitha, passing through the living room on her way to the kitchen, cringing at the mess. Lux was sprawled on the couch, dozens of scraps of paper strewn around him, two holographic screens hovering nearby, a large bowl of trail mix deeply dented in the center, and a very old photo album. Aeneas's sons were not time travelers, but their work habits were remarkably similar.

"Time travel, Mom."

Tabitha paused. "What are you talking about, son?"

"The reason Great Uncle William moved away from any seismic areas," answered Lux. "When Dad and I deduced he must have some abilities, we went to meet him. Being randomly swept into the timestream was traumatic for him. When Dad offered to escort him through his timeline, show him how to enter and exit, all the blood drained from his face. He wanted no part of it."

"You're surprised?" asked Tabitha, flexing her hands in an attempt to not tidy the area around Lux.

"Yeah. I've always wanted to try it."

"It's a blessing and a curse, Lux. I was relieved that you and Tor weren't time travelers. You boys were wild enough as it was for me and your dad."

Lux gave his mother a look and she gave him one back. Twin toddlers speaking their own language with a penchant for mischief were nothing short of a parental nightmare. Fortunately, her parents had stepped in and provided Tabitha and Aeneas with some relief. Lux broke eye contact and returned to the topic he wanted to broach with his mother.

"I've been scanning through your family tree, too, Mom," he said. "You had a Great Aunt Mira. She was the sister of your Italian grandfather."

"Oh, you mean Mirabelle the Magnificent Flier?" Tabitha moved some papers and scooted onto the couch.

"She was a very athletic, agile person. I was reading some old newspaper clippings. Her stunts were harrowing," said Lux, tapping a hologram. A black and white photo of his great grandfather's sister filled the space between them. Luxurious black hair was tied neatly in a bun and her tight-fitting satin, sequined costume was reminiscent of the bathing suits of the 1950s. Tabitha smiled. Mira was a family legend. A flutter in her heart reminded her that what she recalled as a child was now different in the world. She sighed, suppressing the grief that had filled her ever since her father-in-law, Archie, had died, and she turned her attention back to Lux.

"I'm toying with the hypothesis that some athletes might have time-travel genes."

"Well, it would explain some great moments in sports," laughed Tabitha.

"Seriously, Mom, it's likely that Mirabelle could shift space and time to a small extent and capitalized on it during her performances."

Tabitha's eyes went wide. "You think she had time-travel genes? I mean that might explain Uncle Seth, too... He's a champion bowler from a family of limited athleticism!"

Lux stopped talking and tapped his chin thoughtfully. The more he thought about Great Aunt Mira, the more he wondered about his sister who seemed to be outpacing their father. More tests were needed. He was missing something important.

~

Lux pulled the SAIL from his pocket and looked at the flashing green light—it was an incoming call from his twin brother, Tor. The SAIL (Sustainable Autonomous Interconnected Link) was an ingenious piece of self-charging technology capable of recording biometric, climatic, and seismic data within a two-hundred-foot radius, but primarily used for holographic communication. The SAIL also had access to all digitally stored information formerly housed on the Internet and connected anyone in the world who had the same device. His parents often joked it was all the old technology of their adolescence expanded beyond their wildest dreams, wrapped into something the size of a pack of gum.

"So, you think there's some missing genes you've not mapped?"

Tor was soaking in a tub at his hotel in Osaka, relaxing his muscles after back-to-back shows with his band, Puget Funk. He'd been going hard for twelve hours, and self-care was a priority. He never wanted to give less than his best on stage.

"I found a newspaper review of her circus act," said Lux marveling at the spa-like scene that enveloped his twin. "The reviewer described her as 'magically effortless, as if the Earth's gravity had no effect on her.'"

"And you think Mom tossed Cassie a few genes and she's like a super traveler?"

"It would explain a few things. I haven't exhausted all possibilities for genes associated with this ability."

"Ability," scoffed Tor. "That's a light description."

"If Mom has genes, too, then that gives my second hypothesis more traction."

"Which is?"

"Everyone has some genes related to time travel. The more you have, the more skilled you are," replied Lux. "I analyzed open-source DNA samples from the catacombs of a twelfth century Italian monastery. Every one of those monks had time-travel genes, ranging from three to fourteen, and the guy with fourteen could access the timestream."

"Damn!" cried Tor. "That means we have them, too. So, if our partners have a few, our kids could be time travelers?" Tor's face contorted in horror, and he sat up abruptly, splashing water from the tub. "I don't want time-traveling kids!" he yelled. Tor had always been the drama queen of the family.

"It's not a disease, Tor. And besides, we'd have Dad and Cassie to help us."

Tor grabbed a towel and splashed his way out of the tub, just to make it clear to Lux he was not happy. "Lux, it would draw too much attention to our family. Mom has drilled us since birth about protecting Cassie's identity."

Lux nodded in agreement. Tabitha was never one to dictate things to her children because she appreciated her own childhood explorations, but she hammered the wily twins with the one important rule: never, ever tell anyone about your sister or your dad's "unique talents."

"We thought Mom was crazy going on about people taking them away."

"Until Grandma Mimi nearly whipped us for making a joke about it in front of neighbors. I've never seen her so mad," shuddered Tor.

Lux snorted. "Heck, even before she knew she had a time-traveling son, Grandma Mimi was deeply suspicious of government entities. After that, every attempt was made to hide in plain sight. 'Be as scientifically drab as possible'—those were her words to me once."

"Well, you've done Mimi proud," cackled Tor.

"Shut up, man. And hey, get home soon. Dad misses you."

Lux closed the secure connection and cleared the conversation from his SAIL. Harold had advised him never to leave any trace of conversation about time travel.

CHAPTER 3

A Time Traveler
Is Born

September 2028

AENEAS KNELT AT TABITHA'S feet and wrapped his arms around her legs as She puffed through her contractions. She was seated in a very firm leaf-patterned chair purchased by Aeneas when Tabitha had struggled to get off their couch during her eighth month of pregnancy. Aeneas leaned his head on her legs. She raked her hands through his hair.

"I'm okay," she said between breaths.

Martha, Tabitha's mother, bustled in with some herbal tincture to keep the contractions strong. Keniah, Socrates's wife, having recently birthed two daughters, one now age three and the other sixteen months, made her a vitamin smoothie. Tabitha downed the tincture and was sipping the smoothie between contractions. The midwife and her assistant were busy prepping the birth area. Aeneas and Tabitha were renting a condo in West Seattle where Tabitha had found a position at a mental health clinic for her first official job as a licensed counselor. The condo was just barely two bedrooms, but it had a nice open kitchen with a window that overlooked the street. The second bedroom was ready for the baby and Aeneas was proud that he had made it a cozy place for this new person entering the world.

While Keniah and Tabitha talked about something involving Tabitha's cervix, Aeneas still sat at her feet feeling marginal at best; he had no idea what was happening. He didn't understand what Keniah was saying or why Tabitha still had her leggings on. If the baby was coming, didn't those leggings need to be off? His mind went back and forth, resting on three ideas:

Tabitha's doctor said she was healthy and there were no complications with the baby, so a home birth would be just fine.

Keniah is here and she had both her babies at home, and it all turned out okay... besides, she has a lot smaller hips than Tabitha.

And finally, if any of this goes wrong, I will go back and fix it.

He knew the last idea was butting heads with everything Bob North Sky had taught him, but his instincts to keep Tabitha safe superseded anything else.

"Hey, too tight, Aeneas, too tight," yelled Tabitha, as she heaved and let out a grunt that had Aeneas on his feet in two seconds. He'd squeezed her legs too hard. Suddenly there was a lot of movement and Tabitha was ushered into their bedroom. Two hours later, Aeneas was holding a swaddled baby. Archie, his father, stood next to him admiringly as a beautiful baby girl pursed her lips together.

Aeneas brushed a kiss over his daughter's head. "I never knew she would have to work so hard..." He stopped, and his eyes drifted to the bedroom. Tabitha had just birthed the placenta and was being cared for by everyone except the midwife's assistant who had just handed Aeneas his daughter. Archie put his arm around Aeneas, planting a kiss on his head.

"Son, any man worth a damn will soon notice that the female of our species have all but surpassed us on several levels." Aeneas let out a huge sigh, tears streaming down his face.

"What's my new granddaughter's name?" asked Archie, beaming at his new grandbaby.

"Cassiopeia Valentina," replied Aeneas, thinking to himself these were big names for someone so small. "But Cassie for short, Dad."

Archie carefully took his new granddaughter into his arms and whispered softly, "Hello, little Cassie. Tell Grandpa, will you be able to walk through time, too, just like your daddy?"

~

Baby Cassie was chubby with beautiful dark brown curls. At eight months old, her eyes were now the same forest green as her mother's. Those big green eyes followed Aeneas everywhere. To say he was madly in love with his baby daughter was an understatement. Even Socrates, who had two lovely daughters he adored, thought Aeneas was a bit over the top. The thing was, she had Tabitha's eyes and every time he looked at her, all kinds of love welled up inside of him. He felt so lucky to have his wife and baby; nothing in the world seemed greater to him than Tabitha and baby Cassie.

One glorious Saturday morning in May, Aeneas came back from his run to find baby Cassie playing with her stacking cups while Tabitha was busy preparing his favorite breakfast burritos. Aeneas swallowed hard to stop himself from tearing up at the perfection the universe had granted him. Tabitha rolled her eyes whenever Aeneas was overcome with sentimentality. Tabitha loved baby Cassie, too, but she was just beginning to get a full night's sleep and feeling less emotional.

Aeneas sat across from baby Cassie and rolled a plush soccer ball to her. She squealed, crawled toward the ball, and knocked it out of her way. Aeneas glanced behind him. In the corner of the room just to the left of the couch, the timestream was beginning to open. Baby Cassie was making a beeline for it. Aeneas hopped up and scooped his baby girl into his arms. Could she see the timestream? Tabitha could never see it. The day Aeneas tried to bring her with him, Tabitha stayed put while Aeneas was whisked away, flying through his past. Afterward, Tabitha said she noticed the air suddenly felt colder in that spot, but she sensed nothing else unusual.

Aeneas cautiously moved toward the opening and felt the familiar pull to enter. He paused, resisting the pull, which was weak; the earthquake must be small or very far away. Baby Cassie was reaching out at the sparkling lights, so Aeneas took another step, and Cassie squealed again. He scooted just a little closer and whoosh, they were on a timeline, but not his. Scenes passed by. Cassie giggled and reached out to them, but Aeneas kept a tight hold on his daughter as the stream of time slowed down.

"No!" shouted Aeneas covering her eyes. He shook it off, took a deep breath and saw in his mind's eye the apartment and the moment he left. A few seconds later he stepped back into the living room where Tabitha was standing in the doorway to the kitchen.

"Aeneas Entwistle! You took our baby into the timestream?" shrieked Tabitha, dashing across the room to inspect every inch of her daughter. When she sat Cassie down again, the baby happily crawled over to the fading sparkles in the corner. Aeneas grabbed her, blew on her belly, and sat her on the couch with a chunky board book. Cassie immediately scooted to the end of the couch and waved her hands at the corner of the living room.

"She can see it?" whispered Tabitha.

"Yep," smiled Aeneas, wide-eyed.

Tabitha was suddenly stricken with fear. "What if she's swept in and lost?"

She sank onto the couch and cuddled baby Cassie as the opening dissipated. Aeneas sat next to them, kissed the top of Cassie's head, then kissed Tabitha's lips.

"Tab, I am pretty sure she can't enter it just yet, but she can definitely see it. I didn't enter my timeline until I was around thirteen, but I did occasionally slip in and out from the age of four onward. When I was holding Cassie, she could enter the timestream, which means I can train her and keep her safe. And besides, there are things on that end of her timeline that I don't ever want her to see."

"Such as?" asked Tabitha cringing, wondering if her no-video policy during the birth had been useless.

"Well, let's say it goes all the way to the *very, very* beginning of her life."

Tabitha blushed. "You mean before the birth?"

"I covered her eyes, Tab," assured Aeneas.

This made Tabitha laugh which made baby Cassie squeal and Aeneas enveloped them both in a hug.

Later that night Tabitha was snuggled under the covers ready to log in a few precious hours, but her super curious brain was stuck on something. "Aeneas... Cassie's timeline, is it attached to anything? I mean, how does it start?"

Aeneas perked up; he loved to talk about time travel. "Well, my timeline branches off my mother's which was notched to my father's once they combined their DNA."

"Huh," uttered Tabitha, fighting to stay awake a little longer. She was intrigued about the familial connections within the timestream. "So, Cassie is notched to my timeline?"

"Yes. All of our children will be," said Aeneas confidently. He'd seen first-hand the linking of timelines.

"No more babies," yawned Tabitha sleepily. She couldn't imagine managing the care of more than one child. Her career was just taking off.

"Just one more, Tab. They're small," said Aeneas playfully.

"Um, I'll think about it, but right now... sleep," muttered Tabitha, drifting off. Aeneas rolled over and smiled to himself. Just one more baby. A little family of Willoughby-Entwistles.

CHAPTER 4

An Ear-really Recollection

November 2015

C.J. WAS HAVING HIS "down time." This was an agreed upon family norm where everyone took a ninety-minute break from technology of any kind. At first, C.J. found it tough to manage without his iPod or his laptop, but finally decided he would read the sports page in *The Seattle Times* or walk Sput. This evening, after he paged through the rest of the paper, C.J. laid in his top bunk and wiggled his toes. Sput was at Aeneas's house, and it was too dark and rainy to walk him anyway.

Something was bugging him. He fidgeted, trying to settle, then just as he was about to enter his favorite daydream, a thought popped into his head—the story Tabitha had told him a few weeks ago about the woman she suspected was watching her. Tabitha had, quite rashly in his opinion, followed the woman onto the bus. But it was the description of the woman that intrigued him because it reminded C.J. of Aeneas's mother, especially the shape of her ears. After noting Miranda's uniquely shaped ears, C.J. regularly checked out all the ears that passed through his line of sight. And Miranda's ears were rare. Plus, Tabitha said that after the woman got off the bus, she had just vanished. The story would have likely faded from his memory if it were not for what happened the night of his first sleepover with Aeneas.

Aeneas was the first person C.J. had ever invited for a sleepover and this event became an enormous task for his parents, Charlie, and Sakura. He fretted over the snacks, the meals, the games, and every other detail of the sleepover. C.J.'s biggest request was replacing his twin bed with bunk beds for the special event. Sakura knew C.J. would drive her crazy if bunk beds were not purchased. Besides, she reasoned, he rarely asked for new things. And it would come in handy if there were other sleepovers, a point C.J. repeatedly made to his parents. Finally, Sakura and Charlie agreed, and the three of them made a special trip to pick out his new bunk beds.

After consuming three pizzas and several bags of snack mix, competing in a trashketball tournament, and quoting their favorite lines from the *Despicable Me* movies and rewatching the first two, the boys fell asleep just before midnight. C.J. woke with the early gleam of summer sunshine in his bedroom and he popped his head down to see if Aeneas was awake, but the bottom bunk was empty. C.J. climbed down the ladder and tiptoed to the kitchen to see if Aeneas was looking for something to eat. But as he quietly padded through his home, Aeneas was nowhere to be found.

Maybe he left before anyone got up, thought C.J. He trudged silently back to his new bunk bed, plunked face down on his pillow, and cried himself back to sleep. An indeterminate amount of time passed and there was a knock at his door.

His father, Charlie, leaned in cheerfully. "Good morning, boys. Mom will have peanut butter pancakes, bacon, and sliced strawberries ready for you both in about ten minutes."

This was the special breakfast C.J. had requested for his sleepover because he knew how much Aeneas loved peanut butter pancakes.

C.J. was too ashamed to tell his father what happened so he called out weakly, "Got it, Dad," and waited for the door to close. He needed a minute to figure out how he was going to tell his parents—who had gone to so much trouble for this sleepover—that Aeneas had left early.

A rustle below startled C.J. and before he could climb down to investigate, Aeneas was eye level with him. "Bro, thanks for asking your mom to make my favorite breakfast!"

"When... when did you come back?" squeaked C.J., rubbing his eyes and feeling discombobulated. He stared at Aeneas, unsure if he was going to cry again. Maybe the buildup to his first ever sleepover had been too stressful? Maybe he'd dreamt it?

"Come back from where? Bro, I just woke up and I gotta pee bad!" And with that, Aeneas flung open the door and sprinted toward the bathroom.

Later that morning after Aeneas had headed home, C.J. googled waking dreams. After some research, C.J. concluded he must've had an episode of *hypnagogia* and hallucinated the early morning walk through his house. He'd held onto the narrative of that morning's events, thinking it was a bizarre episode in his own life, but now the memory seemed like it could have been something else entirely.

Was it possible Aeneas's nighttime disappearances were happening even before he was waking up with different socks? And could this have any connection to the story of the vanishing mystery lady from the bus? C.J. groaned. His brain was lumping these strange occurrences together, but he wasn't sure why. He pulled up a picture on his phone. It was a secret photo he'd taken last year of Miranda Entwistle's left ear. He'd told himself it was for scientific purposes and never divulged to Aeneas that he'd sneaked a picture of his mom's ear. There were some lines you shouldn't cross and taking a picture of his best friend's mom's ear was probably one of them. He swallowed and sent it to Tabitha with a short message:

Did the ears on the mystery lady look like this?

C.J. lay back and closed his eyes. These two events might not even be related but he had to know. A ping made him jump. Tabitha had replied almost instantly.

Yep! Do you have some weird database of ears?

CHAPTER 5

An Unexpected
Auto Parts
Encounter Alaska

Summer, 2019

BOB NORTH SKY WAS carving a walking stick. His steady hand turned out beautifully intricate designs of salmon, orca, eagles, seals, moose, dragonflies, bowhead whales, ptarmigans and any other animal that caught his eye. Gerry Archambeau walked briskly up his driveway. Bob recognized his long stride and chuckled as he recalled Gerry's childhood nickname, Walking Stick, which had been shortened to just 'Stick' for most of their adolescence.

"Hey, Stick," called Bob warmly. "You look like a man headed somewhere important."

Gerry reached the porch and grabbed a chair, scooting over to Bob and sitting down with a plop. Flushed, he shook his head. "I just threw a white man back into the river of time. He was an old miner from back east and didn't know he could travel the river."

Bob looked up from his carving. "So, he was from the early times of the whites? The Gold Rush?"

"Yes, and I could tell by his smell he'd been a long time from a tub. He crossed over into our time in the worst place. I was in the auto parts store and the river appeared and this fool just came through," said Gerry with distaste.

Bob's eyes widen in amazement. "What did you do?"

"I punched him in the face and told him to get out of here or his god would send him straight to hell. Then I shoved him back into the river."

Bob smiled appreciatively. "Best to give the old miner a good scare. If he ever gets back home, he'll think he's been drinking too much. Make him sober up."

Bob paused, then added thoughtfully, "Moving forward through the river of time is much harder than going back along your own line. Odd that an old miner, who probably never traveled before, managed it."

Gerry pushed around wood shavings with his feet and stared off at the mountains. Bob kept carving. The quiet was what Gerry needed. He had been frightened by the old miner, especially because he, Bob, and other tribal travelers worried what the whites might do if they could enter the river of time.

"If the whites learn they have the gift, they could do real damage to the world if more enter the river," said Gerry quietly.

Bob chuckled. Gerry whipped his head around and barked, "You're laughing at my worries?"

Bob cut short his chuckle and replied gently, "I laughed, old friend, because the whites have already done real damage to the world."

Gerry's face relaxed and he nodded in commiseration.

"I have my own worry, too," said Bob as he blew wood dust off his salmon carving. Gerry watched and waited while Bob took his time. "A young man, not white and not Black, was here a few weeks ago trying to travel the river. He knew the secret and asked for my help. I told him I would think about it. He left me his number."

"You know it's forbidden," warned Gerry, shocked that Bob would even consider such a thing.

Bob raised an eyebrow. "Our ancestors said we must not tell the whites, and he is not white."

"He is not of our people, either," scoffed Gerry.

"No, but he may be descended from the *very* first people, Gerry. My granddaughter told me that human life is said to have come out of Africa," replied Bob, admiring his carving.

"I cannot believe a wise man such as yourself would even consider this!" snapped Gerry, launching off his chair like a rocket. He was known far and wide as a quick-tempered man. He paced in a circle, then walked over to Bob. Gerry figured he would stare him down until he came to his senses, but Bob wasn't easily rattled. He knew Gerry was a fair person.

Bob spoke slowly, never breaking eye contact, "Old friend, I would like for you to meet this young man and give me your opinion. Then I will decide what to do."

Bob lowered his eyes and resumed carving. Gerry let out a huge sigh. He tapped his foot for a minute, thinking it over.

Bob North Sky had asked him to help make an important decision and everyone who was anyone knew that Bob was one of
the wisest shamans who had ever lived.

"Well, get him here soon, because I'm going down south
to fish the Kenai with my brothers in a few weeks," grumbled
Gerry, heading back to his truck. Bob nodded, pleased with
his carving and the outcome of the conversation. If Aeneas
could win over Gerry, he would consider mentoring the young
traveler.

CHAPTER 6

Forbidden Love Meets Looming Panic

Spring, 2053

Soon after Aeneas was released by his medical team to continue his recovery at home, Cassie decided it was time for some solitude. She'd sent Harold a brief message explaining she was exhausted from the strain of repeated time travel and was taking some vacation days. Since then, she'd been staying in C.J.'s cabin along the Payette River in Idaho. The rescue of her father from 2005, coupled with the burden of being the only one who could search for him in the timestream had left her feeling drained and lonely. There was no one she could talk to about the stress she endured all those weeks he was missing, the constant pressure to find him, the shock at finding the past had been changed and the strange romantic entanglement with young Harold.

Missi and her sister Athena, better known as Thena, knew Cassie was hung up on her feelings for Harold and weren't surprised when she notified them she'd be leaving Seattle now that Aeneas was back home. Nia, their younger sister was not included in any private conversations amongst the other female cousins. Cassie didn't feel the same closeness to her as she did Missi and Thena and jotted this in her journal while she gazed down at the river:

Why is my relationship to Nia so different? Why do my memories of her feel like recollections of a dream or a movie?

Cassie had been diligently noting the anomalies in her journal since she came back from 2005. The worst part of all this was the first person she wanted to ask about these inconsistencies was Harold, and Cassie had put a whole state between them.

She woke early from a restless night and was seated in front of a large window that faced a steep canyon scattered with glimmering ponderosa pines reflecting the morning sun. Cassie sensed some possibility had been ripped away from her; thoughts of what might have been kept her awake at night and dogged her throughout the day.

Harold's wedding picture was like a surprise smack in the face. The moment she saw the photograph hanging on the wall of her parents' home she felt a jolt pass through her, shocked at seeing Harold married. Instantly all the memories shuffled in, and she was overwhelmed.

Cassie's SAIL had been flashing cerulean blue for two days. Cerulean blue was the color she programmed for Harold's messages or alerts. She knew he wanted to talk with her and felt badly that she couldn't even bring herself to view his message. Another light flashed violet, and she whispered, "Open message from Thena."

Thena's message appeared in a small holographic frame, a handwritten message, like the letters of old:

Open Harold's message!

"Seriously?" mumbled Cassie heading into the kitchen for her morning cup of tea. Though C.J. had installed a solar powered stovetop, many of the appliances in his cabin were outdated. There was only a stainless-steel kettle to boil water and an ancient microwave oven for heating food, instead of the Nimble Chef, a blend of microwave, refrigerator, pressure cooker, and toaster oven technology. It could be programmed to cook, heat, or cool food to its optimal eating texture and temperature. Nearly everyone she knew had one in their kitchen, courtesy of Harold who had invented the initial prototype. Cassie groaned and muttered to herself, "No matter where I go... there's always some reminder."

Cassie scanned the kitchen cabinets until she found a large ceramic mug. After the water boiled, she poured it over a bag of Earl Grey tea and added a heaping spoonful of honey and some milk. Walking back into the living room she looked skeptically at her SAIL and steeled herself for the inevitable.

"Open Harold's message," mumbled Cassie reluctantly.

A large shimmering hologram appeared with a small blue icon in the center that said, "TAP HERE." Cassie let out a frustrated sigh and tapped the icon. A line of words zoomed onto the screen in bold typed lettering:

Eleanor's House, November 21st, 2015 Seattle, Washington

Suddenly Harold appeared, adjusted himself in the frame, then settled into his chair. Cassie was so surprised to see Harold, *her* Harold, that it was seconds before she realized the ceramic mug had tipped forward pouring hot tea all over her legs. Cassie squealed, swiftly pulled off her pajama pants and hurried into the kitchen to grab two dish towels. Quickly soaking them with tap water, she placed the cold compresses across her thighs, but by the time she'd reseated herself, the video had finished playing.

"Replay," she called out impatiently.

Cassie wasn't sure what the video was about or why it was so urgent, but seeing *her* Harold caused a flutter of excitement in her belly.

Cassie listened spellbound as Harold explained he'd fallen in love with her and that he was making this video because he wanted to be sure she had a happy life.

"I miss you so much, Harold," said Cassie, as tears streamed down her face. She watched the message a second time and paused the video to look at him. Frustrated, Cassie bellowed, "I can visit Harold whenever I want. We can go away for secret romantic weekends. It's my life and if I want to be with Harold, then I'll damn well be with Harold!"

Cassie frantically glanced around the cabin hoping to catch a glimpse of the timestream. She threw off the cold compresses and searched for a pair of clean pants from her travel bag. She finished dressing in silence, grabbed her backpack and headed for the self-driving car she'd rented.

C.J.'s cabin along the Payette River was about a hundred miles from the town of Challis, where enough small earthquakes occasionally opened the timestream. Aeneas and Cassie once had visited C.J. and his son Ryan during summer and were surprised to find the timestream open several times, especially as they drove toward Stanley.

Cassie seated herself inside the silver car and requested her destination, "Stanley, Idaho."

While Highway 21 had been repaved many times, it was still a slow road, winding up through subalpine fir forests before dropping down into the valley near Stanley. The trip took just over an hour. Cassie craned her neck searching both sides of the road for any sparkle of the timestream, but the energy field eluded her. She arrived in Stanley and wandered the tiny town, stopping for a cinnamon roll at the local bakery. After fifteen minutes meandering through small shops, pretending to be a tourist, Cassie decided to search further. Highway 21 ended in Stanley, so Cassie's self-driving car now took Highway 75 north to Challis and Salmon, Idaho.

Cassie had visited Challis a few times in the last three years researching potential investments for Harold's foundation. Some ranching families in the Challis Valley had taken advantage of new geothermal conversion technology, tapping the energy beneath their soil, and selling it back into the grid for a healthy income. The small town, which had languished for years as a forest service/mining outpost, was now booming. Landowners near local hot springs had formed a consortium and installed several greenhouses, shipping hothouse greens and vegetables weekly to restaurants and markets in Boise and

Missoula. Harold had invested in the consortium to promote locally sourced food initiatives.

Cassie had the car pull over at a historical marker just outside of Challis. The sign described how a local man, a former U.S. Forest Service range conservationist, had worked tirelessly to help restore worn out grazing lands by planting native grasses and shrubs for seventeen years before he died. A small path led off the road into an ecological restoration area, a meadow blooming with early spring flowers. Cassie slung her bag onto her shoulder, typed in a code to secure the rental car and headed into the meadow. "There you are," sang out Cassie, passing a clump of snowberry bushes and giddily slipping into the timestream.

Her usual landing spot seemed like the best place to enter November 22, 2015, but Cassie had forgotten it was the Sunday before Thanksgiving and the PCC Market parking lot was alive with shoppers. Hovering above the scene Cassie couldn't seem to find a spot not traversed by people. Finally, she decided the busiest section of the parking lot wouldn't invite much suspicion because people were coming and going in all directions. Springing up as if she'd been tying her shoe, Cassie gazed around, half hoping Harold would be at the market, but concluded he was likely in Queen Anne with Eleanor. Making her way through shoppers, carts, and cars to the nearby bus stop, Cassie felt a prickle on her neck and turned abruptly only to come face to face with her Uncle Socrates, who seemed none too pleased to see her. In fact, she thought to herself, *he looks quite angry.*

"Looking for someone?" he asked sharply. Cassie blushed deeply and felt bile rise in her throat.

"Hello, Socrates," she replied casually, trying to recover herself.

Socrates held her gaze firmly, a tactic he learned from his father, Archie.

"Why are you here, Cassie?" he asked quietly.

"Well, I need to speak with Harold about an issue we are having in the future." Cassie struggled to keep her face impassive.

"Is the timestream still open?"

How could he know that? wondered Cassie, taken aback. The timestream usually stayed open for a few minutes or several hours once the traveler departed the timeline depending on the strength of the event that generated the opening.

Cassie decided the best way to handle this was to dismiss Socrates. After all, he was only seventeen and she was twenty-four.

"I'm going to check the bus schedule. Need to head to Eleanor's house," announced Cassie, patting his shoulder and turning toward the bus stop. Socrates immediately reached out and clamped his hand around her forearm tightly. Cassie was so astonished that she forgot to use her Krav Maga defensive moves she regularly practiced.

Harold had been depressed for weeks before finally confessing to Socrates he thought he'd fallen in love with Cassie. Socrates sensed this could be more dangerous than anything he'd encountered so far regarding time travel, and he'd been worrying about it ever since Harold had confided in him.

Star-crossed lovers could behave desperately, taking risks that might create a disruption in the space-time continuum.

"Let go of me," hissed Cassie.

Socrates leaned in and whispered angrily, "Leave him alone. There will be plenty of other men, Cassie."

"You don't know that," snapped Cassie, squirming to release his grip without causing unwanted attention.

"Harold needs someone in his own time and so do you. Go back. Don't do this to him or yourself," urged Socrates, finally releasing her from his grip. Cassie stepped back, glaring at Socrates as she rubbed her arm where he'd held her.

"I just need to talk to him. I won't stay long. There are a few things we need to sort out!"

Socrates pivoted. From the corner of his eye, he saw Sput pulling C.J. along the sidewalk like the lead dog on a snow sled.

"Aeneas and C.J. are coming! Go now!" ordered Socrates, herding her through the throng of shoppers. Cassie glanced beyond her uncle to see the trio bouncing cheerfully along the sidewalk toward them.

"Dammit!" groaned Cassie through clenched teeth. She turned to go, still cursing under her breath while Socrates stood guard as she merged into the crowded parking lot and vanished.

C.J. and Aeneas waved at Socrates. He returned a half-hearted wave, and he plopped down on the bench at the bus stop, shaken at his sudden encounter with Cassie and overcome with regret. She was right in front of him, and he didn't ask the one question he'd been desperate to know ever since she left to search for her father in 2005. Was it actually Aeneas in the park that day of his attempted kidnapping? He was very certain it was, but as a scientist, he wanted confirmation. And did they make it back safely to 2053 with no repercussions to their present time? Socrates rubbed his forehead wearily. Cassie was so determined to get to Harold that she hadn't even mentioned it, which was odd, really odd. He'd have another word with Harold. Socrates needed to fend off his looming panic over this forbidden love affair.

CHAPTER 7

Tabitha's
First Client

November 2015

HAROLD SAT DOWN ON the bus and closed his eyes. The crisp air of late November usually invigorated his brain, so it whizzed along at top speed. His coding buzzed with innovation in the autumn because it was his favorite culinary season. Consequently, he baked pies: fruit pies, meat pies, sour cream and onion pies, even peanut butter pies—a favorite of Aeneas. But this year his brain was slogging along as if it were the end of February, and he was aching for spring to inspire his tired winter cooking. The bus started and stopped quickly, jarring Harold from his fog. His life had taken twists and turns over the last few years leaving no close friends to relay his troubles. And his troubles were unusual, beyond the expected angst of dating in your twenties. Harold had feelings for a person who wasn't even born and wouldn't be born for another thirteen years. He constantly fought off thoughts about what had happened to Cassie when she returned to 2005. *Did she find Aeneas? Was the rescue a success?* It was as if a riveting novel had been ripped in half and the rest of the story would have to wait until he was an old man.

The bus reached Harold's stop and he made his way down the sidewalk and halted when he saw the open door to Freshy's. Harold was headed for the Entwistle home to begin the morning breakfasts, but part of him just couldn't face it. Several people hustled into Freshy's from the cold, lining up for their morning coffee. Suddenly, Harold decided to take a detour. He needed a triple shot mocha to brace himself for another long day. The Entwistles' coffeemaker was programmed to start seven minutes before he arrived in case Archie or Miranda came downstairs early, so there was no need to rush.

Tabitha had left home early that morning and already had her notes spread out at a table, sipping hot chocolate, working on a history presentation for later that day. She found mornings to be a fruitful time where her mind worked swiftly, unencumbered after a good night's sleep. Besides, Freshy's was much quieter than her home with her mom always after Seth to brush his teeth, get dressed, and collect his school things.

Noticing him as he picked up his order, Tabitha called out cheerfully, "Good morning, Harold." Tabitha always felt more mature when she was on her own in public. It made her feel confident, like a young woman of the world.

Harold took a mouthful of his latte and walked over to her table.

"Bit early for homework, Tabitha," said Harold, scrutinizing all her papers.

"Maybe," replied Tabitha brightly, "but I find twenty-five minutes in the morning is equal to fifty minutes in the evening."

Harold's face radiated approval at this adage. He smiled briefly and marveled at Tabitha's logic.

"I haven't seen you smile in weeks, Harold. Had I known my secret formula for getting my homework finished would cheer you up so much, I would've told you earlier," teased Tabitha.

Surprised she'd noticed, Harold plopped down at the table. "Has it been so obvious?" he asked glumly.

"Aeneas mentioned it and I wouldn't call him super observant," laughed Tabitha.

"I've had a lot on my mind, I guess."

"I told Aeneas you looked lovesick or heartbroken. I thought maybe you'd had a bad breakup or something."

Tabitha's face was all sympathy; and Harold, tall as he was, wilted in his chair. Tabitha, in turn, sat up straight. Her first, real adult client was slumped in a chair before her.

"I'm a good listener, Harold. You can tell me what happened if you'd like."

Harold looked up at Tabitha and thought hopelessly, *I could never tell her what really happened...* but he recalled Cassie mentioning that adult Tabitha had a thriving counseling business. Before he could stop himself, Harold created a story about a woman who had been visiting from overseas. Careful to disguise her origins, he went on explaining he'd developed strong feelings for this woman, but because she'd returned to her home in France, he was struggling to get over her.

"Hang on, Harold. Is there any possibility that you would ever move to France, or she would ever come live here?"

Harold shook his head. "She has family obligations. There's no way she'd be able to leave, and I don't want to move to France," said Harold with a heavy sigh. He took a long sip of his latte as if to steel himself for this reality.

Tabitha sat thinking for a second. "So, what I hear you saying is that while you have very strong feelings for this woman, you are grieving because you know that it's not possible to continue a relationship with her. Does that sum it up?"

"Yeah," nodded Harold, not sure it was all that simple.

Knowing him to be a person who looked at life logically, Tabitha decided to take a practical stance with Harold. "Harold, how long do you think you'll grieve over this?"

Tabitha could see the wheels turning when Harold sat up a little straighter. She'd asked him for a measurable quantity, and he had to think about it. Tabitha had observed when a person was tasked with determining how long they wanted to hold onto something, several thought processes were invoked. She sensed this line of questioning would alter Harold's thinking and her intuition told her all he needed was a little shift.

"I hadn't considered a time. Maybe I should try to figure out my next steps."

"Sounds like a good place to start," declared Tabitha.

"I should go," blurted Harold. He snatched his latte off the table and headed for the door. It was all he could do to contain his feelings of relief. He had a plan, and that plan was to create next steps.

"Bye, Harold," Tabitha called after him.

Harold looked back, gave Tabitha a brief wave, and continued out the door.

"I guess I'll check in again with Harold next week," chirped Tabitha bursting with glee. She'd finally helped someone, and it felt terrific.

CHAPTER 8

Harold Has a Change of Heart

November 2015

HAROLD SAT ON THE pink velvet couch in his bedroom. His tablet and a leather-bound journal were stacked neatly on an adjacent cushion. Lost in a memory, he stared at the green upholstered chair across from him. His bedroom, once belonging to Eleanor and her husband, was the largest of the upstairs rooms. It was more like a suite, with its heavy, well-made furniture, including an old roll-top desk, the pink velvet couch, green chair, and a four-poster bed with an assortment of linens that Eleanor rotated throughout the year to match each season.

The green chair reminded him of Cassie and that reminded him of something he'd done, something foolish—stupid even—that he needed to undo, only he couldn't bring himself to do it. He was stuck, grieving for the loss of a person who wasn't even born yet.

He grabbed his tablet and tapped the screen a few times. Harold scrolled through pictures he'd taken of Cassie in the green chair, the first evening she stayed at Eleanor's when she explained time travel to him. He knew he had to delete them. Cassie would never have allowed her picture to be taken. He'd spontaneously snapped several shots of her as they talked. But now those pictures haunted him. There was also the video he'd made as she entered the timestream, but that wasn't intimate like these photos. He and Socrates would need to decide whether they would keep the footage or delete it after more research was completed. But, if he deleted these photos... he'd have nothing to remember her by.

Harold thought about what Tabitha had asked him. *How long would he grieve?* He closed the photos, grabbed his stylus, and opened a drawing program and scribbled, "How long will I grieve over Cassie?"

He made a list of pros and cons. The biggest con for him was that he would always be waiting for her, hoping she might travel back—and then what? The pros were harder to describe. What if she came back and said she had feelings for him, too? Was that a *pro*? How could that be a possibility? They'd be forced to have long distance relationship that spanned decades. Harold wrote the number 41—the age he'd be when Cassie was born. He sighed, set down his tablet, placed his head between his hands and closed his eyes. It'd been weeks since Cassie left and even if she did come back again it could be years into the future. In the meantime, Harold needed to get on with his life, his life now in 2015, because if he was completely honest with himself, there was a possibility his feelings were infatuation with an attractive, exciting new person. His mother always used to remark he was distracted by bright and shiny new things. And besides, there was already an established future for Cassie and that future did not include him as her love interest. The whole thing was pointless, and it was time he faced up to it.

Harold opened his tablet again and took one last look at the pictures of Cassie and hit delete. In a moment of forward thinking, he grabbed his cell phone, attached it to a tripod, and hit record.

"Hi, Cassie. It's me, Harold, the younger version," said Harold jokingly, trying to steady his voice.

"While you were here, I took some photos of you the night we were talking about time travel." Harold paused and ran his fingers through his hair.

"I know I shouldn't have, but I was so... so awed by you."

Harold took off his glasses and stared into the camera wistfully. "And I think I was falling for you."

Harold brushed a rogue tear from his left eye and pressed on.

"Now it's late November and I've been hoping you'll come back. But I probably won't see you for thirteen years or more and when I do, you'll be a baby."

Harold looked down at his hands thinking of how small she would be, then looked back up into the camera. He swallowed hard, choking back tears. "I'm going to make you this promise... I'll do everything in my power to ensure your life is happy, that you'll have opportunities to learn and explore because I know one day you'll become the brave, stubborn, beautiful, witty woman who opened my mind to a whole new way of thinking about the universe..."

Harold brusquely wiped the tears off his face, trying to hold his emotions in check. "Meeting you was the greatest thing that has happened in my life and even though I'll miss you, I'm happy I get to watch you grow up."

Harold forced a smile and leaned forward to stop the recording.

CHAPTER 9

Solstice Celebration Revelation

December 2015

EVERY SURFACE IN MARTHA'S house gleamed. Seth was drooped across a chair with a smudge of dirt over his left eye. Tabitha sat on the floor next to a pile of clean laundry. George alone remained chipper. He loved a party with live music.

"All we have left is the laundry and decorations," announced Martha.

"Mommy, I need a nap," whined Seth, who received a cool stare from Tabitha. Seth was still young enough to play the 'I need a nap' card.

Seth was given the nod and trudged up his bedroom.

"Go do the shopping," said George cheerfully. "Tab and I will finish the decorating and laundry."

Martha didn't need to be told twice. She grabbed her bags and headed for the door. She loved doing the shopping alone because she could make time for a latte and croissant.

"We should call C.J." said George as his wife pulled out of the driveway.

"Right, Dad!" agreed Tabitha, perking up.

"Remember last year when Mom went shopping? We'll have this finished in no time. He's a pro!"

C.J. ambled over to his cousin's house with a large duffel bag. He saved bits and pieces from all sorts of projects. He collected and categorized them thematically, recycling items normally thrown away for future use. When Aeneas mentioned that Persephone would be interested in his collection, C.J. replied peevishly, "I don't need Persephone involving herself in my hobbies." C.J. was still rankled she'd trained Sput to bark three times at the door when he needed to go out, a constant reminder that she'd managed something he should have done himself.

"Is Aunt Martha gone?" he asked, cautiously entering the kitchen.

"Yep, buddy. She's not due back for a couple hours. She thinks we don't know she takes a long coffee break," laughed George.

C.J.'s superpower was designing spaces. He could decorate any room with maximum efficiency, and he secretly enjoyed it, unless his Aunt Martha was poking around questioning his choices. Last year, he arranged the Willoughby house for their solstice party in under ninety minutes.

"Just direct us. We're ready," said Tabitha, who never minded helping, but didn't have the bandwidth for the whole job.

"Uncle George," began C.J. crisply, "the mantel and banister along the staircase should be draped tightly with garland and lights. No loose ends."

George nodded and headed for the container filled with faux garland.

"Tabitha, polish and reset the candlestick holders. I'll place them when you're done."

C.J. grabbed the box full of holiday knickknacks, frowning. He disliked some of the gaudier ceramic ones, but the hand carved wooden trees, fairies, animals, and children were worth putting out.

Seth peeked out from his room an hour later and called down, "Is C.J. here?"

"Hey, Seth, come help me with the tablecloths," cried C.J., pleased with his work. Seth bounded down the stairs. The staircase banister was tastefully lit up with holiday lights. The mantel over the gas fireplace showcased the small wooden images. C.J. had tucked the garland around them. Real mistletoe hung in the doorway near the kitchen, and it was time to set out the candles.

The solstice celebration started at eight sharp. On her return, Martha jumped right into the preparations and put out a spread of marinated vegetables, bowls of nuts and dried fruit, tiny mince pies, and a rich dark chocolate Yule log cake. Harold walked in with iced sugar cookies in the shapes of trees, sun, moon, and Earth, while Sakura and Charlie brought Chanko Nabe, or Sumo Stew, each year so everyone could bulk up for the winter. All the other guests were asked to bring beverages. The party was in full swing by eight-thirty.

Harold polished off a bowl of Chanko Nabe and was feeling mellow. He clapped Socrates on the back and whispered, "A quick word, Sox."

Socrates edged away from the buffet table with a small plate of food.

"I've got a piece of anomalous data that's bugging me."

Socrates nodded. He didn't want to discuss data, but he was stuck with Harold since there was no one else at the party close to his age.

"That weird shadow I mentioned. Well, I've played around with it a little and it resembles a person, but there's no light source. My thinking is that someone was hovering nearby in the timestream when Cassie was about to enter, and the video picked up their shadow."

"You think someone else was there we didn't know about?"

"Maybe. Or someone was watching her," speculated Harold.

Socrates shivered a little. The idea of someone watching bothered him, but he dismissed it. There was no need to press his panic button.

"It's more important that we continue to train Aeneas. Those messages sent through the mismatched socks are the priority."

"I have good news on that front. I've finished my hypnosis course."

Socrates raised an eyebrow as he slowly finished a cookie. He wasn't completely sold that hypnosis would be the solution to Aeneas's nighttime disappearances.

"I just need to practice a bit," said Harold, giving him a meaningful glance.

"Hell no!" barked Socrates louder than he'd intended. He felt Archie's eyes on him. He turned toward a group of parents where his father was chatting. Socrates shrugged as if to say, 'It's Harold, Dad.' And Archie, full of food and drink, nodded sympathetically. Socrates continued to divest Harold of any notion that he would become his hypnosis guinea pig, and then the room fell quiet.

Martha entered the living room in a stunning floor length black tulle dress embroidered with tiny crystals and announced they'd begin with a Jaiya song called "Yule is Come." Sakura, George, and Charlie readied themselves to play and soon Martha's lilting voice filled the room as she spun and sang with her tambourine. Sakura's snug green velvet dress hugged her growing baby as she deftly moved her bow across the strings of her cello, while George in a bright red vest played the flute and Charlie dazzled with his violin in a black shirt and jacket. Aeneas smiled, awestruck, and whispered to Tabitha, "I forget sometimes how cool your family is, Tab."

Cheers and applause erupted as the foursome finished the first song. George told the guests there were more songs to come but they were waiting on another musician, and he winked at Tabitha.

"What was that about?" asked C.J. adjusting his new knitted cap circled with twelves.

"No clue. What's wrong with Sput?" gestured Tabitha. Sput was sprawled under the Christmas tree with his tongue hanging out.

"He looks a little bloated," worried C.J., heading over to inspect Sput.

"How can you tell?" chuckled Aeneas. Sput was sporting his new navy and green sweater emblazoned with *12th Dog*.

"He might be feeling a little sick," interjected Persephone. "I saw Seth give him a few cookies earlier. Dogs aren't supposed to eat human food."

C.J. gave her a withering stare and roused Sput. "C'mon, boy, let's go for a quick walk around the block."

Normally Persephone would've been annoyed by C.J., but she was having a big night out. Harold had asked her as a special favor to be Eleanor's companion. Miranda had been relieved since it meant her daughter was less likely to eavesdrop on adult conversations. The pair were jolly, giggling, and taste-testing all the treats while Eleanor recounted her childhood Christmases. At the end of one tale, Eleanor's eyes lingered on Harold.

"I wish Harold would find a nice young lady to date... maybe settle down one day. He'd be a good husband."

"Harold's been a little sad lately. He needs to be more cheerful if he's going to find a wife, I think," added Persephone.

"Well, that's because his girlfriend went back to France," remarked Tabitha absently.

"Oh, she was stunning with those emerald green eyes and lovely curls," recalled Eleanor, thinking of Cassie.

"He's grieving, but he'll get over it," assured Tabitha. She started to elaborate but realized she'd just violated client confidentiality and looked around anxiously to see if Harold had overheard her. Persephone tried to contain her excitement at being included in a grown-up conversation and she primed herself to jump in with more commentary.

Nearby, Harold suddenly strung the sentences together and realized his love life was being discussed at a holiday party. He started to quell the conversation, but Socrates leaned into him with a murderous expression and snarled, "What is Tabitha talking about?"

"Let's step outside for a second, Sox," urged Harold, gazing around for the clearest path to the front door.

"Nah. Let's wait," replied Socrates, sensing there was more to come.

"You know," declared Persephone confidently, "if Harold wants a wife he should start searching soon. It might take him a while to find someone who likes all his... his... quirky habits." Persephone beamed after her comment.

Eleanor was at the ready to make her opinions known about what Harold should do to find a wife. She raised her pointer finger and started to speak when Harold blurted loudly, "I've got a date New Year's Eve with an attractive geologist!"

All heads turned in Harold's direction. Aeneas smiled broadly and called out, "Way to go, Harold!"

"Come with me, man. You need to answer my question," insisted Socrates herding him out the front door.

"Well, that was uncomfortable," huffed Harold as they stood in the driveway. Socrates didn't care how uncomfortable Harold was. He wanted to be sure Harold wasn't revealing information to Tabitha that could shift future events.

"So, what've you told Tabitha?"

"It was a hypothetical... about Cassie, but not about Cassie."

Socrates gave Harold his best Archie stare.

"It happened suddenly one morning at the coffee shop. Tabitha asked me a lot of questions about why I was sad, but I framed it as if I was dating a woman from France."

Socrates stayed silent while Harold squirmed under his gaze, trying not to babble his responses.

"Tabitha grows up to become a renowned therapist. It didn't seem far-fetched at the time to take her advice."

"You need to talk to someone, you talk to me. Or you pay a real therapist," barked Socrates, poking his finger into Harold's chest forcefully. Harold hung his head and mumbled an apology. He'd been foolish confiding in Tabitha, that was obvious to him now. He was about to reassure Socrates of his discretion when a small SUV pulled up.

Sput saw Sadie first. He bounded toward her, dragging C.J. in his wake as she collected her guitar and overnight bag from the car. Carl and Catherine grabbed a bottle of red wine, two large poinsettias, and headed for the front door.

"Hi, Sadie!" called C.J.

"Sput looks so cute in his sweater Tab knitted for him."

C.J. pointed at his head.

"Wow, she went all out this year, didn't she?" said Sadie admiring the detail on his twelves cap.

"I didn't know you were coming, Sadie."

"It was last minute. We weren't sure about mom's schedule, but she's not playing anywhere tonight," replied Sadie. "Hey, I'm supposed to make a big entrance. Can you tell Aunt Martha I'm here?"

C.J. tilted his head and stared coldly at his cousin.

"Just tell her I'm here. She's not going to eat you, C.J."

C.J. trudged slowly to the front door. Sadie gave him a playful push and headed around to the back of the house. She was all set to sing "Silent Night."

Sakura settled herself around the cello. She played a few bars of "Silent Night," cueing her niece to enter. Sadie walked in slowly humming along with the music. She wore black skinny jeans, Doc Marten boots, and a sparkling silver sweater. Her blonde hair was secured in the back with a beautifully braided Celtic knot.

C.J. stood alongside Seth who declared, "Sadie looks like an angel."

Tabitha and Aeneas exchanged surprised looks as Sadie started to sway and sing "Silent Night." All eyes in the room were on her. Catherine teared up. Carl videoed the performance with his phone. Suddenly, Sadie motioned to Seth who joined her to sing the last the chorus. Seth hit the high notes perfectly when he belted out "sleep in heavenly peace" and Martha tearfully hugged George. Persephone had to get a tissue for Eleanor, too.

When the song was over, Sadie and Seth were greeted with a round of applause and cheers. Seth took a bow and blew kisses to his parents. Sadie hustled over and hugged Tabitha.

"You were brilliant, Sadie," gushed Tabitha.

"I'd been rehearsing with Aunt Sakura on FaceTime so I wasn't sure how the song would turn out."

"It was incredible," agreed Aeneas.

C.J. walked over and handed Sadie a glass of ginger ale. "For your vocal cords, madam."

"You're such a goof, C.J., but yes, I'll take that ginger ale."

Sadie quickly downed the small glass and gave Tabitha a cheeky grin. "Come with me to the bathroom, Tab. I've got to reset my hair before the next song."

C.J. gave Aeneas a quizzical look. "Her hair is perfect."

"They want to talk in private, man."

"Oh," said C.J. thoughtfully. Aeneas noticed the wheels turning and gave him a stern look.

"Bro, never ask me to go to the bathroom if you want to talk. Just ask me to step outside."

"I knew that."

Aeneas laughed.

C.J. changed the subject.

"What did you get Tabitha?"

"It's a surprise."

C.J.'s face crumpled. "I told *you*."

"Yep, and I'm sure she'll love it, though I think it's a little weird to buy someone shoes."

"They're neoprene insulated galoshes. Tab got her feet wet last time we walked Sput. Plus, they've got little foxes on them," said C.J. defiantly.

The girls returned from the bathroom and Tabitha shyly presented Aeneas with a gift box inscribed 'Happy Solstice' and 'Merry Christmas' in gold lettering. Aeneas smiled and opened the box. Inside was a light brown sweater with leaves, acorns, and squirrels joined together around the neck in green, orange and gold.

"Tab, this is the coolest sweater. I can't believe you can knit like this!" Aeneas stood up and gave her a big hug. Sadie smiled excitedly at Tabitha, anticipating the next scene. She loved people watching, but this was even better. This was like a teen movie.

Aeneas took some time to admire the sweater. He asked about the pattern and type of yarn, which Sadie had to admit was pretty slick conversation for a teenage boy. Aeneas seemed genuinely interested in things Tabitha liked. Sadie supposed this was because they'd been childhood friends before they started dating. Finally, Aeneas reached into his backpack and handed Tabitha a red envelope. Tabitha opened the envelope and carefully pulled out a sheet of paper. A few seconds went by, and Tabitha's eyes were glued to whatever was printed on the page.

"What is it?" asked C.J. impatiently.

"What it *is*," cried Tabitha, "is freaking amazing! I love it, Aeneas!" squealed Tabitha, throwing her arms around him and planting a secret kiss on his neck. Aeneas blushed.

"Glad you like it, Tab."

"Well, what is it?" asked Sadie, who was trying to be cool but was becoming just as impatient as C.J.

"Five ski lessons at Snoqualmie Pass."

"You're coming too, right?" asked Tabitha.

Aeneas nodded. "Yep. Wouldn't miss it."

Sadie glanced at C.J. who was trying to conceal his dread. The last thing he wanted was to go skiing with Aeneas and Tabitha. She gave C.J. a sympathetic look, but he shrugged like he didn't care.

Aeneas wasted no time in grabbing the second red envelope. Sadie eyed the next scene warily. She thought Aeneas was about to blow whatever romantic points he'd scored with Tabitha.

C.J. gave Aeneas a weird look as he opened his envelope, wondering how to appear excited about ski lessons. Tabitha's face had gone slack, and Sadie found herself apprehensive about what was coming next.

But C.J. didn't pull out a paper. He pulled out two tickets.

"No way!" yelled C.J., startling Persephone and Eleanor out of their card game. "Are these real?" demanded C.J., panting hard, trying not to cry. This was the greatest gift anyone had ever given him!

"They're real, bro. Took some work, but I got 'em. The seats aren't great, but we're going." C.J. hugged Aeneas tightly, then started jumping around the living room.

"Who cares about the seats... who cares!! We are going to watch the Seahawks play the Rams in one week. Holy crap! HOLY CRAP!!" bellowed C.J.

"C.J.," barked Sakura from her cozy spot nestled in a chair with a bowl of Chanko Nabe. "Quiet down son and clean up your language."

Usually, C.J. submitted easily to his mother's reprimands, but he bulldozed past party guests and wagged the tickets in front of her.

"I can go, right, Mom?"

She smiled. "Yes, it's all been arranged."

"Finally!" yelled C.J. rushing back to hug Aeneas again, knocking a plate of someone's food onto the floor. Sput quickly darted over to tidy up. He always liked it when C.J. knocked over plates.

In the end, Tabitha loved her galoshes. Sadie was delighted to receive a lacy, blue cashmere knitted scarf, the same color as her eyes, and a vintage Neil Young album C.J. had proudly purchased in an online auction.

Aeneas was programming his bright green fitness watch from C.J. when Sadie left to get a bowl of stew and cookies. Once she was out of earshot C.J. spoke to him in earnest.

"These gifts they're... expensive. How could you afford them?"

"I got money saved up. Besides you and Tab... well, you've been helping me with my *project*, and I wanted to do something special for you both to show my appreciation."

Tabitha smiled. One thing she admired about Aeneas was his generosity. And she was secretly relieved he'd chosen activities that she and C.J. would both enjoy.

The grand finale, "O Christmas Tree," was sung by Martha, Sadie, and Seth. The trio came together along with Sakura on cello and Charlie on violin to give the partygoers a warm, cheery send-off. While Martha loved to celebrate the winter solstice, she liked her party to have a beginning and an end, so by ten-thirty, the house was empty again. She and George were briefly cleaning up what couldn't be left until morning.

Martha was putting away leftovers when George leaned against the kitchen counter and remarked thoughtfully, "I think Sadie's voice and performance seemed improved, even since Halloween. She's talented, that one."

Martha smiled. "She'll surprise us all."

CHAPTER 10

Aeneas Shifts Gerry

Late Summer, Alaska 2019

Bob North Sky mulled over how to introduce Gerry to Aeneas. Gerry was deeply suspicious of outsiders and rarely made a good impression when meeting new people.

"He will be gruff and standoffish," sighed Bob, mumbling to himself as his daughter, Sheila, opened the door to his log house, her arms loaded with containers of soup. She'd made a large pot of salmon chowder and brought him several portions.

"A good daughter always feeds her father well," said Bob, smiling.

Sheila laughed. "I heard you mumbling to yourself. Something on your mind, old man?" Bob had been sitting in his recliner staring out the window when she arrived.

"That boy from Seattle, you know the one I met on the trail. I have a good feeling about him, but he needs mentoring, or he could go astray."

"So, you train him up," said Sheila matter-of-factly, making her way to the kitchen.

Bob shrugged. "Gerry is making a fuss about it. He worries the boy will not respect our rules because he is not of our people."

"Isn't Gerry leaving soon to fish down south?" called Shelia from the kitchen.

Bob eased out of the recliner and stretched his aching hip.

"He'll been gone in a week with his brothers. He wants to meet the boy before they go."

Sheila returned to the living room with a knowing look and held up her pointer finger. This meant she had an idea, and her father was glad of it.

"Take the boy to him instead. When he's on the river, Gerry is like an old bear."

Bob let out a hard laugh. Sheila was right about that. Gerry was distracted when the salmon were running, especially along the Kenai. "Less fish for the tourists," he would cackle maniacally.

~

Aeneas fidgeted nervously waiting for Bob to arrive; he'd been staying in a spare bedroom at Sheila's house. She had kindly made him a big breakfast, but the pancakes and bacon were souring in his stomach. Bob was going to introduce him to an important time traveler, his friend Stick. But Bob had said to call him "Mr. Gerry."

Aeneas and Bob were heading south to the Kenai Peninsula where Gerry and his brothers had a fishing camp. Aeneas tossed his gear in the back of Bob's pickup truck and hopped in the front seat.

Bob pounded him on the back and smiled. "Don't worry. Just be yourself."

Aeneas smiled back weakly. "I'm never myself. I have this big secret that I can't tell anyone about. Even my parents don't know."

Bob gave him a sympathetic look. Seeing as how Aeneas had no family to guide him, Bob felt it was his duty. But whether he liked it or not, Gerry's approval would make the process easier.

A few hours later, Bob eased his pickup into a gravel roundabout. Cell service was spotty here and Bob had no plans to call ahead anyway. Best to just show up. Shelia had baked three white fish pies for him to bring along with two quarts of duck soup. They were Gerry's favorites.

"Hey, hey, brothers," called Bob. Aeneas had slept most of the way with his face pressed against the window. Groggy, he got of the truck and started unloading Bob's gear. He felt it was best to keep a low profile until Bob was ready to introduce him.

The camp was an old A-frame cabin with four picnic tables out front loaded with buckets, knives, a long chopping board and an old tackle box. Bob strode up to the door, peeked in and said, "Any fisherman in here?" But the cabin was quiet.

Bob motioned Aeneas.

"Bring in the cooler. We will unpack our food, then head down to the river." Aeneas and Bob unloaded the truck and repacked their fishing gear into a tackle pack. Then the pair walked down the trail to the Upper Kenai River. Bob smiled as they ambled along. In his old age, it was good to have a tall muscular young man to carry his things. Plus, the boy never complained and never seemed to tire. He was always respectful and kind. Bob hoped Gerry would see these good qualities.

An uproar reached their ears before they reached the river. Aeneas sprinted off, leaving Bob to quicken his pace as best he could. When he reached the riverbank, the scene was grim. Gerry's brothers were on the shore whooping and waving their arms trying to get the attention of a large male grizzly who was fishing near their capsized boat. Gerry was atop the boat, frantic.

Aeneas eyed the situation. He had little experience with bears, but it was obvious the guy on top of the capsized boat was in trouble and no one could reach him.

"What can I do to help?" cried out Aeneas, dropping the tackle pack. Gerry's two brothers, Reg and Russ, turned around surprised. Reg gave him a quizzical look.

"Who are you?"

"I'm with Bob," replied Aeneas motioning behind him. Bob hurried toward them and winced. This wasn't exactly the meet and greet he'd hoped for.

"Get me out of here!" squawked Gerry loudly. The boat would shift off the shoal into the main current soon and he wasn't about to hop off and swim to shore with a big griz feeding a few feet away. Bob, Reg, and Russ huddled up, conferring.

"Best to let the boat float away from the bear," said Reg.

"What if we lose the boat and Stick falls in the river?" bleated Russ.

"Stick can swim. Tell him to hop off and enter the current. One of the tourists will throw him a line," assured Bob, adding, "then we go back for the boat once the bear moves on."

Keeping an eye on the bear, Aeneas skirted the riverbank until he reached the shallows downriver from the capsized boat. A deep swirling vortex of water backed by two large boulders was between him and the trapped boat. Aeneas waded out to the boulders, found a foothold, and climbed on top of the flattest rock. He focused on the spot next to Gerry and gracefully leaped onto the hull of the boat.

"Who the hell are you?" yelped Gerry, who had been focused on the huddle happening onshore.

"I think I can get you out of here," replied Aeneas breathlessly. The bear huffed and cast a glance in his direction. The hair on Aeneas's forearms tingled.

"Get off the boat, you idiot," demanded Gerry. "You are pissing off the bear!"

Bob called out to Aeneas anxiously, "What are you doing, boy?"

"He is going to get himself and Gerry drowned," yelled Reg, running toward the shallows where Aeneas had entered the river.

The bear huffed again and that was all the warning Aeneas needed. Before he could protest, Aeneas locked his muscled forearm around Gerry's waist, which was awkward given how skinny he was, and made a leap for the shore. They cleared the boulders but missed the riverbank, landing in the shallows. All in all, Bob estimated Aeneas had leapt twelve feet with Gerry in tow.

Reg waded in and quickly grabbed his brother, hauling him ashore as the bear grunted loudly and scratched himself against the side of the boat, releasing it into the main current.

"What about my boat?" hollered Russ as the craft headed downstream.

"Who cares about your damn boat," spluttered Gerry. "Who in the hell is this boy? Is he part of the Olympic long jump team?"

Aeneas, coughing and spitting, hurriedly sloshed ashore and flopped next to Gerry who was sprawled on the riverbank struggling to remove his waders. Reaching out a wet hand he smiled broadly. "Aeneas Entwistle, from Seattle. I'm very pleased to *finally* meet you, Mr. Gerry."

Bob suppressed a chuckle. "I told you about him, Stick," crowed Bob cheerfully.

Gerry gave Bob a cold stare. "Yeah, you did," grumbled Gerry, taking Aeneas's hand, and giving it a hard squeeze.

Bob eyed the pair with amusement. There was no going back now. The boy from Seattle had saved him; and Gerry, despite his gruff exterior, always paid his debts.

CHAPTER 11

Under Fed, Under Pressure

Spring 2053

TABITHA SCOOTED IN NEXT to C.J. with a little more force than was necessary, and faced her husband, who was recovering from weeks of living homeless.

"For years I've wondered if it was possible to go back in time and save a life. But you've always been adamant to leave events as they unfold, so I haven't asked you about saving Sadie. But Aeneas, you were saved!" cried Tabitha, slapping her hand on the table, jostling the silverware.

Then she leaned in and whispered, "And if what I'm hearing from Cassie is true, before you left, Nia never existed, and Harold never married Meg."

Aeneas paled. "She told you?"

"I called last night after her abrupt departure to C.J.'s cabin. She confessed she was struggling coming to terms with all the changes!"

C.J. dropped his fork with a clang. "Is this true? Did all these things change?"

Aeneas went to scratch the beard he'd had for weeks and realized it was gone. He looked to each of them, both still his best friends. He had no answers. Nothing this big had happened before, even when he'd screwed up a few times before Bob North Sky took him on as an apprentice.

"I've got a long list of questions that Lux and I will begin working on for the next few months, perhaps even years, but I don't have any definitive answers. I know Cassie and I can sense the changes, but I'm not sure why you don't. It's been worrying me ever since I came back."

"Nia was never born before Cassie went back?" said C.J, stunned. "That's a whole other life that didn't exist before Cassie went back. Does Socrates know?"

Aeneas nodded. "Cassie told him."

C.J. downed his coffee and politely indicated to the server he'd like another cup. Without missing a beat, he abruptly turned to Tabitha, leaning in close. "What you're asking could change the present, Tab. Your own life could be upended. Cassie popped back to 2015, met up with Harold and Socrates, and Nia is born, and Harold married Meg. And none of us knew any different because that's how it's always been for us. You see how risky what you're asking is?"

Tabitha waved her hand dismissively at this idea, an adolescent gesture that still annoyed C.J., and replied, "He could at least find out what happened to her. It's a small thing to ask after all these other changes have happened."

Keeping his voice low, trying to control his outrage, C.J. retorted, "You're asking him to go back and watch her die? Then what? He's seen this devastating event and comes back with PTSD or who knows what psychological trauma!"

Aeneas tapped C.J. on the hand reassuringly. "I'm here, bro. I'm okay."

The strain of his disappearance had been hard on him, too, and Aeneas could tell that C.J. was feeling protective.

Tabitha placed her hand on top of theirs. Her tears came easily. She whispered, "They never found her body. What if..."

"What if she didn't die, has amnesia, and is living somewhere in California in a mental institution?" C.J. finished her sentence, the same scenario he'd heard teenage Tabitha expound on for years. *The what-if scenario.*

Aeneas kicked C.J. under the table and shot him a warning look.

He leaned over and kissed Tabitha's forehead and said gently, "Tab, Sadie's death was painful for all of us. I'm not sure knowing what happened will make it more bearable."

Tabitha sighed, wiped her tears, grabbed a sausage link off C.J.'s plate, and stood up to leave, her grief shifting to anger.

"I guess you two would like to continue catching up. Wish Sadie and I could have breakfast together sometime," she said coldly. It was an underhanded comment, but C.J. didn't go for it. He knew when Tabitha was trying to wind him up.

"And I suppose you might like to go get your own breakfast," remarked C.J. peevishly. Tabitha rolled her eyes as she walked away. Aeneas watched her go, unsure if her parting shot was directed at C.J. or meant to guilt him into accepting her request.

C.J. finished his cold pancakes, but Aeneas had gone quiet, save for the tapping under the table. The foot tapping would normally annoy just about anyone, but C.J. knew his best friend only tapped his foot when he was grappling with a problem. Aeneas flagged the server and asked if there were any cinnamon rolls left.

"A cinnamon roll plus an omelet with hash browns and sausage gravy, and my fruit cup!" exclaimed C.J. in disbelief.

"Bro, I need to restore my physique after all those lean weeks. Besides, you know the only thing to really satisfy me is pastry," said Aeneas patting his belly.

C.J. leaned across the table, lowering his voice. "Would you be able to go back and watch what happened to Sadie? You'd feel obligated to save her. Look at what happened when Cassie simply visited 2015. I still can't believe Nia was never born!" C.J. shut his eyes and placed his forehead on his palm.

Aeneas gave a faint nod and rested his hands on his chin. It was a big ask and one that he would likely decline. There was no way he'd be able to watch Sadie be swept out to sea, if that was what happened.

"Aeneas, this thing you can do... it's been my life, too," said C.J. quietly.

"I know, bro, but it's hard to say no to someone you love. You heard her. She's missed out on a life with Sadie and now she thinks I can give that back to her."

CHAPTER 12

Aeneas Has a Change of Heart

Spring 2053

A FEW DAYS LATER, Aeneas sat on a bench at Hamilton Viewpoint Park and gazed across the bay, studying the city. The Space Needle, an icon of Seattle, still marked the skyline, but the Great Wheel had been moved after an earthquake in 2032 and now resided in Magnuson Park. The ferries, still running on their same schedule, were filled with people and bicycles now that fewer cars clogged the roads. Large areas of Seattle had been reconfigured to maximize pedestrian access to green spaces, modeled after Barcelona's superblocks. The conversion had been completed in 2035 and the city was populated with more families than ever before. Seattle streets still bustled with pedestrians, public transit, and electric self-driving vehicles of all kinds, but fewer cars meant the city was quieter and cleaner.

Aeneas was pleased that he and Tabitha had stayed in West Seattle. His childhood was the best of both worlds and he'd been happy to give that to Cassie, Lux, and Tor, too. And that thought made him gasp for air, nearly causing a panic attack. This family he had made with Tabitha, the life they had built together that allowed him to be who he really was, could not be gambled away, despite the goodness of the deed.

"I love you, Tab, more than anything," whispered Aeneas to himself, "but I don't want our life to change if I go back for Sadie." Aeneas stood, grabbed his bike, and took one last look across the bay. A voice in his head wondered if he might be able to give Sadie back to Tabitha, but then he remembered the warnings Bob North Sky had seared in his brain when he was just a young man about resurrecting the dead. He couldn't reconcile either because Tabitha's plea and Bob's warnings were playing tug of war in his psyche. He was pedaling toward home when he suddenly detoured to C.J.'s house.

~

While Tabitha and Aeneas had torn down a decaying old home and built a new one on their lot, C.J. moved into his parent's home when they retired to Sequim. Aeneas parked his bike and knocked at the door. He'd been surprised when C.J. wanted to work as a freelance architect but, he surmised, those wily Willoughby genes could not be completely denied. C.J. took on projects he liked, such as earthquake-resistant home designs similar to the one he'd devised for Tabitha and Aeneas. He was his own boss, and in the early days, he might be gone for months at a time working on projects all over the world. Aeneas had been surprised at his willingness to accept the uncertainty of irregular employment, given how C.J. liked to have his life plans secured well in advance.

C.J.'s schedule slowed down when he met Lyla. She was a cellist, just like his mother, Sakura. However, she had an essence of Aeneas's own mother, Miranda, an observation that Tabitha spent weeks analyzing after she met Lyla for the first time. Though Lyla wasn't a mirror image of Miranda, like his daughter Cassie, she was a biracial beauty with hazel eyes and a dazzling smile. Tabitha admitted, after spending more time with Lyla, that she could see the attraction. She was easygoing and fun, whereas C.J. still retained his seriousness.

Aeneas reached in his pocket and pulled out a small, clear rectangular device, his SAIL. On this particular SAIL was stored every piece of information about his life. He'd recorded Tabitha making breakfast that morning, and a conversation he had yesterday with Tor who was touring with his band in Japan. He blueprinted every piece of information from his existence—financial information, medical records, research projects, even the book he was reading. Coming back from his past to find so much changed surprised Aeneas, even though he'd always hypothesized that the smallest shifts in the past could create an entirely different present. Still, Nia had been born and Harold had gotten married. Those were not tiny shifts. And yet he could also recall the before—when there was no Nia; when Harold had never married.

Aeneas stowed his bike just inside the front door as C.J. motioned him into the house. A hologram of C.J.'s son, Ryan, paced along with them. Ryan and C.J. were just wrapping up a discussion about a family reunion that his mother Sakura was planning. Ryan Jones Willoughby, not ever known as R.J., but just Ryan, was an only child whose name C.J. decided would be the least unusual thing about him.

Aeneas sat down on the couch and fiddled with his SAIL. In his mind, he knew going back to discover how Sadie actually died was risky at best, but the voice in his head kept at him, the voice that said why not at least resolve this mystery for Tabitha, give her some peace of mind?

C.J. came back with a bowl of his special mix—pretzels, macadamia nuts, spicy rice crackers, and seaweed snacks—and handed Aeneas a kombucha.

He grabbed a handful of the mix, munched on it, swallowed, and cleared his throat, all the while never breaking eye contact with Aeneas. He had a feeling something was coming that he wasn't going to like. He'd been worried since that morning at the bistro that Aeneas might have a change of heart and do something risky; it had happened before when they were young. "I think whatever you are here to talk to me about is a bad idea."

Aeneas hung his head, still struggling with what he thought was his duty to his wife and his adherence to the careful set of rules Bob North Sky had given him.

"Bro, a whole other person was born and Harold has a wife! When we came back to our present, all that stuff just filed into my brain like someone overlaid an entire new reality over the old one."

C.J. tossed out a question he'd never had a chance to ask but thought rather important. "Have you ever wondered why your rescue from the past impacted whether Harold married or not?"

Aeneas grabbed a handful of mix and threw a few pieces in his mouth. "Maybe Cassie hinted to him that he was unmarried in the future, so he decided he wanted a wife."

C.J. turned his head, stifling a chuckle. "I think you may be overlooking the obvious. Besides, Cassie would know better than to reveal something like that."

Aeneas made a *pfft* noise and waved his free hand (the other was holding snacks) at C.J. "Bro, Harold would know in the future that he would be an old man and she'd be a young woman."

C.J. gave him a thumbs-up as he drained his kombucha. Exhaling, he responded, "You're right. Simple as one, two, three."

Aeneas narrowed his eyes and spoke in an uncharacteristically formal tone, "You're terrible at concealing your patronizing disdain for my opinion."

C.J. chuckled at this impression of himself, as Aeneas placed the SAIL nearby to record.

"In case I decide to go, I want to document my life on the SAIL. For whatever reason, the data collected isn't impacted in the timestream. And if something is changed, at least I have proof."

C.J. sat diagonally across from Aeneas. He knew this was a bad idea from start to finish. But he reasoned that maybe if

Aeneas thought about the life he might lose it would become more obvious how ridiculous and dangerous this scheme of Tabitha's really was.

Aeneas sat up and gazed into the holographic lens. "I'm happily married with three great kids. My son, Lux, works for me while he attends college, and we research genetic markers associated with time travel. My other son, Tor, is a musician and inventor and is currently on tour in Japan. My daughter, Cassie, is an accomplished time traveler. She works as the public relations director for Harold Torkelson's foundation that supports sustainable industries, and often partners with my sister, Persephone, a famous eco-engineer. My wife, Tabitha, owns her own counseling business and is consulted worldwide as a strategist in supporting egalitarian work environments." Aeneas paused and took a breath. He was shaking.

The SAIL kept recording as C.J. leaned over and whispered, "You alright? This is upsetting you, isn't it?" And he meant it to sting.

"You're damn right it is," snapped Aeneas. "Too much has changed because of Cassie going back to find me after the earthquake. She went back twice and in those brief visits, a new human being was born, and a marriage was forged. These are enormous differences that never existed before she left." Aeneas shook his head, still in disbelief. C.J. stood up and paced about. He was fuming.

"This is asking too much of you. Tab has no idea what the consequences could be. She is only thinking of her *own* pain, which is ironic given her profession."

C.J.'s tone was harsh, but Aeneas knew he was right, only he couldn't say no to her. Aeneas mumbled something and crumpled. C.J. walked over and patted his back.

"I didn't catch that. What'd you say?"

"I said she almost died."

C.J. looked out the window, then returned his gaze to Aeneas. "But she didn't die, and the twins were fine. There were a couple of scary minutes before the boys were born and we were all ushered from the room except you, but everything worked out. You don't owe Tabitha anything," said C.J. with finality.

"I do, though. She didn't want another baby. Tabitha was happy with just Cassie. It was me who insisted we have another. The look on her face when the scan revealed two babies..."

C.J. walked back to his chair and sat down with a sigh. They all knew Tabitha was shaken up by the idea of having twins, but once they were born, she loved them heart and soul, especially their genius quirks. Aeneas's reasoning wasn't sound and C.J. went right at him without a second thought. His friend needed the truth behind his own motivations.

"So, you're going through with this because *you* feel guilty?"

"Maybe?" said Aeneas, fighting back emotion.

"So, you're proceeding with this risky scheme because of three minutes in your marriage when things got a little scary?"

Aeneas had the decency to look sheepish. "Well, when you roll it out like that, I do sound pathetic."

C.J.'s face morphed into his I've-now-stated-the-obvious configuration of one eyebrow up and the merest smirk.

"Just help me finish the recording, bro," pleaded Aeneas.

C.J. settled back into his chair and asked the next question. "Aeneas, why are you traveling back to 2016?"

Aeneas's face changed, replacing a neutral countenance with one of sadness. "Sadie Willoughby died in early spring of 2016. The Coast Guard investigation concluded she was washed away by a rogue wave resulting from an offshore earthquake. After a long search, Sadie's body was not recovered and even to this day, her remains have never been found."

It was quiet except for the faint sound of Lyla's cello playing a sad melody. C.J. broke the silence. "Are you planning to save her?"

Aeneas didn't pause to think before he answered. "No. It could alter the course of many peoples' futures. I'm only going to witness the event so I can put an end to any speculation about what happened. For Tabitha."

This response puzzled C.J. because it sounded too practiced, so his next question was meant to be sharp. "So, why are we recording every detail of your life if you have no intention of altering the past?"

That hit him right in the solar plexus. Aeneas groaned, "Save her? Don't save her? I have no idea what I'll do!" His face contorted in anguish as he folded in half, his head resting on his knees.

"Look, if I tell you this... well, I guess we're recording it anyway," said Aeneas as he sat up wearily.

C.J. stayed quiet. Whatever it was, Aeneas would get to it when he was ready. He carefully removed his glasses, cleaning the lenses and returning them back to his face. A few minutes later, Aeneas began to speak.

"I'd wanted to go back and save her for years, but I never discussed it with Tabitha. When I brought it up to Bob North Sky, his eyes teared up and he told me the story of his brother."

C.J. continued to wait. Aeneas cocked his head. "It was short, bro. I've never forgotten it."

My brother was killed in the Vietnam War when I was a young boy. My whole life I wanted to go back and save him, but our shaman, Soaring Hawk, told me that the river of time was not for my own use. It was a gift from our creator so that we could watch over our people and the consequences of bringing someone back from the dead could lead to the greatest of unhappiness for those who attempt it.

CHAPTER 13

Dancing Dilemma Smackdown

Spring 2016

SPRING ARRIVED IN TRUE Pacific Northwest fashion. The occasional bright sunny day with blooming daffodils and budding trees was followed by three rainy days with whipping winds. Aeneas was hanging out with Everett—his teammate and former rival for Tabitha's affection—at Hiawatha Playfield on one of those sunny days, laughing and messing about without the formality of team practice, shooting free kicks while the other tried to block.

Aeneas had texted C.J. to join them at the park. It was Sunday afternoon and time for Sput to go to C.J.'s house for a few days. The dog-share schedule was informal, but each of them had Sput on a weekend day and part of the week. Sput never seemed to mind going between homes as there were things to appreciate at each place. At the Entwistle home, Harold was quite liberal with samples when he cooked, always including Sput in his taste tests. Aeneas took him for early morning runs and Persephone secretly spent time teaching Sput new words, few of which he learned, but reveled in the peanut butter treats she used to reward him. At the Willoughby home, Sput was able to exercise his musical talents as he was an aficionado of Bollywood music. He'd also become quite attached to Sakura, who in her seventh month of pregnancy had Sput as her constant companion. "He knows the baby is coming soon, Mom," said C.J. proudly. While Sakura had been slow to warm to Sput, she now found his company quite soothing as they napped together in the afternoons. They'd also been known to share the occasional pint of salted caramel ice cream.

Everett, Aeneas, and C.J. headed to their respective homes as the sunlight waned, walking together for a few blocks, with Sput leading the way.

Everett was excited. He had big news. "Hey, so are you and Tabitha going to the spring formal together?" asked Everett eagerly.

"Yeah, I guess so," said Aeneas haltingly. Until Everett mentioned it, Aeneas had completely forgotten there was a spring formal at his school.

Everett gave a nod. "Cool. I've asked Bethany Purvine and she said yes, so we could double."

"Sure," said Aeneas, cutting a sideways glance at C.J. who was listening intently to their conversation. He kept quiet so as not to embarrass his best friend, but C.J. knew two things that were significant impediments to this double date idea.

First, he had tried to teach Aeneas to dance last year—tried being the operative word—and second, Aeneas hadn't even asked Tabitha to the spring formal. As Everett turned to go down his street, he called back to Aeneas, "We'll sort out details later, Entwistle. See ya, C.J."

"Bye, Everett," yelled C.J. who always felt he needed to be louder around Everett who was very tall and had a personality to match his size.

Aeneas and C.J. walked along in silence. C.J. felt he had to say something. He was pretty sure the spring formal was only two weeks away.

"I think you should talk to Socrates about this as soon as you get home. He's bound to have some ideas," said C.J. sympathetically.

~

That evening the family was gathered around a fragrant dish of pasta primavera, with sautéed vegetables in a cream sauce and homemade linguine noodles. It was Harold's ode to spring as well as his weekly requested vegetarian meal. Aeneas was busy twirling linguine around his fork when his mother interrupted his love affair with the pasta, startling him back to reality.

"Aeneas, are you and Tabitha going to the spring formal? I received some information about it in the weekly parent email from your school."

Miranda looked at her middle son earnestly and waited for an answer. Persephone noticed the reddish color creeping up his face.

DANCING DILEMMA SMACKDOWN

"Yeah, I guess so." Aeneas stopped twirling his pasta. He might as well ask his mom now since she brought it up.

"I might need some new clothes," announced Aeneas shyly.

"We can go shopping this weekend and find you something snazzy," said Archie pointing at his middle son, "and you will look hot."

"Dad, you aren't supposed to refer to your offspring as 'hot,'" interjected Socrates sternly. A look of exasperation passed between his sons.

"And nobody says snazzy anymore, Dad," added Aeneas with snort.

"Your father is just excited for Aeneas's first school dance," chided Miranda. At this break in the conversation, Persephone decided to ask the question in her mind most pertinent to the situation.

"Excuse me, Mommy."

Miranda turned her attention to her youngest as Persephone continued matter-of-factly, "How will Aeneas be able to attend the formal without embarrassing himself and Tabitha? His dancing is rudimentary, unlike me and Socrates, who are excellent dancers. Remember, you said Aeneas inherited his dancing genes from Dad?"

While Persephone waited patiently for her mother's response, Archie puffed up, exclaiming, "I *am* an excellent dancer! Your mom loves to dance with me, right, Miranda?"

Miranda never responded to his challenge, instead fixing her gaze on her daughter in such a way as it had never been before. Her eyes bored into Persephone's, and Socrates discreetly nudged his brother.

Persephone, being the youngest, was normally exempt from their mother's criticism, but it appeared, in this moment, she'd surpassed that level altogether. Socrates mouthed to Aeneas, "smackdown." All was silent at the Entwistle dinner table as Miranda locked eyes with Persephone. Archie leaned toward his wife expectantly waiting for her to confirm he was, in fact, a good dancer. The boys dug into their plates and Aeneas smiled to himself just a little. While he was embarrassed that his dance moves were, as his sister said, rudimentary, it appeared that young Seph was about to get a real piece of their mother's mind and that cheered him immensely.

CHAPTER 14

Aeneas Attempts an Overture

Spring 2016

AENEAS KNOCKED ON SOCRATES'S bedroom door and waited. It was a family rule their parents insisted be respected. Knock and wait. So, he waited. A few moments passed, then Sox opened the door. He'd been expecting his younger brother after the remarks made at dinner. No words passed between them. Aeneas plopped onto the computer chair adjacent to Socrates's multi-screen panels. Socrates raised an eyebrow expectantly.

Aeneas was in agony but tried not to let too much emotion escape. There was only so much humiliation he could take in one night from his siblings.

"I haven't even asked Tabitha and the spring formal is less than two weeks away. Everett assumed I'd asked her and invited us to double."

Aeneas squeezed his temples. Socrates grinned at his little brother.

"Aeneas, you have nearly two whole weeks. I once asked a girl to be my date two days before a dance," boasted Socrates, clapping him on the back.

"Yeah, but that's you!" Aeneas scoffed at his brother. "You've got slick dance moves and you're... you're experienced at dating. It's easy for me with Tabitha because I don't have to be somebody I'm not, but this formal... My dancing *is* rudimentary. You heard Seph, and mom didn't disagree, did she?" squawked Aeneas.

"No, but the look she gave Seph was epic," chuckled Socrates.

Aeneas's face relaxed and he laughed too. "She's no longer exempt from the smackdown. Did Mom ever say anything?"

"Not within my earshot, but she asked Seph to help her wash the dishes and afterward little sister was teary-eyed. Mom took her down a few pegs, as Dad would say."

Socrates let out another chuckle that lasted a full minute by which time he was wiping his eyes. He'd laughed so hard he'd cried.

"Seriously, bro, have you got it in for Seph?" Aeneas didn't quite understand the extent of Socrates's humor at the situation.

"Nah. I'm just relieved she's on the radar instead of me," sighed Socrates, reminiscing.

"You're more sensitive, Aeneas," said Socrates, squeezing his brother's shoulder affectionately.

"You haven't gotten many smackdowns, not like me."

Aeneas rolled his eyes. His siblings were occasionally tact-less. Socrates returned to his advice-giving as he reached into his wallet and handed Aeneas a ten-dollar bill.

"Go to PCC Market—they're still open. Buy a small bouquet of flowers. Hand Tabitha the bouquet first and ask her if she would like to accompany you to the eighth-grade spring formal as your date. Don't say 'go' because that's not the best term. Say *accompany* and use the word *date*. No slang. Make your invita-tion sound prepared."

Aeneas was wide-eyed at these instructions. Socrates rat-tled them off like an expert. He was so relieved that he grabbed the money, gave Socrates a quick fist bump, and hustled down the stairs.

Later that evening as he knocked on the Willoughbys' door, Aeneas started to get nervous. This was all second nature for someone like Socrates who had the magnetism to pull off a romantic overture. At least that was the term C.J. used when he texted him on the way to the market, "a *romantic overture* is a great idea." Aeneas started to sweat. He heard footsteps at the door and realized he should have texted Tabitha that he was coming over, so she'd be more likely to answer the door. When the door swung open, George raised an eyebrow, gave Aeneas a nod of recognition, said, "Just a moment," and closed the door.

About thirty seconds passed and the door swung open again. This time it was Tabitha. Her smile grew as she noticed the bouquet. Aeneas smiled back, took a breath, and held out the flowers, "Tabitha, would you accompany me to the spring formal as my date?" That was it. One sentence and he got it off without any fumbling. Now all he had to do was wait. Tabitha took the flowers and said teasingly, "Aeneas, this is really sweet, but I was hoping to go with my boyfriend."

Aeneas grinned and stepped in closer. He placed his arm around her waist and whispered in her ear, "We don't have to tell him."

Tabitha whispered back in his other ear, "I'll let him down easy."

~

C.J. looked down at the text message from Aeneas with dread.

Bro, can you give me more dance lessons? I need to learn some moves before the spring formal.

C.J. groaned and his mother, Sakura, looked up from her book. She and C.J. were in the living room reading their respective novels.

"What's the matter, son?" asked Sakura, yawning. There was only seven weeks until a new baby would be born, a surprise baby.

"Aeneas wants more dance lessons," said C.J. with another groan. Sakura looked at him for a moment then dispensed her advice; she found that her pregnancy brain was either spot on or way off, and today it was on.

"Find another person to give him lessons. That way you can support rather than instruct."

C.J. blinked then cried out enthusiastically, "Mom! That's a great idea. I have a few people in mind already."

In two steps, C.J. had made his way to the recliner where Sakura sat cuddled with her book and kissed the top of her head.

"Mom, you give excellent advice."

Sakura teared up and waved him away. C.J. had seemed ambivalent, even standoffish when he found out a new sibling was coming to their family, so the kiss meant a lot. She made a mental note to tell Charlie when he came home from rehearsal.

Meanwhile, Aeneas hunkered down in his room searching YouTube videos looking for a dance style that he felt comfortable to practice. He scrolled through dozens of video clips. Nothing popped up that he felt he could attempt. He leaned back on his bean bag and looked up at the poster of his soccer idol, Clint Dempsey.

"Clint, your bro here needs some advice. Where can I find dance moves that are simple, but... will look cool to my girl-friend? Spring formal is in less than two weeks, Clint." All was silent as Aeneas gave Clint a long stare, willing him to speak.

Then from nowhere a deep voice yelled, "Try the Uptown Funk video!" Aeneas scrambled up from his bean bag. He looked around his room, back at the poster of Clint Dempsey, dashed toward his door and threw it open. No one was there. *Some practical joke*, thought Aeneas as he shot into the hall to find the culprit, but the hallway was empty. Socrates wasn't home. Aeneas quietly tiptoed to his sister's room and peeked through the keyhole. She was reading an ecology textbook and eating a bag of pretzels. Aeneas shrugged. It wasn't the weirdest thing that ever happened to him.

"Maybe," he whispered, "I imagined the whole thing."

Aeneas went back to his bedroom and loaded the Uptown Funk video. He watched it all the way through, feeling relieved.

"You know, Clint, Bruno has some smooth moves. They aren't too complicated either."

Aeneas propped the video in front of him while he mimicked Bruno's footwork. He liked this song; the rhythm was easy for him to follow. Aeneas had worked through the video several times when, unbeknownst to him, his bedroom door opened. C.J. watched Aeneas for thirty seconds and decided it wasn't hopeless. But there was serious work to be done before the formal. He'd already contacted Jesús Catalina, a tenth grader who specialized in rehabilitating the choreographically challenged. C.J. had texted Jesús and paid him twenty dollars for Aeneas's first lesson. They could squeeze it in on Saturday between soccer games, but as C.J. would soon tell Aeneas, sacrifices had to be made for the greater good.

Jesús to the Rescue

Spring 2016

JESÚS CATALINA MADE EXTRA money giving secret dance lessons, and he was extremely popular because his services were discreet. He helped those with real need, teens who required extra support on the dance floor before a big event. Spring was his busy season and he worked non-stop, occasionally in between his own soccer games. His practice location was an enclosed old garage with walnut flooring that he acquired through a barter agreement, trading a weekly chicken coop cleaning for unlimited use. Working in old Mrs. Monetquin's enclosed garage gave him the privacy he needed, especially since his own house was infested with little sisters who wanted to watch the lessons.

"You paid how much to Jesús Catalina?" yelped Aeneas, shaking his head in disbelief.

"Calm down. He charges an extra ten bucks for emergency services. And yours is a real emergency," said C.J. standing his ground.

Aeneas deflated. "I was just practicing and I've gotten a few nice moves from Bruno." Aeneas demonstrated his snap, step, head bob improvisation he'd mimicked from the Uptown Funk video.

"I saw you when I walked in and you've definitely improved, but given the time crunch, I thought it was best to call in a professional."

He reached up and awkwardly placed a hand on Aeneas's shoulder. "Let this guy help you," urged C.J. "The dance will be here before you know it."

Aeneas flopped into his bean bag and C.J. sat on his bed. Neither said anything for a minute. Finally, C.J. broke the silence.

"This will be a big deal for Tabitha. Girls get really excited about this stuff. I know for a fact she is having her dress custom-made by a friend of Aunt Martha's."

"C.J.," sputtered Aeneas, as he backpedaled out of his bean bag. "What am I supposed to wear?"

Aeneas looked petrified and C.J. realized it was time to step up and take Aeneas in hand before he became unhinged by this whole experience. *Besides,* thought C.J., *at least I'll have some practice before my first formal dance.*

"Aren't your parents taking you shopping for something to wear?"

"They are," mumbled Aeneas, who'd started bouncing his miniature soccer ball off his knees to soothe his nerves.

"So, do you want me to come along to help pick out the clothes?"

Aeneas bungled the ball, and it went rolling across his room. "Yeah. That would make me feel much better about this shopping trip. I was worried I'd end up in some fancy suit and look ridiculous."

"Oh, you definitely would!" C.J. hooted with laughter.

Aeneas caught up with the soccer ball and sent it hurling toward C.J.'s head as he called out, "It's a date, bro."

~

It was the Saturday before the spring formal. C.J. had texted Jesús and told him Aeneas would be biking from Walt Hundley Field in between soccer matches.

Aeneas walked in shyly. The garage was bare except for a few folding chairs, two stand-alone vertical mirrors and some speakers. Jesús was sitting on the floor, texting furiously when Aeneas walked in. He gave him a nod and held up one finger. Aeneas hung his backpack on a hook and waited.

"Sorry, man," said Jesús as he walked over and shook Aeneas's hand. "Super busy right now with so many formals and weddings coming up."

"Thanks for working me in," said Aeneas. He looked around the garage uncomfortably.

"I hear you have a formal next weekend," said Jesús as he opened two of the folding chairs and motioned for Aeneas to have a seat.

"Yeah. I've practiced a little, but my buddy thinks I could use some extra help." Aeneas shifted in his chair and let out a sigh, a familiar sound of many of Jesús's clients before they received their lesson.

"Hey, man, relax. This will be painless," chuckled Jesús. "Given the time crunch, we need passable dancing, not perfect dancing. Can we agree on that?"

Aeneas nodded vigorously, relieved that Jesús understood his predicament.

"So, C.J. told me you've been practicing. I downloaded your song, just to see where you are. Don't be shy. All the blinds are closed. Show me what you've been working on so far."

"Uptown Funk" came blasting out of the speakers and Aeneas started his side steps and head bob. Jesús smiled and joined him, and they moved back and forth together.

"You've got a nice rhythm," commented Jesús, clapping him on the shoulder. Jesús had an older brotherly vibe about him that put Aeneas at ease. They worked through the whole song. Jesús added some moves that weren't in the video. Aeneas followed along and started to have fun. They played the song one more time and Aeneas learned a spin and some hip moves from Jesús.

"Nice to see you smiling," grinned Jesús, high-fiving Aeneas.

"Before we try another song, just some man-to-man info for your upcoming dance." Jesús motioned to the chair, and they sat down again.

"So, girls care less about *how* you dance and more about *will* you dance," said Jesús. Aeneas nodded, taking it all in to share later with C.J.

"I checked around and I know for a fact that the DJ will be playing the new Timberlake song at your formal. Good news is that anyone can dance to it. This is what we'll practice next."

Aeneas stood, blew out another long breath, this time of relief, grateful that C.J. had been right about Jesús. This guy did his homework and was proving extremely helpful.

"Can't Stop this Feeling" came on and Aeneas started the moves he learned while Jesús mirrored alongside him. Suddenly, Jesús grabbed his hands and Aeneas stiffened.

"Relax, man. This is a song where you can do some mixed dancing with your date. Follow along. No one can see us."

Aeneas and Jesús held hands and rocked from side to side. Jesús, who was a bit shorter of the two said, "Twirl me, man." Aeneas hesitated for a moment, moved in closer and twirled Jesús awkwardly.

"That's it! Now, let's break apart and do some of our own moves, then try the mixed dancing one more time."

As the song continued, Aeneas practiced with Jesús moving forward and backward so he could change position on the dance floor. Jesús stepped in again and grabbed his hands. This time Aeneas didn't hesitate.

"You've got it, man. Now let's—" but before he could finish Aeneas twirled Jesús with slightly better form and they continued dancing.

"Right on, man. Your date will love this!"

C.J. had slipped in and was watching inside the doorway. He couldn't believe what he was seeing. Not only could Aeneas dance, but he could also dance with another person. He nodded appreciatively. *Money well spent*, he thought to himself.

As the song ended, Aeneas noticed C.J. in the corner by the door.

"Bro!" he yelled, running toward him, wrapping C.J. in a huge hug as Jesús started to laugh.

"Thank you, C.J.!" Aeneas whispered. C.J. could hear the emotion behind it and knew finding Jesús to help Aeneas was a big deal.

"Hey, Aeneas. I'd like to meet with you…" Jesús grabbed his phone and quickly scanned his calendar, "on Thursday at six-thirty. Will that work? We need to recap these moves and practice some slow dancing."

Aeneas beamed. "Sure, Jesús." Aeneas had soccer practice until seven, but he'd figure it out. These dance lessons were a priority.

CHAPTER 16

Formal
Preparations

Spring 2016

TABITHA WAS READING A reply from Sadie when Martha knocked on her door. She had messaged her cousin about the spring formal, seeking advice on just the right style of dress to wear. Tabitha was a little uncertain as to her own personal style regarding formal attire, and she wanted her cousin's opinion.

"Hi, sweetheart," said Martha, glancing over at the small bouquet of flowers Tabitha had placed in a mason jar on her desk. Martha had been working late at her school, finishing up the second round of student conferences and was just informed of the big news by her husband, George.

"Hi, Mom," said Tabitha with a big smile. "Did Dad tell you already?"

Martha nodded, taking a closer look at the flowers.

"Pretty exciting. Your first formal. Any idea what you want to wear?"

Tabitha showed her mother a photo of a dress style Sadie sent to her. It was an off-the-shoulder fit and flare dress. Martha raised her eyebrows and said appreciatively, "Nice choice. I think that'll suit you well."

Her niece, Sadie, did have an eye for these things. The dress was not extremely elaborate. It was tasteful, though a little shorter than Martha or George would have liked for their thirteen-year-old daughter, but lovely and suitable, nonetheless.

"The color is the problem, Mom," sighed Tabitha, frowning.

"Yes," agreed Martha. "It's the spring formal after all and it would be nice to have a lighter color." They stared at the picture together for a few seconds, then Martha asked, "When do you need the dress?"

"Two weeks," said Tabitha, biting her lip.

"You know my friend Ysabel, who makes the costumes for the school plays, is a phenomenal seamstress." Martha sat on the edge of the bed next to her daughter. "All she needs is a pattern and I bet we could find one easily for a dress like this," indicated Martha tapping the screen.

Tabitha was so excited she flung her arms around her mom. Martha smiled, giving her a squeeze.

"What about cerulean blue, Mom?"

Martha's fingers rested on her mouth for a second as she imagined the dress in the color Tabitha suggested, then she murmured, "Absolutely perfect, Tabby."

~

"Mom, does everyone have to come with us?" groaned Aeneas. He was trying to whittle down his entourage to just him, his mom, and C.J. If his dad came, then they'd have to bring Persephone and his mom would suggest Socrates come along, too, in case he felt left out which Aeneas was certain he would not. Nevertheless, she would insist upon it and that was too many people watching him try on clothes.

"I suppose not. Your father is adjusting his design for a large-scale enzymatic plastic digester. He has a deadline for a company in Japan that wants to purchase his prototype." A small smile escaped Aeneas for two reasons. First, his parents were remarkable people, and he was proud to be their son and second, Archie with a deadline was like a man possessed and there was no way he was leaving the lab this weekend.

"So, can it just be me, you, and C.J.?" asked Aeneas hopefully.

"Well, mostly," replied Miranda lowering her voice, not sure where Persephone might be in the house. Her daughter had bat-like senses. Miranda and Aeneas were sitting in the living room side by side on the couch.

She leaned in closer and whispered, "Your little sister has specifically asked to come along. She feels she can be a great help to you, and your father needs uninterrupted time to finalize his prototype."

Horrified, Aeneas whispered back, "What about Sox? Can't he watch her?"

Miranda shook her head. "Have you forgotten? Your brother has an interview at Stanford this weekend."

"Mom, please," begged Aeneas.

"Please what?" asked Persephone as she magically appeared before them, startling the pair. The two were so ensconced in their discussion that they never saw Persephone walk into the living room. The real reason that you had to knock before entering someone else's room in the Entwistle family was largely due to Persephone and her stealth-like movements around the house.

"Oh, hey, Sephie. Your brother was asking me if we could have lunch at Serious Pie when we go shopping for his new suit."

"That's my favorite," squealed Persephone enthusiastically, clapping her hands.

"C.J. is coming, too," said Aeneas coldly. He wasn't about to give Persephone the impression that she was welcome.

"Oh," uttered Persephone, as if she'd just gotten bad news.

"I'm sure we'll all have a great day together," said Miranda, looking back and forth from her middle to her youngest child. Aeneas mumbled something under his breath, got up off the couch, and stomped off toward the pantry.

~

Aeneas, Persephone, C.J., and Miranda were all seated together on the bus heading across the West Seattle bridge toward downtown. Another Entwistle family rule in navigating the greater Puget Sound metropolitan area was to take the bus during the day but get a cab after dark. The Entwistles rarely used their car, preferring public transit during peak traffic hours.

"Aeneas, do you know what color Tabitha's dress is?" asked his mother, causing a jolt of panic to shoot through his solar plexus. Aeneas jerked his head sideways to make eye contact with C.J. who replied for him, "Tab said it's cerulean blue when I spoke with her yesterday."

Just as C.J. finished his comment, Aeneas chimed in casually as if he'd known along. "Yeah. It's blue, Mom. Why does it matter what color her dress is?" he asked trying to hide the alarm in his voice. He was so relieved that C.J. was there because he knew these kinds of details.

"Well, it's customary that your shirt and tie don't clash with your date's dress," said Miranda carefully. She knew Aeneas was a little on edge and hoped he'd take her comment as a gentle nudge in the right direction. Aeneas was processing this tidbit when Persephone looked up from her book and joined the conversation.

"I brought a swatch from Tabitha's dress," offered Persephone, digging into her small green backpack embroidered with sea turtles. She carefully removed a blue swatch from an envelope with Tabitha's name on it.

Aeneas's eyes bulged and he started to sputter, but before he could say anything his mother intervened. Miranda held out her hand and Persephone surrendered the piece of blue cloth.

"Seph, how did you come to have a swatch of Tabitha's dress?" asked her mother, locking eyes with the youngest Entwistle. At this juncture, C.J. discreetly whispered, "I think your sister is toast."

Aeneas responded with a barely perceptible nod as Persephone began her explanation. Even though he loved his little sister, she was definitely in need of another smackdown.

"Well, Mommy," began Persephone with a pause. She hoped using 'Mommy' might soften her mother's glare, but Miranda remained stoic.

"I called Mrs. Willoughby and explained I'd be assisting Aeneas in his purchase of a suit for the spring formal. Prior to that, I checked an online etiquette source and noted the information you mentioned about the clothing not clashing."

Persephone gave Aeneas a benevolent smile as if her assistance to him was invaluable and continued, "She was extremely helpful and contacted the dressmaker. Then Seth gave me the swatch at school yesterday."

She smiled triumphantly at the group. C.J. raised an eyebrow. As much as Persephone annoyed him and she really did *annoy* him at times, he had to admit she was incredibly efficient.

Much to everyone's surprise, C.J. complimented Persephone while Miranda thought how to soothe her rattled son.

"Persephone, that swatch will actually be extremely helpful today. Glad you thought of that."

Aeneas whipped his head around, aghast at the words coming from his best friend. Miranda forced a smile and Persephone beamed.

"Thank you, C.J.," said Persephone brightly. Aeneas, stunned into silence, exchanged a look of bewilderment with his mother as the bus motored toward Seattle.

Aeneas shuffled into the Men's Warehouse, already burnt out from shopping. They'd been to several department stores and his mother had been insistent that they would visit one more store before stopping for lunch. Aeneas's stomach responded with a yowl, and he shot a weary glance at C.J. who returned a sympathetic face.

"Mom, can we just come back after lunch?" moaned Aeneas.

"Aeneas, they have a huge stock of clothes here," said Miranda, smiling encouragingly. "We just might find something."

Persephone and C.J. had been indispensable at the last two department stores and Miranda realized it required a team effort to complete this task. They had found several suitable options. The issue was Aeneas himself. He'd never been a careful, particular dresser. In fact, any store with a sporting goods section could outfit him easily, but suddenly everything had to be just so! Miranda sensed this was a rite of passage for Aeneas and he wouldn't be satisfied until he closed in on perfection.

C.J. was the self-designated tie expert and as soon as they entered the Men's Warehouse, he walked briskly to the tie section. Miranda oversaw pants and Persephone collected shirts of all shades and styles requested.

C.J. was quickly sifting through the ties when a squirrel print caught his eye. The silk tie was orange with gray squirrels, but when he flipped it over, he winced. It was a designer tie, discounted to sixty-seven dollars. He held it in his hand, wondering how they could ever match an orange tie when Persephone walked up behind him.

"What do you have there, C.J.?" she inquired. Her tone, as usual, was tinged with curiosity.

"It's a squirrel tie," said C.J. without enthusiasm.

"Really? Aeneas loves squirrels," exclaimed Persephone as C.J. passed her the tie. Persephone carefully examined it and walked over to her basket. She placed it next to a charcoal-colored shirt and C.J. raised his eyebrows. "Not bad, but will he go for it?"

"Honestly, if this doesn't satisfy him, I don't know what will," lamented Persephone.

"He's definitely been channeling his inner prima donna," smirked C.J., holding back a laugh. Persephone started to giggle.

"C'mon, Seph," gestured C.J. with a friendliness that made Persephone smile. "Let's see if we can get Aeneas dressed for that formal and eat some well-earned pizza."

When the pair arrived with their choices, Aeneas was scrutinizing a pair of pants with a matching jacket as Miranda eyed him with the ire she usually reserved for politicians. She was tired and hungry, too. Her middle son, who'd never given her a moment's trouble, had become impossible.

"Aeneas, we found a shirt and tie combo I think you should try," said C.J.

Aeneas nodded glumly, grabbed the shirt and tie, and headed for the dressing room.

"Are you alright, Mommy?" asked Persephone. Her mother had a stony look about her that was concerning. C.J. knew that look. He'd seen that same expression on his mother's face before and knew they had to bring this expedition to an end. Aeneas was shuffling around in the dressing room and uttered a loud, "Yes!"

C.J. called to him, "What do you think?"

"I think I love this tie. It's awesome!" yelled Aeneas. This pronouncement made Miranda snap to attention, and she called Aeneas to come out of the dressing room. The charcoal shirt and pants contrasted nicely with the orange tie and Aeneas's smile lit up his face.

As Miranda was placing the suit into her basket, she checked the prices to see what the final total would be. She gasped when she saw the price of the tie. C.J. grimaced. He'd forgotten how expensive it was and decided if there was any issue, he would offer to buy the tie for his best friend.

Persephone, too, saw her mother's reaction. She'd also noted the price of the tie, but thought it was worth every penny to get her brother ready for his big date. "I'll buy the tie for him, Mom," said Persephone quickly, opening her sea turtle backpack and producing a tiny wallet. She counted out seventy-four dollars and handed it to her mother.

"It should cover the cost plus the sales tax!" exclaimed Persephone, smiling brightly, happy that she'd been able to help her brother.

C.J. gave Persephone a look of astonishment mixed with admiration, and she beamed back at him. They'd finally found something in common—their love for Aeneas.

CHAPTER 17

Jesús Secures a Stand-In

Spring 2016

JESÚS THUMBED THROUGH HIS song collection, waiting for Aeneas to arrive. He knew that some guys often blew it with the slow dance. They got nervous sweats or made the dance into a three-minute death grip. The worst, though, was when they tried to get fancy and started flipping their date all over the place. What was needed was moderation.

Aeneas opened the door with a hello. He placed his backpack in the corner and walked cheerfully over to Jesús.

"You look confident, man. Feeling ready for the big dance?" asked Jesús.

"Yeah, I got my clothes and I'm double dating with a buddy," replied Aeneas, feeling he'd finally gotten a handle on things. Jesús nodded.

"So, we're going to work on the slow dance first and later we can recap some of last week's dance moves. How does that sound?"

Aeneas gave Jesús a thumbs-up. "I've practiced all the moves you showed me and my buddy, C.J., says I'm like a thousand times better than before."

Jesús raised his eyebrows. "Good to hear."

"Before we begin, let's talk," said Jesús, his voice taking a more serious tone. Here was where he probed for the impediments to a successful slow dance.

"Have you ever slow danced with a girl?" asked Jesús, eyeing him skeptically.

"Er, uh, not really," replied Aeneas, worried this was something he should have already tried at least once in his young life.

"That's okay. I can teach you," said Jesús reassuringly, then added, "Do you have any concerns about it?"

A whoosh of breath left Aeneas. "I, uh, I'm not sure, like, where things go," confessed Aeneas, panic crossing his face.

"You mean where to put your hands?" This was a common concern among first time slow dancers. Aeneas nodded vigorously. Jesús tapped his phone and said, "Don't worry. We'll practice this. Hold on for a minute."

Soon the door opened, and a girl walked in wearing a black satin party dress. Jesús introduced her.

"This is my friend, Sasha. She is going to practice hand placement and distance with you."

Aeneas's eyes widened. The girl gave him a warm smile.

"Relax, man, you'll get this," insisted Jesús, all business.

Sasha walked over to Aeneas and whispered, "Don't worry, I help Jesús with this all the time." She smiled and Aeneas finally looked at her. Her glossy black hair was piled up with curls falling down the back of her neck. Sparkly earrings dangled next to her neck. Her dress was strapless, and she wore low heels.

Aeneas exhaled and nodded. He was doing this for Tabitha. He wanted their first dance together to be special. Jesús walked over to the pair and started his instruction.

"Girls want you to be close, but not too close. It needs to seem as if you like them but are not trying to smother them, so as a gentleman you set the distance," stated Jesús firmly as Sasha rolled her eyes behind his back.

"Is that what you say to your female clients, Jesús?" asked Sasha teasingly.

"I tell them to find their comfort zone and maintain it," replied Jesús, adding, "It's important for both parties to feel the space between them is the right distance."

"Oh, girls get lessons from you, too," said Aeneas, surprised.

Jesús chuckled. "Yeah, about forty percent of my business comes from girls."

Sasha suppressed a grin. She thought Aeneas was just adorable. "Aeneas, girls want to make sure they can dance in their dresses, don't fall over in their shoes, and can deal with any unforeseen events," said Sasha.

"Girls and their shoes," grumbled Jesús, starting his anti-heel rant. "If it were up to me, high-heeled shoes would be outlawed. I tell girls, find matching flats. No one's looking at your feet!" squawked Jesús irritably.

Aeneas listened intently. He'd never really considered it. High-heeled shoes must be uncomfortable.

"Aeneas, move your hands to Sasha's waist and keep them straight. Now, take one step forward, then bring the other foot along." Jesús was scrutinizing the distance, using a ruler to measure his client's foot length, and checked Aeneas's arm distance again. Jesús shot a questioning glance up at Sasha.

"He could be another inch closer and that would be perfect," said Sasha, responding to Jesús's nonverbal request.

"Okay, start again, Aeneas, increasing your step inch by an inch."

Aeneas placed his hands on Sasha's waist, then took a step forward as Jesús measured the distance on the floor.

"Okay, man, once your hands are at her waist, you need to move seventeen inches, so take the same step and just edge forward an inch."

"Aeneas, watch your feet the next time. It helps," encouraged Sasha, making him blush. After a few tries, Sasha and Aeneas agreed he was hitting the right distance consistently.

"Hands should stay on the waist for now until you learn more advanced dance moves," instructed Jesús, starting the music.

"Your DJ has plans to play this slow song so let's practice it."

Aeneas smiled as he recognized the tune. He liked the song.

"Aeneas, move your feet," reminded Sasha.

"Sorry," cringed Aeneas, blushing again.

Aeneas eased into a slow sidestep avoiding Sasha's gaze.

"Let's try a twirl," said Jesús, tapping Aeneas on the shoulder and stepping in front of Sasha. The song was on repeat and started again.

"Watch how I change positions when I twirl Sasha."

Jesús took a step back, released his left hand from her waist, lifted their right hands together and gently spun her, giving her shoulder a gentle push. Sasha twirled perfectly, returning to face Jesús. His hands were back on her waist, and they were moving in time to the music together again as if they'd been dancing partners for a long time.

"Wow, that was fast," exclaimed Aeneas.

"Give it a try," said Jesús stepping aside for Aeneas to practice.

Aeneas awkwardly began the movements.

"I'll talk you through it," reassured Jesús.

"Step back. Now hands up and... spin Sasha."

Aeneas pushed a little too hard and Sasha came back around nearly knocking him over. "Oh, I'm so sorry, Sasha," blurted Aeneas, mortified.

"No worries. Less force on the twirl. The shoes will help with the spin," stated Sasha lifting her foot to show him how little traction her shoes had.

They gave it another try. Aeneas used less force and Sasha stopped on point.

"Again," directed Jesús.

They practiced a few more times until Aeneas was consistent with his technique. Jesús called for a break.

"You were great, Sasha," grinned Jesús.

She shot back a flirty smile.

"I'll..."

"Take me to the Cinerama on Saturday night," she murmured, walking past him seductively.

Now it was time for Jesús to blush.

"I'll pick you up for the second movie," called Jesús as Sasha grabbed her bag to leave.

"So, do you plan on kissing this girl while you're dancing?" he asked, causing Aeneas to sputter like a tea kettle.

"So, yes," answered Jesús.

"Well, I've kissed her before," replied Aeneas defensively.

"Just some pointers I tell all the guys. Choose a favorite slow song. When it's nearly over, lean in, kiss your date, and don't make a big production of it. One nice kiss is best." Jesús smiled and punched Aeneas playfully in the arm. "Hey, it's a formal dance."

Aeneas returned the smile. "Got it."

As he walked to his bike, Aeneas texted a message to C.J.:

Bro, I owe you big. Jesús is top notch. Come by later for more details.

CHAPTER 18

Kissing Cousin Catastrophe

Spring 2053

A BLUR OF FARMS and forests flew by. Sadie glanced out the window, wiping away the tears puddling in the corners of her eyes. She'd decided to take the new electric *Coast Starlight* from Portland to Seattle. Flying would've been faster, but she was embarking on a new journey and a train seemed more fitting. Life with her husband Dylan had ended abruptly in a short, tense conversation. He was tired of her being on tour for half the year; she didn't like his pettiness, always correcting her when she overlooked something small. It was her second failed marriage and Sadie, heartbroken and ashamed, called Tabitha who encouraged her to come for a visit.

Aeneas woke the next morning feeling sick to his stomach. C.J. had been right. There was no way he could witness Sadie's death and not react. After a harrowing rescue from the jetty, Aeneas dropped Sadie in a heap and sprinted down the beach toward the mouth of the Columbia River in search of the timestream. Panicking, he darted into the trees to take cover and regroup. A few minutes passed and he caught his breath and slowly looked around. Surely Carl had reached Sadie by now. All he had to do was leave. Aeneas closed his eyes then opened them a few seconds later, sighing with relief. The sparkling lights were just beyond a small copse of trees.

A day had passed since his return and Aeneas had cautiously checked his SAIL. The major pieces of his life were intact, but as he went about his day, Aeneas kept encountering slight alterations, like the living room furniture and some of the family photos. Even the cookware was different. Despite these changes, he was genuinely shocked to see Sadie, more shocked than he could let on because Tabitha had no idea she was living the remake instead of the original. Part of him felt he should say something. The other part was still feeling his way through the newness of having Sadie back, the replacement memories not feeling as strong as the original ones. For now, he decided to say nothing, but log the changes on his SAIL. He'd speak with Cassie soon and explain to her what had happened, though he doubted that conversation would go well. He'd violated every rule he'd been taught and passed onto her from Bob North Sky.

Tabitha and Sadie took a long walk along Alki Beach while Aeneas made them dinner. Then the trio gathered around the dining room table to eat dinner and share a bottle of wine.

"I'm never getting married again," said Sadie, downing her glass of wine, sneaking a glance at Aeneas under her long black lashes. There were times when a dark presence entered her psyche and she wished she'd pushed harder to keep Aeneas for herself back when she'd had the chance.

"You never know," quipped Aeneas, refilling everyone's glass. "You might find the next love of your life in an unexpected place." He was trying to sound upbeat, but he was increasingly worried about the changes Sadie's extended life had created.

Sadie beamed at his comment. At fifty-three she was still the most beautiful woman in any room. Her long blonde hair was streaked with silver, making her appear even more glamorous. Tabitha felt a tinge of jealousy. Her cousin had aged so well, having no children and more time to take care of her own needs.

Dinner wound down and Aeneas went into the kitchen to chop nuts and fresh fruit for hot fudge Sundays. Tabitha and Sadie remained at the table engrossed in their conversation.

After a brief search Aeneas called out, "Hey, Tab, I need to run to the market. We're low on vanilla ice cream and I can't find any chocolate sauce."

Tabitha got up from the dining room table and called back cheerfully, "I'll do the market run."

Aeneas was glacially slow at errands, and she needed a break. The last few hours felt like a marathon counseling session. After Tabitha left, Sadie casually wandered into the kitchen, leaned against the counter, and gazed at Aeneas while he meticulously chopped fruit. An intense desire welled up inside her. It had always been there she supposed, but now it consumed her watching him in the kitchen. Oblivious, Aeneas smiled pleasantly, trying to conceal his worry about the implications of

Sadie's resurrection. Suddenly Sadie shot forward and kissed him passionately, wrapping herself around him tightly. Aeneas jerked back and dropped the knife, trying to disentangle himself from her grip, but Sadie was surprisingly strong.

"What the hell, Sadie!" hissed Aeneas just as the back door slammed shut. Sadie whipped around to see Tabitha's face purpling with rage.

"Pack your things and get out, Sadie!" shouted Tabitha. Rage was wafting off her and Aeneas felt his skin prickle.

"Oh my God, Tab. I'm so sorry. I don't know what's wrong with me," stammered Sadie, trying to shake off whatever had possessed her. She walked toward Tabitha extending her arms for an embrace, but Tabitha slapped them away, screaming, "I don't care what you are. I don't ever want to see you again."

Sadie fled the room in tears, but Aeneas was rooted to the spot.

"You aren't welcome here anymore, either. Go stay at C.J.'s until you can find another place."

"Tab, no," pleaded Aeneas, shaking his head. "It's not what it looks like. Sadie had too much wine or something."

"Oh, it was something alright. Something that's been going on for as long as I can remember!" she screeched. Tabitha reached for the vase on the dining room table and hurled it into the kitchen. Aeneas leaped back as it shattered at his feet.

"Let me explain," yelled Aeneas, side-stepping the shards walking toward her, but Tabitha burst into tears, shouting, "I just came back for the grocery bags!"

Aeneas looked wrecked when he showed up on C.J.'s doorstep with his duffle bag. He quickly explained to C.J. and Lyla what happened, omitting his intervention that brought Sadie back to life. They had said very little, and Aeneas took this to mean they didn't want to take sides. Later after he was settled in Ryan's childhood bedroom, Aeneas rehashed the scene in the kitchen trying to make sense of it.

"What the hell have I done?" he groaned, gripping his stomach, and curling into a ball on Ryan's bottom bunk. He'd already thrown up once before he left his house, and more was on the way.

Just as he reached for the trash can to throw up again, it hit him. Tabitha's reaction was fueled by a lifetime of jealousy. When Sadie died at sixteen she'd been frozen in time as Tabitha's cousin and best friend who'd tragically died. But now forty years of resentment, likely made worse by those few weeks when he and Sadie briefly dated, had built up. That was all the *remake*. And the remake had re-made Tabitha.

~

The thing that bothered Cassie the most in this whole mess with her parents was her mom's reaction. Sure, Aunt Sadie had kissed her dad in their kitchen, but it had been fleeting, momentary—and nothing had come of it. Why throw him out of the house?

Tabitha Willoughby Entwistle, sought-after Seattle therapist, could trace any behavior back to previous incidents in a person's life. She always had an answer for knee-jerk reactions, but like many astute people, when it came to her own behavior, all her unique insights vanished. And hadn't she and Aunt Sadie always been the closest of friends? Aunt Sadie— who wasn't her aunt at all, but her second cousin—felt like an overlaid memory.

Since traveling to 2015, Cassie was aware of the sensations when new memories were added, and she felt it keenly when Tabitha told her why she and Aeneas had temporarily separated. Something was off. Cassie's spidey sense had been pinging for a couple days, but she couldn't quite pinpoint what was triggering it until she found out about her parent's split. Cassie pulled the SAIL from her pocket and recorded a message to Missi and Thena:

Mom told me today why she and Dad have separated, but something is off. The memories of Aunt Sadie feel recently added. Something in the past was changed. I glanced at my diploma from U.W. a few minutes ago and I know this sounds crazy, but isn't my middle name Valentina? Why does my diploma read Cassiopeia Eleanor Entwistle? Am I losing my mind? My initials are CVE, not CEE!

Cassie set the SAIL down on the kitchen counter and called out, "Send now as urgent."

Within a minute her SAIL announced, "Incoming calls from Missi and Thena."

"Answer," said Cassie sliding into a chair at her kitchen counter. She was at her condo in Ballard and had been throwing together some leftovers for a quick breakfast when the sensation hit her again.

Missi's hologram appeared first. She was sitting on a yoga mat in her living room shaking her head, arms folded, far from relaxed. Suddenly, Thena popped in from a commuter train and appeared equally exasperated. Cassie often forgot Thena was teaching classes at Santa Clara University.

"You busted in on my morning yoga because your middle name suddenly sounds weird to you?" asked Missi, eyeing her cousin with rancor.

"I'm not busy, either!" snapped Thena, holding up a satchel and a lunch box, gesturing to her surroundings.

"Hey, wait a sec," cried Cassie holding her hands up in defense. "My mom just kicked my dad out of the house for kissing her cousin! That's worth a little sympathy, isn't it?"

The sisters instantly softened and started to talk at once.

"You go first, Thena," said Missi, deferring to her sister who only had a limited time to be with them.

"When Mom messaged me last night, she mentioned there'd been something between Sadie and Aeneas in the past and even though Tabitha had been cool with it, she'd always wondered if that was just a facade."

"Aunt Tab had every right to boot Uncle Aeneas out," snapped Missi, who'd once been duped by a cheating boyfriend. "And why would Sadie and Aeneas be kissing anyway? I'm surprised you aren't upset about *that!*"

"You know if I wasn't so stuck in this sensation, I might be," mumbled Cassie, rubbing her temples. Her head felt like she was riding on an old, dirt washboard road.

"It all feels too new. And it seems unlike my mom. Tabitha would normally want to analyze it all before acting, but maybe it's like your mom said, maybe it's been lying dormant all these years."

Cassie grabbed her chopsticks and pulled a bowl of left-over rice and veggies toward her. Missi and Thena exchanged looks. They knew what was coming next and why she'd really called. Cassie wanted to go snooping in the past and was feeling guilty.

"So, Cass, what's your plan?" asked Thena, adding, "Make this quick. I get off in three stops."

Cassie looked sheepish. "I thought maybe I could take a peek back into the past and see what prompted this, then maybe I could…"

"Hold on!" interrupted Missi. "I know I wasn't trained in time travel etiquette or whatever you call it, but I'm pretty sure you are not supposed to interfere in the past, especially with something this delicate."

Cassie shrugged. "I wasn't planning on actually doing anything, just observing."

"Mmhmm," responded Missi doubtfully, uncrossing her legs, walking her hands forward, moving into downward dog, then walking her hands back and standing up, giving her favorite cousin a knowing look.

Thena chimed in, "Cassie, you can't change what's just happened between your parents. I think you should focus more on why you sense the past was altered. Is it possible that Aeneas has gone back in time and made some changes?"

"Dad? Mister follow-these-shamanic-rules or else?" scoffed Cassie.

"Well, what do Lux and Tor think? Shouldn't you call them and get a consensus?" asked Thena, trying to get in her best advice, before she departed the train.

"Lux and Tor are busy with the twits," grumbled Cassie, making no attempt to disguise her disdain for her brothers' sudden girlfriends. She was skeptical about the road trip romances her brothers had landed themselves in.

Missi cleared her throat. "You mean the twins, Lana and Lanna?"

Cassie put down her chopsticks and shook her head.

"Lana and Lanna are another puzzle. They seem recent, too. And what's worse, I can't remember how they even met these girls! I mean one minute they up and leave on a road trip and the next they're dating twin sisters?"

"After your mom caught Sadie and Aeneas kissing in the kitchen, there was a huge blow up between them and Lux decided he needed to take a road trip to remove himself from the situation," said Thena, stepping off the train. "Tor rushed back from Japan to join him, and they met Lana and Lanna at some campground in the Grand Canyon."

"Listen, I have to go, Cass. I'll call you after class this afternoon. Bye Missi," called Thena as her hologram quickly closed.

"Well," sighed Missi, waiting for the final word from Cassie who'd suddenly deflated.

"Well, something isn't right," sniveled Cassie, wiping away a tear.

"Then start asking some questions," said Missi, pushing back into another downward dog.

Cassie's Close Call

Spring 2053

CASSIE WALKED ALONG ALKI Beach. A cold wind pressed against her face making her eyes water. She knew she'd be in the timestream for longer than usual, so she ate a substantial lunch—two turkey burgers and a pile of sweet potato fries. Time travel was a strenuous business, especially when you were hunting for something.

A shiver passed through her as the sparkling lights flickered near the water. She made a beeline for the opening, glancing around for anyone who might notice her sudden disappearance. There was a couple behind her sitting on a blanket, but they were deep in conversation and the other beach walkers were farther ahead of her on the boardwalk. Cassie pursed her lips together in anticipation. *I'll just peek on mom's timeline and see if there is anything that might have set her off. Aunt Keniah mentioned Sadie and Aeneas had dated briefly in college. Maybe there's more to it.* Cassie slipped into the timestream and focused her thoughts: *Tabitha timeline college years 2021.*

She flew through swirls of people and places surrounded by a golden pink atmosphere that filled the timestream like a soft mist. She followed her timeline all the way back to Tabitha's which was notched to hers.

As she homed in on Tabitha's college years, gigantic scenes appeared before her, like massive photographic slides, depicting Tabitha's life. Cassie smiled at all the familiar faces and thought to herself, *I love these people!* Once she fixated on a scene, she'd enter, and it would expand into a period of Tabitha's life. She was about to step into the spring of 2021 when Cassie noticed something odd in the distance. There was a strange aberration—colors were distorted, and the golden pink atmosphere of the timeline was disrupted by a large pulsating, sphere-like shape. Curious, she flew toward it ignoring the pinching sensation in her stomach as she closed in on the object. A faintly glowing sapphire blue sphere the size of an old water-tower tank stretched open Tabitha's timeline. Attached to it were dozens of offshoots giving it a parasite-site appearance. Cassie was taken aback with a mixture of curiosity and fear. *What in the hell is this?* she thought to herself.

As the thought entered her mind, a whooshing sound filled her ears, and she was sucked in with a small POP! Immediately Cassie struggled to escape but her spidey senses indicated there was no immediate danger. The energetic atmosphere inside the sphere was a beautiful silvery blue that felt slightly warm. Each offshoot was a narrow timeline of Tabitha's life.

Cautiously, Cassie peeked inside one. She watched as a scene played out and spiraled off, but the clarity wasn't as defined as other scenes. Cassie peeked in another where a slightly different version was playing out. It also spiraled off.

These are all possibilities, alternate realities that can play out in Tabitha's life. But how did it get here? I've explored past this point before, but I've never seen this...

Cassie glanced around the sapphire sphere for any clues as to why this temporal aberration had appeared on her mother's timeline.

"I'll just enter this one," whispered Cassie aloud, leaning into the offshoot with her usual determination. As she transitioned from the boundary of the sphere, the atmosphere changed and sounds like radio static filled her ears. The scenes were pixelated compared to the clear, well-developed ones she usually viewed in the past and suddenly Cassie felt queasy. She attempted to go further, but the sensation worsened, and someone bellowed sharply, "Get out now!"

She was stunned to hear a man's voice not belonging to her father inside the timestream. In a flash, Cassie was sucked out. She looked all around Tabitha's timeline for the person who must be nearby. Instinctively, she flew to the notch connecting their timelines, entered her own line, gazed around for the source of the voice, then took the unusual tack of peering upward. The timestream consisted of infinite layers, but Cassie focused on the linear lines of single lives so as not to be overwhelmed. She sensed someone above her in a series of timelines connected to her family. She glanced left and was startled by a face peering back at her, as if it were magnified through binoculars. A young Asian man with a square jaw, spiky black hair and alluring dark eyes gave a nod of bemusement and vanished!

When Cassie stepped out of the timestream, returning to her present, she felt like she'd been on a ride at the state fair. She reached for a nearby chair in her living room to steady herself. The cells in her body were vibrating at a different frequency. Her SAIL was nearby and Cassie called out weakly, "Help me."

Even though they joked about it being something out of a comic book, Cassie and Aeneas had their own emergency signals. These could be sent to their families to let them know when they were in trouble, especially if they'd come back from a particularly troublesome or strenuous episode in the timestream. It was part of the safety protocols they'd developed once Cassie began time traveling without her father when she was a teenager.

Cassie's SAIL had an override so when the message came back, she didn't have to decide whether to open or answer it. Instead, the hologram opened immediately once the emergency signal was activated.

"Cassie!" yelled Aeneas. He moved the hologram closer so he could see her. Cassie, pale and trembling, collapsed on the floor gasping for air as if she'd been drowning. Her optic nerves were still vibrating at the wrong speed. The room seemed to be spinning.

"Blue sphere," groaned Cassie weakly.

"Hang on, baby. I'm dispatching the team. Why didn't you come to the lab?"

Cassie shook her head. "Could only think 'home.' Worse when I left the stream."

Minutes passed while Cassie clung to the edge of the carpet, hoping the spinning would cease.

Tabitha had been working minutes away in her downtown Fremont office and came charging through the door straight to her daughter's side, quickly placing her hands on her.

"She's freezing!" Tabitha yelled to Aeneas's hologram. He was running to hail an electric ride-share car. He'd kept his SAIL open to monitor Cassie while he rushed to get to her condo in Ballard.

"House!" called Tabitha brusquely.

"Madam?" answered the virtual butler. Harold had installed it as a birthday gift last year.

"Run the tub to a hundred and ten degrees."

"Certainly, Madam," responded the virtual butler.

"House!" called Tabitha again, "Turn the heat up to seventy-eight."

"Done, Madam."

Tabitha disliked the idea of a smart home. She'd declined Harold's offer to install one for her and Aeneas, but now noted that during an emergency, it was enormously useful.

The door flew open again. Amy, a retired nurse who lived nearby, helped Tabitha carry Cassie to the tub. Aeneas kept several medical personnel on retainer who would not ask questions for these types of emergencies.

Once Cassie was immersed in hot water, Tabitha rushed into the kitchen and pulled some bone broth from the freezer, placing it in the Nimble Chef. Amy poured two cups of magnesium sulfate in the tub with Cassie and took her temperature.

"She's at ninety-five point eight degrees, Tabitha," said Amy, taking the cup of broth from her. Cassie's teeth were chattering. Amy carefully handed her the hot soup, and Cassie weakly swallowed the warm broth.

Amy grabbed a wool hat from the closet, shoved it on Cassie's head, and took her temperature again.

"Ninety-six point seven," she said quietly. The color started to return to Cassie's face. As her body temperature continued to rise, Tabitha tried to question her, but Cassie, shrugged, feigning comprehension. She was waiting for Aeneas. After about ten minutes, Amy and Tabitha helped Cassie from the tub and wrapped her in a fluffy pink robe. They pulled thick socks onto her feet and carefully guided her to bed. Amy was checking all her vital signs, which were approaching normal, while Tabitha went to refill the cup with broth.

Aeneas walked in quickly and was relieved the SAIL had recorded the incident. He was curious if her body temperature was lower than usual. He reminded himself to check the database later.

Seeing Tabitha in his daughter's kitchen caused a gut-wrenching pain in his belly, but he kept his face impassive.

"Hi," said Tabitha flatly.

Aeneas responded gently, "She's okay now?"

Tabitha nodded. "I think so. She won't say much. She's frightened and exhausted. I can't get anything out of her."

"Is she out of the tub yet?" asked Aeneas hoping for some small connection with Tabitha. He'd missed her so much.

"Yes. Amy is checking her vitals again. I am going to scramble her a few eggs and make some sausage gravy and toast for her before I go," replied Tabitha, giving him a hard stare as if to say, 'don't ask me to cook *you* anything.' Aeneas swallowed. He was missing Tabitha's cooking, too, and it caused more emotions to well up inside.

"Sounds..." he started to say 'delicious,' but he felt he had no right to, so he said, "sounds nutritious. I'll go see her." He hurried toward the hall. Amy was just leaving Cassie's bedroom.

"Everything stable?"

"Getting there. I'll be in the living room if you need me," replied Amy. Aeneas nodded. He closed the door. Cassie sat up in bed and gave him a withering stare.

"Hi, sweetheart," whispered Aeneas, returning her gaze questioningly.

"What have you done?" she hissed. Cassie's cheeks flushed and she plopped back onto to her pillow, feeling weak again.

"I'm not following..." said Aeneas slowly.

"Mom's timeline has some weird pulsating blue sphere with alternate realities. I tried to enter one—it was all pixelated and I started to feel sick. Then some guy yelled at me to get out of there."

Aeneas sat on the edge of her bed, unsure of how to proceed. He *had* done something three days ago and now everything was a mess. He pulled his SAIL from the pocket of his pants and tapped it. "Play the backup video," he said.

A hologram bloomed in front of Cassie, and she watched the conversation between her dad and Uncle C.J. along with the video he'd made documenting his life days before, occasionally glancing over at her father incredulously. The story aligned with her other memories, but now a new reality seemed to exist on top of those memories. Cassie shook her head in disgust.

"I made this just in case," he said, choking back a sob. "I had no idea it would, would be like this..." his voice trailed off and he broke down.

Aeneas bent over, weeping into his knees. As much as he loved each of his children, as much as he loved Tabitha, he loved the family they were the most, and now it was fractured by some idiotic moment in the kitchen.

Cassie looked over at her father, and as weak as she was, forced herself up and whispered, "There has to be a way out of this."

Aeneas glanced furtively at her bedroom door for signs of Tabitha or Amy and wiped his face.

"Were you unhappy? Is that why you went back and saved her?" asked Cassie.

Aeneas shook his head.

"It was all good for me, except..." Cassie waited as Aeneas hesitated, he felt weird talking to his daughter about his marriage, "... except Tabitha wasn't happy... there was a tragedy from our past she asked me to go back and change. Bob had always warned me about ripple effects, and I swore to him I'd never do something like this."

"So, why now?"

Aeneas shrugged. "Because of Harold and Nia. A new person was born. A marriage was forged. Tabitha saw that nothing seemed to have been damaged in the present... and because it's tough for me to say no to your mother."

A hard knock at the door startled them both. Amy popped her head in.

"Your mom wants to know if you're up for eating in the kitchen?"

Aeneas got the hint.

"I'll be going. Call you later."

CHAPTER 20

A Clandestine Confession

Spring 2053

ARCHIE AND MIRANDA'S ORIGINAL laboratories in the Industrial District had been reconfigured to accommodate a new generation of scientists. Persephone used the first two floors of the original building for her environmental engineering firm while the third floor was used by Aeneas and Lux for their research.

Blandly named Western States DNA Research Inc., it was home to a highly secured lab that stored all the time travel data, including DNA samples from Cassie, Aeneas, Bob North Sky, and some of his grandchildren. A magnificent skyway bridge housed an art gallery that linked this building to the former spare warehouse where the family lived at one time. Socrates and Harold were housed in this building; Harold's offices were on the first floor and Socrates used the rest of the building for his physics labs. During the extensive remodel, Persephone insisted that their companies utilize the latest solar rooftop technology and include rooftop gardens. This resulted in two state-of-the-art solar-powered buildings tastefully topped with solar panels, vertical gardens, raised vegetable beds, and cozy park-like spaces.

Aeneas, Harold, Socrates, C.J., and Cassie sat inside a small enclosed stained-glass gazebo filled with specimens of native plants, a space usually rented out for small weddings and other events. The stained-glass scenes were designed by a local artist and highlighted all the ecosystems found in Washington State. The idea had been Archie's. He'd camped around the state as a young boy and it was a special place for all the Entwistle family and their friends.

Cassie had arrived last to ensure she could choose where to sit in case Harold plopped next to her—they still hadn't spoken about the video he sent, and she felt uncomfortable.

"Aeneas, don't you think this is a little over the top?" asked Socrates, annoyed at being pulled away from his work for a clandestine meeting. His brother had sent him an urgent encrypted message a few hours ago insisting they must meet in the gazebo.

Harold was quiet. He sensed things were shifting. Cassie had received the video clip from 2015 and he wondered if an awkward, painful conversation was going to take place between five people instead of two.

"I think it's best if I just show you this video I made," Aeneas said looking down at the floor. "And before I do, please know I accept full responsibility."

Aeneas turned to C.J. and murmured apologetically, "Bro, you were right."

Just as this comment was sinking in, C.J. was startled to see a video of himself urging Aeneas to not undertake a risk that could tear his future apart. Socrates kept looking from the hologram back to his younger brother shaking his head in disgust. Harold was the first to speak.

"Aeneas, you made this video before you went back in time a few days ago? And in the present you left, Sadie had been dead for what... thirty-seven years?"

Tears welled in Aeneas's eyes. All he could do was nod.

Cassie moved her hand to her forehead and rested it there for a moment to get her bearings; she was still not fully recovered from her jarring experience in the timestream. Seeing her distress, Harold reached into his pocket, took out an herbalboost lozenge, and silently slid it in front of her. C.J. glanced toward Aeneas who'd missed the gesture but logged it into his own cache of things to ponder later.

"You violated the shamanic rules of time travel?" thundered Socrates. Aeneas shivered hearing the undertones of his father Archie's voice.

"Tabitha has struggled so much with Sadie's death. It took so long for me to pull her from that dark place," whispered Aeneas.

"Tabitha can be a bully sometimes," snapped C.J. getting up from the cushioned chair, nearly cracking his head on a hanging pot full of ferns. He walked over and scanned back through the holographic video to the conversation he'd had with Aeneas before he traveled back in time, scowling as he watched a rerun of a life of his he didn't even recall.

"I can't believe I didn't just knock you out as soon as we had this talk," grumbled C.J., his fury building. *This was just like Tabitha,* he thought to himself. *She always had to have her own way; now her life is in chaos, and she has no idea it was all her fault.*

"I can see how upset you all are," acknowledged Harold crisply, as he stood and opened a hologram from his own SAIL. "But we need to log everything that we know has changed and work from that point onward to do whatever we can to right the situation, if that's possible."

Cassie held back a smile as she thought to herself, *That's my Harold. The younger version; less sentiment, and more action.*

"Well, Sadie isn't dead," said Socrates flatly.

"Mom and Dad have split up," added Cassie softly. The sadness in her voice made Aeneas wince like he'd been stabbed, and C.J. put his hand on his shoulder.

"The twins are talking about getting engaged," barked Socrates, shaking his head.

"To some twits," mumbled Cassie. Harold cut his eyes her way, trying to hold back a grin. The seriousness of the situation had to be maintained, at least until he could get more data.

"Cassie's middle name has changed," said Aeneas quietly.

"I knew it," yelped Cassie, startling the group.

"Tabitha named you after Sadie to pay homage to her memory. Her real name *is* Valentina. She was born on Valentine's Day."

"Ha!" yelled Cassie, nearly upsetting C.J.'s coffee. "Mom told me this story so many times!" Cassie rubbed her eyes as more scenes from the original past flew through her mind. "I keep having memories of the same time period that don't match up."

"I'm not sure how the process works for time travelers when the past is altered," said Aeneas, pausing, "but I think Cassie and I have dual memories."

"Anything else?" asked C.J. wishing the list would be short. He was suddenly worried that his own life had been changed without his knowing.

"Anything at all is possible," said Socrates, glaring at his brother.

"Think of all the people Sadie interacted with who otherwise would never have met her," fumed Socrates as his hands flew to his temples. "All the shows she played, all the people she dated, the life she lived that impacted others—the permutations are endless! You are a fool, Aeneas. How you thought saving one person's life—no matter how tragic—could leave little unchanged defies logic." He, too, was worried what else might have changed.

Harold glanced around the table, saw Cassie was in tears, and stepped in to slow the eruption of emotions.

"Socrates, take two laps around the building and come back. We need you focused, not furious."

Socrates looked at Harold and deflated. Though Harold had mellowed as he aged, he could still command a situation which required a logical, calm thought process. Socrates's anxiety had been triggered and he needed to clear his mind.

"Alright... I'll go for a walk," replied Socrates through clenched teeth. He stalked out of the gazebo heading for a well-worn path.

Aeneas placed his head on the table and let the weight of his body slump forward. He knew there was something he could do before anything else was attempted, but his idea might not go over well. A few minutes passed and C.J. felt like he was about to burst.

"Aeneas," said C.J. shaking him. "You can fix this with Tab; I know you can. The video you made, the change that's happened... she'll believe you."

Aeneas grunted something unintelligible then said, "But will she believe I had nothing to do with that kiss in the kitchen?"

"About that," interjected Cassie tersely. "What in the heck were you thinking, Dad?"

Aeneas became a little defensive. "There was no thinking. I was chopping fruit for hot fudge Sundays, and she suddenly planted one on me."

"And you pushed her off?" asked Harold, scrutinizing Aeneas's face. He'd wondered how much of this was due to a misunderstanding between Aeneas and Tabitha versus Aeneas and Sadie.

"I was attempting to," said Aeneas blushing under the stringent gaze of his daughter, "but she's surprisingly strong."

Socrates returned and Aeneas sat up straight.

"There's something I'd like to do before we make any plans moving forward," said Aeneas, standing as Socrates sat down.

"Go on then," barked his brother irritably.

"I'd like the team to allow me to go talk to Bob North Sky," pleaded Aeneas earnestly.

"Oh, so you intend to confess to your mentor and hero that you violated every rule he ever taught you?" asked Socrates. The chill of this comment was felt by everyone. Socrates's anger hadn't dissipated, and Aeneas could feel generations of Entwistle men seething through this brother.

"I'll do anything to fix this mess," said Aeneas humbly. He turned away from them and accidentally inhaled a face full of orchids.

CHAPTER 21

A Matter So Grave

Summer 2019

Bob North Sky sat in his living room watching a makeover show. He liked how simple changes made people happy, even if they were sad about it at first. He especially enjoyed the show where people had to throw away all their old clothes and get new ones, mostly because he could never imagine doing just that. Bob kept and wore all his clothes until they were thread-bare, occasionally adding a few new things each year.

His new apprentice, or "that city boy you brought here from down south," as Gerry Archambeau referred to Aeneas, was busy splitting firewood for his winter cache. Gerry had slowly warmed to Aeneas's presence in their community after his river rescue but was still skeptical of Bob's desire to teach him to use the river of time. Aeneas was a thoughtful kid, helpful, kind, and was always asking if Bob needed any chores done. Splitting rounds of cedar was the first thing that came to Bob's mind when Aeneas asked today.

Bob sensed a small shift in his timeline. He muted his TV and looked out the window. The timestream had recently opened. This was one reason he had the boy chopping wood— to teach him to focus on a task and ignore the pull of the sparkling lights. "You can't always cross into the river of time when it opens," he told the boy. "Sometimes, even a shaman must stock up on firewood for the winter."

Aeneas was hovering along his timeline, just above this scene from his past. He was taking a risk, but there was a substantial pile of cedar to be split which would give him enough time to speak with Bob. He slipped in, knowing full well that Bob would be expecting someone, but perhaps not him. Aeneas had often resisted the urge to coast back down his timeline and drop in on Bob North Sky, missing him terribly when he died. But Bob had told him not to come back "unless it's a matter so grave that you cannot see the way through it."

Bob squinted as a man stepped through the sparkling veil into his living room. His black curly hair was cropped short around his head, graying at his temples. But his eyes and smile were unmistakable. Very little surprised Bob, as he'd lived a long life. He'd been many places along his timeline and those of his ancestors but seeing Aeneas as an older man nearer to his own age gave him a start. Bob's eyes widened. He pushed himself up from the recliner, casting a quick glance outside to be sure his apprentice was still chopping wood.

"Old man, I've missed you!" cried Aeneas grabbing Bob tightly, giving him a huge hug. Bob returned the hug and thumped Aeneas on the back laughing.

"Who's old now, young puppy?" chuckled Bob.

"Oh, I guess I am," agreed Aeneas, tears welling in his eyes.

Bob nodded. He knew for Aeneas to take this risk something had gone terribly wrong. Holding up his wizened pointer finger, he tapped his lips and motioned Aeneas back into the kitchen.

Bob walked over to the door and peeked out. "Hey, hey, young time traveler. I need to make an important call," said Bob with an air of authority. "When you're done, start stacking the firewood under the tarp around back."

"Got it, Bob," called young Aeneas cheerfully, wiping the sweat from his face. Alaska in July could be warm on a sunny day.

"Now, let's have some tea and you can tell me why you've come," said Bob walking into the kitchen and motioning Aeneas to the kitchen table as he drew the blinds. Bob grabbed two cups and poured hot water over the tea bags. He kept a kettle of hot water throughout the day for his tea.

"Life is good?" asked Bob, handing Aeneas a cup of black tea with milk.

Aeneas took a sip, and a brief smile crossed his lips. Bob had served him black tea with milk many times when he was apprenticing with the shaman.

Aeneas sighed. "Life has been good, Bob."

Bob eyed Aeneas. "So, what brings you here?"

Aeneas waded in, figuring a confession was in order. "Some circumstances occurred and I felt I needed to change the past. I know I shouldn't have." Aeneas hung his head in shame, shaking as he fought back tears. "And I know this is what you taught me not to do and are likely teaching me even now."

"Just get it out, man. What have you done?" barked Bob impatiently as he downed his tea. Normally he was the soul of patience, but Aeneas had surprised him.

"I saved Sadie," croaked Aeneas. Tears erupted and he reached for a napkin. Bob was quiet. The story of Sadie was still fresh in his mind. She'd died only a couple years ago, and young Aeneas had told him this tragic story; they'd even discussed why going back and saving her violated the shamanic rules of time travel. What he'd told Aeneas just a few weeks ago popped into his head, like a TV rerun.

The river of time has great power. We travel on her bringing peace to our people by listening and helping them move forward through their lives, but it's not to be used for our own purposes or to change one's pain. Bringing someone back to life has caused consequences so terrible, all the shamans and travelers before me have forbidden this practice.

Aeneas continued with his confession, overcome with emotion. "She's alive. She kissed me in the kitchen a few days ago. Tabitha saw us and kicked me out. My sons met some identical twins from Canada and are now thinking of getting married. And Tabitha's timeline has an enormous blue pulsating sphere that almost killed my daughter."

Bob took this all in as he got up to make himself another cup of tea. One detail stood out. He absently rubbed the space just below his bottom lip.

"You and Tabitha have a daughter who is a traveler?" asked Bob, his grandfatherly pride getting ahead of the problem.

Aeneas nodded. "Yep. She's traveled since the age of three. Cassie is remarkable. Recently saved my life. Her stamina within the timestream is greater than mine, too."

"There are a few who were always stronger than others," remarked Bob, thinking back fondly on his grandfather as he sat back down with a fresh cup of tea. "Tell me about the damage to Tabitha's timeline."

Aeneas, now spent from his emotional unloading, explained what Cassie had told him about the multiple realities.

"You likely have this sphere-like temporal anomaly, too," said Bob staring out the window. He turned to Aeneas. "I suspect this anomaly emerged when Sadie was brought back to life. Have you visited Sadie's timeline yet?"

Aeneas shook his head.

"Go back and check her timeline. Watch for your young self when you return to my house," warned Bob gesturing toward the window. "He must not see you."

Aeneas stood up to leave but hesitated. There was a piece that did not make sense after his resurrection of Sadie had gone awry.

"Bob, there is something I don't understand. When your people travel, haven't they issued warnings that might have saved a life?"

Bob thought on this for a moment. "Shamanic travelers may give advice or most importantly just listen, because people have free will, Aeneas. They choose their own paths. When a traveler has gone back and raised the dead though, bad things have happened. This is what my uncle and grandfather told me when I wanted to go back and save my brother who died in Vietnam. It was very hard for me to accept this."

Aeneas looked down at his now cold tea and realized it had gone quiet outside.

"The chopping has stopped," he whispered.

"Check Sadie's line, Aeneas, but be careful to avoid any anomalies," cautioned Bob, worried Aeneas might not survive what Cassie had endured.

Aeneas walked into the living room. The timestream was still twinkling near the woodstove and he knew it was fading on his end. He slipped through just as his younger self tapped on the door to let Bob know he had finished his chores.

CHAPTER 22

Orbus Eruptus

Spring 2053

AENEAS HAD VOWED TO keep his team apprised of every step
to restore the present back to what it had been, or at least to
a version that was more closely aligned to the previous reality. It was in everyone's best interest, they concluded, to keep
a *consensus*. As soon as he returned from Alaska and fortified
himself with a bowl of soup, he pulled out his SAIL and called
the team. Their faces appeared in multi-paneled holographic
screens and as soon as they were settled, he shared his conversation with Bob North Sky.

"We all need input for the next steps—like the old saying 'no
man is an island unto himself,'" said C.J.

"But some men might need to be banished to one," added
Cassie.

Aeneas met her eyes as she stared him down, but there was
nothing to do but move forward.

"These sphere-like anomalies, Aeneas, do you think they are on all the timelines? For instance, would they be on mine?" asked Harold, wrinkling his brow.

Aeneas paused, shook his head, and said slowly, "I'm not sure, Harold. And for you, my old friend, it would be too risky for me to check."

"I think before we proceed, Cassie and Aeneas should investigate," said Socrates. "Perhaps Tabitha and Aeneas were more affected, but it's likely the immediate family has been impacted in some way."

"Sox is right," agreed C.J. giving him a nod of affirmation.

"I think so, too," added Harold. "More data on this temporal anomaly needs to be gathered."

Harold pulled out what looked like a small wand but was actually a specialized stylus and began writing notes that he quickly sent to the team.

"When do we leave, and do we go alone or together?" asked Cassie impatiently. She was ready to make some headway, especially since her brothers were making noises about getting married in Las Vegas, and she hadn't told her parents about their plans.

"It *would* go faster if we split up," continued Cassie, transferring her gaze from person to person assessing their reactions. Harold was the first to respond as he scribbled notes, avoiding eye contact with Cassie.

"You have to go together," he said firmly and was seconded by Socrates.

"We saw the medical data collected by your SAIL," said Socrates. "You were in bad shape, Cassie. There's no going alone. These temporal anomalies contain fragmented pieces of time or alternate realities. They're very dangerous," warned her uncle sternly.

"Yes, but if I hadn't wandered down one of the paths..." she stopped as her father was shaking his head determinedly.

"No way, sweetheart. We go together."

~

Cassie suited up for her extended journey wearing snug-fitting silk long johns she used for cross-country skiing. One thing she'd learned about the timestream was conserving heat was essential but being weighed down with extra clothes was cumbersome. Aeneas did the same as they prepared to depart. A quick trip here or there was fine in just regular clothes, but prolonged searches would require more preparation like wearing layers, eating high protein meals, and consuming electrolyte drinks.

Without traveling to Alaska, the quickest way to access the timestream was to check the seismicity of the two nearby volcanoes, Mount Rainier and Mount St. Helens. Aeneas scanned the UW seismology databases and told Cassie Mount St. Helens was their best option. Three small tremors had been logged daily in the past week, so they headed south down I-5, then turned east on Spirit Lake Highway, passing through rural scenes and forested areas as they approached the mountain. Cassie spotted the timestream near the town of Toutle and they stopped the car next to a pullout by the North Fork of the Toutle River.

"Dad, we should check your timeline first," said Cassie, pulling on a bright blue and purple beanie her mother had knitted that housed all her curls. Aeneas silently pulled on his favorite navy-blue wool ski hat embroidered with miniature squirrels around the headband. His demeanor was an easy read for Cassie.

"You're dreading this aren't you?" she asked as they walked toward the sparkling lights a few feet from the riverbank. Aeneas didn't respond and glanced around for a place to sit. Cassie ran along the swiftly moving river in both directions to be sure no one was hiking or fishing nearby. Aeneas waited pensively on a log, fidgeting with his hat, oblivious to the beautiful valley.

When Cassie returned, she gave him two thumbs-up, and they slipped into the golden pink atmosphere, launching themselves down Aeneas's line. As expected, a similar sapphire blue sphere bloomed near Aeneas's adolescent years. Arms locked together, they moved back up his timeline and branched onto hers. Cassie's timeline remained intact until just after the point when Aeneas went back, meaning her life had been the same until recently. Several small pathways branched just after that point, meandering into the hazy golden fog of the future. Cassie noticed at once there were too many possibilities. Undamaged timelines moved into the golden fog where multiple possibilities existed, but now the possibilities were opening too early. For reasons she could not articulate, Cassie knew these pathways had to be merged back into one. A deep urgency to repair her timeline welled up inside her along with bristling anger toward her father. Cassie and Aeneas slowed as they came to the notch where Aeneas and Tabitha were connected.

"Dad, I'll take the lead from here," said Cassie as they maneuvered onto her mother's timeline. The next set of transitions was quite complicated. Cassie would navigate from Tabitha's line to Grandpa George's and once she reached his, she would enter her great grandmother's line and slip over to Catherine's, then pass through her birthing notch to access Sadie's timeline. Cassie had explored much of her mother's history and had mentally mapped the path back to her great grandmother, Leona, mother of Catherine, George, and Charlie.

Cassie inhaled deeply and closed her eyes, envisioning the path. Holding this in her mind, she whispered, "Sadie Willoughby, age fifteen."

In a blink, Cassie and Aeneas flew through the timelines, passing through birth notches, making twists and turns like a rollercoaster. Entire lives of family members flew by; the lines of the deceased ended with glowing polished orbs and lines of the living glowed with murky possibilities. The futures were sidestepped at all costs, though Aeneas and Cassie both agreed the future had already happened in some ways, but also existed in other ways in a state of possibilities. Sadie's future had ended when she died and her line should have a polished glowing orb, an ethereal tombstone near her sixteenth birthday.

Aeneas and Cassie arrived at Sadie's timeline, winded from the intensity of travel, and barely had caught their breaths when they both gasped.

Keeping a tight hold on Cassie, Aeneas gestured toward what they were both staring at in disbelief, "Is this a new timeline? Did the orb burst?"

Sadie's timeline was branched. It looked abnormal, like nothing Cassie ever seen inside the timestream. Sadie's glowing end-of-life orb had erupted, like a swollen seedling sending out its first new shoot. The line wasn't clean and clear like other timelines. Cassie sensed an instability she couldn't explain and an urgency to repair it.

"Something's not right about this," muttered Cassie frowning, as she and Aeneas hovered near the entrance. "The atmosphere inside the new line is fractured, weak even."

She felt a pinching sensation in her stomach, the kind of sensation her mother always reminded her not to ignore.

"We need to leave now, Dad," said Cassie.

CHAPTER 23

Tough Love,
& Weird Stuff

Spring 2053

AFTER DISCOVERING THE ERUPTION of Sadie's end-of-life orb,
Cassie and Aeneas decided to return to their present, regroup
with the team, then visit Bob North Sky. Aeneas spent the return
journey home in the self-driving car taking one of his famous
naps, while Cassie struggled with an upset stomach. The sensation she felt near Sadie's orb was like eating spoiled food. *I'm
guess I'm sensitive to temporal disruptions*, thought Cassie, recall-
ing the physical beating she took in the sapphire sphere.

Cassie closed her eyes for a little while then felt fidgety,
overwhelmed by an urgency to confront Harold over the video
message he sent from 2015. Quietly, she opened a small holographic panel and checked Harold's calendar. He was at the lab
but nothing formal was scheduled, so she had the car drop her
there and sent Aeneas on to C.J.'s house.

Cassie paused outside the Entwistle Enterprises buildings and messaged Missi and Thena.

I'm going to talk to Harold. I can't stand it any longer!

She felt a boost of courage as she sent the message. Within seconds her SAIL flashed violet and gold, and Cassie tapped the top. Two holograms appeared side by side.

Thena's one word response appeared in gigantic, sparkling discotheque lettering:

FINALLY!!

Missi was on her yoga mat again, holding side plank position and yelled, "It's about time!"

With a flick of her hand, Cassie cleared the messages and rolled her eyes, bemused; the support of her beloved cousins was never in short supply.

"Harold," called Cassie loudly as she entered the reception area of The Torkelson Research Group.

"In the back," replied a distant voice. Cassie drew herself up and gently pulled out her hair tie so that her curls fell freely around her shoulders. She wasn't exactly certain what to say, but she wanted to look commanding when she said it.

Harold was feverishly making notes on a holographic screen when Cassie walked through to his spacious office adorned with photographs. Inventions he'd patented, new companies he'd invested in, special charity events, and the people and places he and Meg visited were showcased on the walls.

As he looked up, a pause fell between them, and the old and young versions of Harold merged. Unsettled, Cassie blurted, "How could you marry someone else? How could you, Harold?"

Cassie stopped short of announcing her true feelings, tears flooding her face. "I came back for you, but Socrates..."

Harold was rooted to the floor. His stomach gurgled. It was uncomfortable being confronted like this, but he knew he had to send the message from his younger self so Cassie would move on. Harold loved Meg and was grateful to have found her and he had Cassie to thank for that; her visit to 2015 changed him and brought Meg into his life. Harold centered himself. He only had one shot to explain this without sounding pathetic, or worse, disloyal.

"Cassie, I spiraled into a depression after you left. I worried I'd be alone forever waiting for you to pop back into my life..."

Harold gestured for her to sit as he gingerly slid into a chair keeping his left hand pressed against his belly. Cassie ignored his offer to sit. She was fuming.

"Socrates knew I'd been unhappy," said Harold quietly. "I was losing myself in grief. I finally talked to a counselor, and she asked me how long I planned to grieve over losing you."

Sounds like something my mother would say, thought Cassie irritably, taking a few steps closer.

"It could have been managed, Harold. We could've spent time together, been in each other's lives..." Cassie faltered and stopped speaking.

Harold held her gaze. "No, Cassie. I spent hours and hours researching this possibility. I consulted Socrates, other physicists, the most brilliant minds of my generation. They all agreed... too many disruptions in your parents' timelines could've generated a reality where one day you might abruptly disappear."

Cassie slowly edged closer and plunked into the chair across from him. Harold inhaled deeply before he spoke again. "I had to move on with my life for both our sakes."

"For both our sakes?" scoffed Cassie, wiping tears from her cheeks. The unbearable grief of lost love made her want to collapse. She never realized how lonely her life was until she met young Harold. Cassie folded forward and wept, her luxurious curls spilling over her knees. Harold winced watching her sob. Her hurt was stingingly fresh, but he'd lived a lifetime with a person he loved and had no regrets.

"And, Cassie, we do spend time together. We are very much in each other's lives, and I cannot tell you how much I treasure that." Harold was old enough to be her grandfather now and it was up to him to help Cassie through this piece of their past. Just as he had to make it through it himself. He'd made the right decision for them a long time ago.

~

Cassie slept in late the next day with no plans to go to the lab, needing time to reset herself. She woke slowly, feeling out of sorts and knew she needed to talk about what happened with Missi and Thena.

"Did either of you know what was in the video message from 2015?" asked Cassie. The cousins were meeting for coffee semi-virtually. Cassie was wrapped in a red silk kimono bathrobe wedged in the corner of her couch with a cup of freshly brewed coffee. Missi sat next to her. She had decided the night before that an in-person meet up might be needed and had taken the Vashon Island ferry plus a bus to get to her cousin's condo. Thena, still in California, was seated in her office space at Santa Clara University having an espresso between classes.

Missi answered first, "I knew he had something important to tell you, but I had no idea it was a video he'd made in 2015."

Thena followed. "He told me what he had to say to you was extremely important, which is why we agreed to use our influence."

"So, neither of you remember Harold *not* being married?" asked Cassie, still puzzled on how memories filtered in for non-travelers. She and Aeneas needed to analyze their dual memory phenomenon.

"Meg has always been around for as long as I can remember," replied Missi leaning over and squeezing Cassie's hand supportively.

"Ditto," affirmed Thena who was still grappling with why Cassie was so devastated. Nothing had happened between them that seemed to warrant a broken heart. Even so, Thena proceeded carefully as she inquired about their interactions in the past.

"Cass, did anything at all transpire... between you and young Harold?" Thena raised an eyebrow ever so slightly and leaned closer to the screen.

Cassie shook her head sadly. "There was nothing physical. It was more..." she paused trying to find words to convey the intensity. "There was this overwhelming attraction like we were about to fall in love."

"Oh," murmured Missi, struck by Cassie's lovesick expression.

"Some love affairs never make it past the almost together stage, but the emotions behind them can be intensely passionate," stated Cassie defensively, wiping away tears.

No one spoke for a few seconds. Then Thena attempted to sound sympathetic, keeping her voice even. "I can see where it could be incredibly tempting to go back and dig into the what-ifs, but that's already caused major upheaval in our family."

Cassie was about to respond but a nearby sound caught her attention. Missi was rapidly tapping her toe on the floor. The hard part about supporting Cassie in her confusion and sadness was no one had been privy to the contents of the message. She cut a quick glance at her sister and plowed ahead.

"It would give me a clearer picture of how you're feeling if I could watch this video message," offered Missi, carefully controlling her voice so as not to sound too eager. Thena rolled her eyes and hid a smile behind her hand. Missi wouldn't rest until she'd seen the video from Harold.

Cassie assented and tapped her SAIL.

"I'm going to the bathroom. I can't watch this again," mumbled Cassie sullenly, getting up from the couch.

Missi and Thena watched the message, each wiping away tears as the video ended. Cassie stopped in the kitchen to refresh her coffee and trudged back to her seat on the couch across from Missi.

"Was this necessary?" asked Thena.

"It's heavy stuff and I'm not sure it's helpful to you, Cass," added Missi. She and Thena exchanged a look that conveyed their mother's family motto 'we don't need any drama.'

"I thought about that, too," grumbled Cassie, feeling a little anger rise in her belly at Harold unloading all this on her.

"But it was a loose thread and Harold hates that. Besides, he'd feel guilty if I was forever wondering or thinking my feelings weren't reciprocated."

"So he was falling in love with you!" exclaimed Thena looking from her sister to her cousin. "Can you imagine how complicated that could have been? Even life threatening? Didn't he say as much last night?"

"I'm not sure that's completely true," replied Cassie stubbornly.

"Would you've gone back again without the video though?" wondered Missi before downing the last bit of her coffee.

"Maybe or maybe not. I've felt so mixed up. Some weird stuff has been happening that I haven't told anyone about."

Missi sprang up from the couch unleashing a rant that startled Cassie, who shrank back as far as she could into her corner of the couch.

"Weirder than a person being brought back from the dead, your parents splitting up, your brothers about to marry some giant red-headed twins from Canada and you falling for a guy from the past that's like a grandpa to you and who is also your employer?"

"Yep," nodded Cassie. "Weirder than that."

Missi stalked into the kitchen to pour another cup of coffee muttering to herself as Cassie's comment sunk in when, suddenly, Thena cried out, "Hold on, hold on! You mean there is more than this?"

Cassie swept a sheepish glance between the two cousins, biting her lip and wondering if now was the best time to mention the guy she saw in the timestream.

"When I was on Tabitha's timeline I found an anomaly, a strange looking blue sphere that turned out to be a temporal portal to multiple realities," Cassie explained. "Someone warned me to get out. It was a masculine voice. After I escaped, I saw this face staring at me from a distance."

"Was it Bob North Sky?" asked Thena, her first thought being the old shaman swooping in to save Cassie.

"I don't think so. He was young, Asian, with a very attractive, chiseled face," said Cassie, struggling to hold back a smile.

"Wait a sec! There are hot guys flying around the timestream?" deadpanned Missi.

"Have you told anyone else this, Cass?"

"No way. My dad is in bad shape and if he thought anyone was watching me... well, I don't think he could handle that right now."

"My oh my, a hottie in the timestream trying to save your life..." chirped Missi, bobbing her head and winking at Cassie.

Thena tapped her lip. "Like a dashing hero..."

"Or a creepy guy spying on me," countered Cassie.

On that note Thena decided it was time for some tough love. "Cass, you need to bury this thing with Harold. For him it was a long time ago. You need to move on."

The mood suddenly changed. Missi's smile faded. She knew Thena was right, but Cassie was not a person easily swayed. Her personality contained a mile-wide stubborn streak.

Just Say No

Spring 2053

HAROLD CALLED SOCRATES AFTER Cassie left and asked if they could meet on the rooftop gardens in their usual spot for private conversations. SAILs were commonplace in public spaces and conversations were easily recorded without special encryption protocols. Socrates had supported Persephone's grand renovations because he needed a quiet place to think. His panic attacks were rare now, but when he sensed tension building, the gardens were a welcomed retreat.

"What happens now?" asked Harold. They were seated on a bench near a copper tree fountain with native ferns and aquatic plants nestled around it.

"I told you not to send the video, man," chided Socrates, unwrapping a brownie. Keniah had made zucchini brownies that morning and though they weren't exactly his favorites, they tasted mostly of chocolate.

Harold looked over at Socrates. "Are those Keniah's zucchini brownies?"

Socrates reached in his backpack. "Here. I cut you an extra-large one."

Harold smiled briefly and opened the wrapper, breaking off a large chunk and chewed it thoughtfully.

Socrates grabbed a thermos and poured two cups of hot, milky coffee.

"Did you pack all this?" asked Harold, taking his cup.

"Yep. I had a feeling we'd need something for this conversation."

"She's probably going to quit," sighed Harold. Socrates popped the last bite of his brownie into his mouth and thumped Harold on the back.

"It's time for her to move on anyway."

"It hasn't felt right since she came back the first time," agreed Harold.

"We've got bigger issues than you and Cassie's forty-year-old thwarted love affair," said Socrates dryly. Harold winced. His stomach gurgled again. He wondered when this awful feeling would finally dissipate.

"We need a list of options," stated Socrates, placing his thermos back in the bag. Harold reached in his pocket and pulled out his SAIL.

"New working board, titled *Repair Project*, full encryption."

"Now?" asked Socrates wearily. It was getting late, and Harold's request had pulled him back to the lab when he'd planned to have an early night. His anger at Aeneas was exhausting him and he hadn't slept well.

"I always find it helpful to have some ideas outlined to get the collaboration under way."

"Yeah, but we still need to hear what Bob North Sky has to say," yawned Socrates, stretching his legs out in front of him.

"You're right. But aren't we meeting Aeneas and Cassie in the gazebo at ten tomorrow morning?"

"Yes, and I'll need some sleep before I go, so make this quick."

Harold gave him a brotherly nudge. "Ten minutes. Let the brownies digest."

Harold grabbed his stylus and began writing and recited his ideas back to Socrates.

"The most obvious option is to have Cassie go back in time and prevent Aeneas from saving Sadie."

"Great. We'll just kill her off?" mumbled Socrates. Harold ignored the sarcasm.

Socrates plowed on. The sooner he got home, the sooner he could sleep.

"What if Aeneas just comes clean to Tabitha, and we can work to help them repair things moving forward?" suggested Socrates, hoping to avoid any more disruptions in the space-time continuum.

Harold scribbled on the holographic screen murmuring, "Option two, Sadie lives, Aeneas comes clean, works to fix his marriage without continued tampering of timelines." Harold clapped Socrates on the back. "So that's two down... what about a third?"

"I can't think of anything else at the moment," groaned Socrates, getting up from the bench. Then he paused and shook his head.

"What I can't understand is why my brother, who apprenticed himself to a shaman and diligently trained for years, would undertake something that might undermine his own existence?"

Harold closed the screen with a gentle swipe of his index finger and turned to Socrates. "He couldn't say no to Tabitha."

"Couldn't he? Sometimes it's easier for me to understand how Persephone thinks than Aeneas," sighed Socrates.

"It's not easy to say no to someone you love. You and Seph are tougher than Aeneas. He's more sensitive. Maybe even more easily guilted."

Socrates closed his eyes and tried to imagine Keniah guilting him into changing the past. And then he laughed out loud. His wife was physicist.

· CHAPTER 25 ·

Deliberating
Sadie

Spring 2053

THE NEXT MORNING AENEAS took the unusual step of sending Cassie a message reminding her of their meeting in the
rooftop gazebo. Normally Cassie was the reminder, but he'd
noticed that she'd seemed quieter and more withdrawn since
they returned.

"Super. Can't wait," mumbled Cassie sarcastically. After a
light breakfast of coffee and toast, Cassie slipped into her rock-
climbing gear, ensuring she could claim a previously booked
lesson and slip out early if things got uncomfortable. She
opened a hologram and ordered a car to take her to the Industrial District. She wasn't feeling up to public transit.

Harold decided that the best approach was to focus on
developing options for the team to discuss. He woke early
and meditated for fifteen minutes to clear the clutter from his

mind. He grabbed a bag of his famous almond apricot granola, bowls, spoons, a quart of yogurt, plus napkins, and placed it all neatly in his vintage picnic basket he'd gotten from Meg on their six-year wedding anniversary.

Aeneas and C.J. arrived together since Aeneas was staying in Ryan's old bedroom. Socrates arrived last. His late-night chocolate brownie had given him indigestion and he trudged in, giving Harold a cold eye. Harold knew the tension in the room might prove a deterrent to collaboration, so he set the table and filled the bowls as the group filed into the gazebo.

Aeneas, beleaguered by guilt, was the first to smile.

"Harold, man, what a great feast," exclaimed Aeneas, sitting down to a bowl of granola and yogurt.

"You've already eaten two eggs, four sausage links, a stack of buckwheat pancakes, and a banana," remarked C.J. coolly.

Aeneas's appetite had not waned with the stress of his estrangement from Tabitha and C.J.'s pantry had taken a hard hit from his house guest.

"I know, bro, but this is my second breakfast. Time travelers need to eat more than other people," replied Aeneas with his mouth full.

"That's categorically untrue," said Cassie, plopping in a seat next to her father. "We eat the same as anyone else but need to pack in a few more calories before a long journey. You still eat like you're sixteen, Dad."

Cassie looked at the bowl in front of her and decided she would eat, too. It *was* her favorite granola. Harold stood and positioned himself as far away from Cassie as he could. *No need to make either of us uncomfortable,* he thought, opening a new screen, and turning to face the group.

"We need to discuss options moving forward, but first, the big question is... what happened to Sadie's timeline?"

Harold focused solely on Aeneas who was just finishing his last spoonful of granola. He met Harold's gaze and the cheeriness vanished from his face.

"Her timeline is damaged," said Aeneas evenly, wiping his mouth with a napkin. He continued to meet Harold's gaze not wanting to see the expression on his brother's face when he revealed the next piece.

"I've never seen anything like it," confessed Aeneas. "Her end-of-life orb has burst open, and a new weaker timeline is branching from it."

Harold quickly wrote Aeneas's comments, and they appeared in large golden letters on the holographic screen. As a backup for later review and for Lux's historical database, he programmed his SAIL to record their meeting.

"Anything else?" Harold was poised with his stylus.

"My spidey senses tell me the timeline is unstable and fractured, like Mom's, only different," added Cassie, stirring her granola as she spoke, focusing on her food rather than risk catching Harold's eye.

"Describe what you mean by 'different,'" muttered Socrates wearily. Cassie glanced at her uncle. He appeared exhausted, but she had no sympathy for him, though part of her felt silly for it. Their conflict over Harold was long ago in his past, but stingingly fresh for her.

"When I'm in the timestream, I can sense its composition, like a salmon can detect the chemistry of its home stream." Cassie glanced around the table. "I can sense the quality of the timestream... how it feels." All eyes were on her, with expressions of varying states of confusion.

She continued, "Have you ever felt a piece of cloth and it felt thin or thick? Maybe the consistency of the weave is tight or open? Or the threads used to make the cloth are more or less dense?" Heads nodded.

"I can sense the atmosphere and structural integrity inside the timelines. And my best explanation is that I know when it feels like the others and when it doesn't. And Sadie's doesn't feel right to me."

Harold wrote all of Cassie's comments, even though the SAIL recorded everything. He willed himself not to ask more about her 'spidey senses' even though he could feel himself twitching with curiosity. It was clear Cassie was in no mood to talk with him after their awkward conversation.

"Aeneas, do you have these 'spidey senses,' too?" asked C.J.

For C.J., there were times when he felt he grasped the phenomena of time travel, but then something new would emerge and once again he was struggling to bring these concepts into his understanding.

"A bit, bro," responded Aeneas. "I don't notice differences in the timestream as well as Cassie. I know what things should look like, but I can't sense the subtle atmospheric changes like she can."

"Huh," said C.J. making eye contact with Harold, then Socrates.

"Isn't Lux SNP-typing your familial genomes to search for certain genes related to time travel?" asked Harold.

"Yes," replied Aeneas. He hadn't spoken to either of his sons since they left for their road trip. They weren't speaking to him, and he was too ashamed to say so in front of his brother.

"Can we get back to the purpose of this meeting?" said Socrates irritably. He was nursing a headache and wanted desperately to go home and talk to his wife. She had strong opinions about all this, too.

"What are the options?" asked Cassie. Her tone was all business.

Harold responded lightly, "Socrates has a couple of ideas."

Socrates glowered at Harold.

"I can present them, of course," continued Harold hastily.

A new screen appeared in the hologram, lit up with light blue letters.

Option 1: Cassie goes back to prevent Aeneas from saving Sadie

Option 2: Aeneas explains the truth to Tabitha

No one said anything for a few seconds.

C.J. took a breath and dove in, "So... in option one, Sadie gets, uh, re-erased?"

"Option one, murder one," announced Socrates sarcastically. Aeneas's eyes bugged out. He automatically leaned back and placed a stout kick on his brother's shin, just like when they were children and Sox said something tactless.

"Ouch," yelled Socrates, grimacing.

"You deserved it, Uncle Sox," snapped Cassie, glaring at him like some strange inter-dimensional mixture of his mother, his sister, and Tabitha. Socrates leaned under the table to rub his shin. The comment *had* been a little over the top.

Harold shrugged. "Actually, it's not a bad title for this option. Until recently she had not been alive past the age of sixteen."

"How about Option Reset," suggested C.J. No one disputed this title and Harold added it.

"What would the consequences of this option be?" asked Harold, scrutinizing the short list of options.

C.J. pushed back his chair and paced around the edge of the enclosed gazebo. His brain worked better when he was on his feet. "So, Sadie's gone, she's revived, and she's gone again... how will that work, Aeneas? Would we even remember it?"

Aeneas shuddered, closed his eyes tightly, and thumped his forehead. After he met Bob North Sky, Aeneas was careful never to change the past to impact the future, that is—until recently.

"I'm not sure. I've thought about that kind of fix, and it worries me, especially because of what I've seen in Tabitha's timeline."

Harold's stylus started flying across the holographic screen. He had an idea. "It'd be great if Lux could start tracking all these possibilities. We could do something like what you did with the SAIL when you traveled back to save Sadie—basically the time traveler's SAIL could store the real data, so nothing was lost."

Aeneas stared at the table and fiddled with his spoon, too ashamed to reply. His sons, deeply hurt by their parents' separation, had decided to take a road trip, and weren't answering his messages.

"We need Lux back, Dad," whispered Cassie softly.

Aeneas shrugged. "They aren't speaking to me..."

"Or Tabitha," interrupted Socrates. This small comment made Aeneas feel better and he gave Socrates a gentle nod.

Cassie grabbed her SAIL from her backpack and headed out of the gazebo. "I'm going to send them a message and those two better not ignore *me*."

Cassie marched over to the alcove where Harold and Socrates had met the night before. She placed her SAIL on a nearby rock and voiced the instructions.

"Record message, full size."

The SAIL recorded her in a large screen format so that the whole background was contained in the message. As well as the twins knew Cassie, she also knew them. Her brothers were masterful in reading body language, and they needed to see all of her to tune into the seriousness of her request. She began with her usual acerbic wit.

"Hello, Lux and Tor. Hate to interrupt the international love festival, but here's the thing: the situation between Mom and Dad is a sort of by-product of something Dad changed in the past... because Mom asked him to. And now we are trying to repair it without doing any more damage to the present. I know you're both pissed at Mom and Dad, but we need you both back as soon as possible. Like today. So, hop a plane and get here. And it would be best if you came alone." Cassie ended her message with a knowing look.

"Send message to Lux and Tor."

The SAIL didn't flash a reply right away, and she felt a twinge of anger as she made her way back to the gazebo. She held it in her hand for a few more seconds, hoping for a quick response, but none came. As she approached the door, she heard raised voices.

"I think option two has merits, Aeneas," argued Harold. Aeneas's hangdog expression told Cassie some new conversation had occurred in her absence.

"What's the problem, man?" squawked Socrates. "Just tell Tabitha what you did; show her the SAIL, show her the *before...*"

"Tabitha should see she is just as responsible for this mess as you are," added C.J. hotly.

"What is it, Dad?" asked Cassie softly.

Aeneas swiveled around, unaware his daughter was in the doorway.

"I'm the one who broke the rule Bob said never to break," mumbled Aeneas. "I'm so ashamed and I dread facing your mother again."

A new screen shimmered, and Persephone appeared. "Once Tabitha hears the whole story, I doubt *all* the blame will stay at your feet, brother dear."

"Ahhh!" screamed Socrates, leaping from his chair, stumbling into some ferns, and clutching his chest. "What the hell, Persephone!" This was the final straw for his nervous system. It was widely acknowledged in the Entwistle family that Persephone had missed her calling as a covert operative.

"Hey, Seph," called out Aeneas, giving her a wave. All eyes were on the holographic image of his sister.

"Um, just out of curiosity, how is it that you knew we were here?" asked Aeneas. He, like the rest of the group, was taken aback when she popped in as if she'd been listening, which was exactly what Aeneas was worried about. *Had* she been listening?

Persephone cast a tight-lipped grin over the group.

"Recall I handle all the security for our two buildings?"

Everyone nodded as she continued, the grin replaced by a small frown. "Last year we lost several plants from the gazebo after it was used for a few wedding receptions."

"Who steals ferns?" cried out C.J., looking around as if the last thing he'd want to take home was a fern.

"They are native, some of them rare and they aren't all ferns; there are other species," corrected Persephone a tone that always rankled C.J.

"You've got surveillance in here now, Aunt Seph?" asked Cassie, trying to smother her amusement. Aunt Seph never disappointed.

"Yes and a good thing, too, or else I'd have no idea the crisis our family is facing right now," she said, clenching her teeth as she glared from Aeneas to Socrates.

Old wounds from her childhood had bubbled up. She'd been one of the last to know that Aeneas was a time traveler. Harold cleared his throat, and everyone turned toward him. He pointed to his holographic screen.

"We do need to get back to this," he said sternly. "If Persephone is involved now, we can receive her input, too."

"It'd be best to regroup later," groaned Socrates wearily, edging toward the door. Persephone popping in like some phantom had sent a surge of adrenaline through his body. It was all he could take first thing in the morning.

"And Aeneas still has to report back to Bob North Sky which requires additional time travel, so we should all head home for now," added C.J., who'd felt this meeting wasn't making progress.

Harold tapped the screen again. "We need to develop several contingency plans to limit the impact right now."

No one seconded his proposal. The energy of the meeting was shifting toward action. C.J. grabbed his SAIL and pulled up the regional earthquake database.

"A small earthquake just hit south of Edmonds four minutes ago."

Cassie perked up. "What size?"

"Two point six. I can drive you both up the freeway, then pull over when you spot it," offered C.J., anxious to be done with the meeting. He could tell Aeneas was getting worn down from these familial interactions and giving him a task to do would be the best thing for him right now.

"Let's go, Dad," urged Cassie.

Aeneas gave her a thumbs-up. "Let's get Bob's take on what to do next."

Persephone gave Harold a sympathetic look. He sighed and sat down with a plonk. So much for his contingency plans. "Okay, everyone, contact me when you are back; I'll set up secured screens."

CHAPTER 26

Under Advisement in a Huckleberry Thicket

Summer 2019 & Spring 2053

THE TRAFFIC ON I-5 had dramatically decreased with the expansion of several flexible employment initiatives using new holographic technology in addition to on-demand self-driven cars. Fewer and fewer people opted to buy personal vehicles, except C.J. He loved to drive and was still hanging onto his now nearly vintage electric car.

His small green car, circa 2029, sped up the interstate while Cassie and Aeneas scanned the roadside for any flicker of the timestream.

"Get off here, bro," pointed Aeneas urgently. "Pull into the parking lot near the lake and we can hop out."

C.J. guided his zippy, green car into the Ballinger Lake parking lot as Cassie and Aeneas jumped out.

"Should I wait here?" he called after them.

"Yes!" yelled Cassie as they made their way toward some trees. "Dad, you take the lead."

Aeneas gave her a nod, feeling more confident now that he had a task. Cassie clung to her father tightly as they flew down his timestream and hovered just above Bob North Sky's cabin. A minute passed and there was no sign of Bob or his young apprentice, which meant they both had to be inside. They landed in the forest just north of the cabin, crouching in a small thicket of huckleberry bushes and watched the door.

"We need to take this timestream opening back, Dad, so we've got to make this quick," whispered Cassie.

"Okay. Pull up your hoodie, hide your hair, and go knock on the door."

"Why me?" she hissed.

"I'm *in* the cabin, Cass," reminded her father. "It has to be you."

Cassie hurriedly walked toward the door and gave a series of sharp knocks.

"Hey, hey, dinner's ready soon; come on in," shouted Bob to whoever was knocking on his door.

Cassie knocked again with more intensity. Bob groaned, lifted himself off the recliner, and flung open the door, wondering what fool was taking the paint off his door. Cassie quickly flipped her hoodie off her head and back on again.

"Oh," gasped Bob. A quick glimpse told him all he needed to know.

"Hey, young time traveler, I need to take a meeting outside," he said to his young apprentice inside the cabin. "I'll be back soon. Keep an eye on the food, but don't eat it, yah!"

Bob closed the door and smiled at Cassie. She smiled back, a flutter of excitement passing through her. The legendary Bob North Sky in person! His thick white hair was stylishly cropped, and his brown eyes were lively. She noticed a heavy silver bracelet on his right arm. His face was leathery but inviting. Cassie's immediate thought was that he looked very distinguished. Motioning behind her, she whispered, "I'm Cassie. My dad is over here hiding in the huckleberry bushes."

Aeneas popped out and gave a quick wave. Cassie quickly darted to the cover of the huckleberry thicket as Bob made his way over to them.

"We don't have much time, Bob. Our window will close soon," said Aeneas, piling another big hug on Bob.

But Bob was only half listening. His eyes were glued to Cassie, and he was smiling appreciatively. Of course, Aeneas and Tabitha would have a beautiful, time-traveling daughter.

"Bob," repeated Aeneas gently, shaking his shoulder. But Bob was still mesmerized by Cassie.

"Yes, yes, tell me what you found," replied Bob, grinning at Cassie.

"Sadie's end-of-life orb has burst," said Cassie, staring straight into Bob's bemused face. She figured she might as well deliver the information to speed things along. Her spidey senses estimated they had less than ten minutes left before the timestream closed.

"And a second timeline has erupted from it, but it's weak and lacks the consistency of a normal timeline," added Aeneas.

"Hmm," muttered Bob, his left eyebrow gently raised. "This is very bad, Aeneas," said Bob sternly.

"We know," said the pair in unison.

Bob thought about what his father had said regarding resurrecting the dead using the river of time. *Disrupting the path of the river caused heartache among our people and the person most disappointed was the traveler who'd made the change.* Shamanic travelers knew the river of time was to be traveled as a guest, not as a mercenary for personal, monetary, or emotional gain.

Bob's stillness was worrying Cassie, but Aeneas was used to it and waited patiently. Cassie cut a glance at her father. He signaled for her to wait.

"When Sadie died, she was alone. She walked out onto the jetty to watch the ocean and was taken by a rogue wave," said Bob. "Her actions were her choices. Free will, Aeneas, as I told you, is a special power given to us by the great spirit."

Bob had always imparted his wisdom in small stories like this and left Aeneas to ponder the meaning. He looked skyward for a moment, wondering if he was making a mistake in training young Aeneas. When his eyes were level again, he asked Aeneas how he'd changed the past.

"When you traveled back to save Sadie, what actions did you take to prevent her death?"

Aeneas shut his eyes. He'd not told anyone, even C.J., how Sadie's rescue had unfolded.

"I saw Sadie heading toward the jetty and called out to her. I thought the best thing to do would be to change her mind with an urgent message."

"What was this message?" asked Bob absently stroking his silver bracelet.

"I told her that her father, a guy named Carl, wasn't feeling well and asked her to head back to the parking lot."

"Did she turn back?"

"No," groaned Aeneas, anguished.

"What the heck?" sputtered Cassie in surprise.

"Why wouldn't she go back to the parking lot if someone told her that her dad was sick?" Cassie couldn't conceive of such a strange response.

"I'm not sure she heard me correctly because of the wind, or maybe she didn't believe me," shrugged Aeneas, pulling his hands down his face. Bob crossed his arms, deep in thought and urged Aeneas to continue.

"What did you do?"

Aeneas kept his view trained just above Bob's head. It was easier to focus on the tree just behind him than make eye contact.

"I ran after her. She kept walking onto the jetty, making her way toward the middle. She didn't even look back to see me try-ing to get her attention. I saw her sit and face the ocean. I wasn't sure she could hear me over the wind and surf, but I kept calling to her anyway. Then my spidey senses detected a vibration..."

Cassie turned her face away; she was tearing up. Memories of what Tabitha had told her they thought had happened to

Sadie came flooding back. She now had two distinct memories of this story in the spot where one had previously existed. It was an odd sensation.

"Suddenly, I saw this massive wave rolling toward the jetty," Aeneas continued. "Sadie must've had her eyes closed because it was easy to spot. I yelled to warn her and scrambled across the jetty as fast as I could. Out over the water the timestream bloomed; it tugged at me, and I was just close enough to leave if I'd wanted to." Aeneas stopped and hung his head. Part of him wished he had jumped into the water and swam to the timestream, letting the past be.

Cassie tapped his arm and motioned him to finish the story. Her eye was on the current timestream opening and her thoughts were of C.J. waiting for their return.

"The wave was starting to crest right when I reached her," continued Aeneas. "I grabbed Sadie around her waist and carried her over my shoulder. She was startled, kicking and screaming, but I held onto her tightly. I scrambled back over the jetty. We cleared about thirty feet from where she'd been sitting just as the wave broke over the rocks. You know I'm able to close distances when the timestream is open nearby. Time stops and I can just zip through the space. Anyway, I stumbled, nearly fell as the wave hit, but I never let go of Sadie."

Aeneas heaved a huge sigh and Cassie nudged him to continue. Their opening was closing soon.

"I'm certain of one thing now: the force of that wave knocked Sadie off the jetty and washed her out to sea... that's why they never found her body."

Aeneas leaned against a tree, slowly slid to the ground, bile creeping up the back of his throat. It made him sick to know that was how she'd died.

Bob reached down and placed his hand on Aeneas's shoulder; he knew why this had gone so badly for Aeneas.

"She had no free will," said Bob with a sigh.

Cassie looked anxiously over at the timestream and decided she needed to move things along.

"Bob, are you saying if Sadie could have decided to head out to the jetty or stay on the beach, she would have determined her own destiny?"

"Correct," said Bob, eyeing Cassie. *This is Tabitha's daughter alright*, thought Bob, *sharp as a tack*. Despite the circumstances, meeting Cassie gave him a warmth in his chest, a glow of pride and hope.

"So, if I went back and stopped Dad from saving Sadie, maybe I could offer her some piece of guidance. Maybe I could mention that rogue waves had been spotted and that it might be dangerous to go out on the jetty. Wouldn't that constitute free will?"

Bob smiled again. He couldn't help himself. She was delightfully quick witted. "Hmm... letting *her* choose wouldn't violate shamanic rules and—"

"But would that really make any difference, Bob?" interrupted Aeneas pushing himself up from the ground. He felt a twinge of panic. His life had been altered too much by Sadie not dying and now, selfish as it was, he worried about any possibility of keeping her in it.

Cassie yanked Aeneas's arm and tilted her head toward the nearby opening in the timestream.

"It was wonderful to meet you in person, Bob. I've heard so much about you my whole life," gushed Cassie leaning in and planting a kiss on his wrinkled cheek. "We have to go now or wait for another earthquake and we must get back to our own time."

Bob touched his cheek where Cassie had left a nice warm kiss. A goofy grin crossed his face.

"Wait, Cass! Bob, what will happen if she dies again?" Aeneas needed this answer. They all did. But Bob just shrugged.

"That, as they say, is uncharted territory."

Cassie grabbed Aeneas's hand and pulled him into the timestream. Aeneas reached for Bob's hand and gave it a good-bye squeeze. For a moment he was suspended between the two of them like a paper doll chain.

"I miss you every day, old man!" Aeneas called over his shoulder as he stepped into the timestream.

"You will find the path, boy!" thundered Bob, letting go of his hand, then thumping his heart in solidarity.

CHAPTER 27

Three Bowls of Pho & Two Sides of Conversation

Spring 2053

THE CAR RIDE SEEMED uncharacteristically quiet, and this had C.J. worried. Aeneas was sprawled out uncomfortably in the backseat with his eyes closed. C.J. kept glancing at him in the rear-view mirror. Cassie, too, was broody and asked to be dropped at the nearest light rail station that would take her back to her condo in Ballard. C.J. had asked about Bob's advice but gave up after the pair deflected his question, citing they wanted to wait and share with the group.

After Cassie left, C.J. pushed a little harder on Aeneas.

"What the hell is going on, man?"

Aeneas shook his head, refusing to answer.

"Geez... how bad could it be? Is there a permanent tear in the space-time continuum? Have you set in motion some catastrophic end to our world?"

Aeneas, still sprawled across the backseat, opened his right eye, fixed it on C.J. for a moment, then closed it again.

"Aeneas!" yelled C.J., flushed with frustration. "Forty damn years, bro. You can tell me this. It can't be worse than what's rolling around in my imagination."

Aeneas groaned, lifted his head, and said wearily, "Feed me and I'll talk."

"Well, why didn't you say so!" snapped C.J.

C.J. pulled off the I-5. Within minutes, his SAIL navigated him to a Pho restaurant.

"Pho?" exclaimed Aeneas cheerfully. Revived by the promise of a steaming bowl of beef pho, he hopped out of the backseat. *The man's stomach hasn't changed in forty years*, thought C.J.

Slurping his hot noodle soup, Aeneas explained what little they had gleaned from Bob North Sky.

"So, the vital info you two got from Bob was that letting Sadie choose to head out to the jetty or not constitutes free will?"

"That's what Cass and Bob determined," sniffed Aeneas, wiping his mouth then blowing his nose on a napkin. Aeneas liked his pho loaded with aromatic spice and jalapeños, for a full sensory experience.

"Now we can clarify option one the list," said C.J. using chopsticks to roll rice noodles and transfer them onto his soup spoon.

"Yeah, but it's risky, bro. Cassie would intercept me, send me back to my own time, wait a few seconds and return to hers."

C.J. paused mid bite. "How would that work? She goes back in time to prevent an event that you've already gone back in time to prevent?" C.J. dropped his spoon and waggled his head. Aeneas's existence was foreign to him. He felt he could never know him as a time traveler, only as a best friend.

"We may need to back things up again, but this time on her SAIL," said Aeneas thoughtfully.

"So, this conversation will never have happened?" asked C.J. in disbelief.

"Well, it probably happens for me. Cass and I have been noticing what we're calling 'dual memories phenomenon.'"

"Layman's terms?" said C.J., slurping broth and noodles.

"Well, we think that your experience will be replaced, while ours will be accumulating."

"Break it down a little more, man," grumped C.J.

"You get a new memory, but we get to keep them all."

"Aeneas, this seems like a tangled mess. How will any of us ever know if our experiences are the first or second version?"

"Well, bro, once this is cleared up, I have no plans to change anything ever again so it shouldn't be a regular occurrence," explained Aeneas. "I'll focus on my work with Lux. I'm certain Cassie has more time-traveling genes than me and we need to conduct more genetic tests to identify the entire genetic range associated with time travel."

C.J. snorted. "I'm sure she'll be delighted to be the subject of more scientific investigation."

~

Cassie's sail was flashing dark green and cherry red. Lux and Tor had finally responded to her message. By sheer coincidence or some yet undiscovered time traveler telepathy, Cassie, too, had grabbed an order of pho and was busy navigating a spoon and chopsticks while slurping beef, fresh herbs, and hot noodles at her kitchen counter. She reached over between bites and tapped the tiny rectangular device. Her mouth was too full to use the voice command.

Lux's message appeared first.

Hi, Cass.

Super busy with Lana & Lanna. Will arrive as soon as possible.

XO XO Lux

Cassie rolled her eyes. *This situation couldn't get any more complicated,* she thought to herself.

Tor's message was next. Of the two, he was the most loquacious, but his message was uncharacteristically short.

Cassie,

Lux and I are headed home ASAP like you've asked. We've had an amazing experience with Lana and Lanna. I think this might be it for us. Who knew? Twins and twins! Lux will have us all on the next flight to Seattle. Love, Tor

PS Check out this picture of the four of us!

Cassie wiped hands onto her pants, then floated her finger across the right side of the hologram to enlarge the picture. She leaned in. "How in the world do they tell them apart?"

Lana and Lanna were identical twins who placed great emphasis on the identical portion of their twinness. They wore matching clothes, right down to their socks and hiking boots; their hairstyles were the same, too.

"Geez, I hope there's some weird freckle or scar, or maybe they wear name bracelets," cackled Cassie.

At first, she'd been upset about these sudden relationships, but now it was so surreal that all she could do was laugh. Lana and Lanna wore their strawberry blonde hair plaited in braids tied with matching ribbons. Their great big, toothy grins reminded Cassie of the fictional Pippi Longstocking character.

"Send picture to Missi and Thena," said Cassie, activating her SAIL.

She shoveled in a few more spoonfuls of pho, expecting responses from her cousins any minute. Missi joined her first.

"Cass, can *you* tell them apart?" giggled Missi.

"No," said Cassie, shaking her head, twisting some rice noodles around her chopsticks to get one last bite before the conversation took off.

"Well, they appear to be... cheerful, healthy young women," remarked Missi, diplomatically.

Thena arrived a minute later. She knew Cassie wanted commiseration, but all she added was, "Meh. The heart wants what the heart wants."

"They're bringing them. I asked them not to and they are bringing them!" said Cassie. "Dad even mentioned they were thinking about getting engaged, which is strange now that I think about it. How did he find out? They aren't even speaking to him."

"I think Lux mentioned it to Nia who told my mom and dad, and they passed it onto your parents—through separate channels, of course," reported Missi, not stopping to take a breath.

Cassie sighed and fiddled with her spoonful of broth and noodles.

"What's wrong with you?" asked Thena, squaring off at Cassie who was acting as if her brothers had committed some horrible breach of family etiquette by getting girlfriends.

Cassie pursed her lips for a moment. "Why would Lux tell Nia about maybe getting engaged?"

Thena and Missi exchanged a quick look.

Missi scoffed, "The same reason you tell us stuff and not them. They all hang around together and have their own little clique, just like we do."

"We don't have a clique," protested Cassie, slipping off her chair and carrying her bowl into the kitchen.

"Don't we?" laughed Thena. "We still treat them like little kids."

Cassie slurped down the last bite of pho, reached for a cloth napkin, then turned to face Missi and Thena.

"I treat them like younger brothers, which they are."

"Okay, then, what would you have said?"

"Well, I would've asked a lot of questions about these girls and—"

Missi threw up a hand and cut her off. "Yep, precisely why you were not informed, and Nia was, Cass. The lover boys didn't want you to ruin their party."

"Okay, you two can laugh it up, but you aren't about to inherit two farm-fed, toothy identical twins as sisters-in-law. I can only take so much. This year has been..." Cassie caught her breath then deflated, "it's been a lot and I want things to slow down and get back to normal."

"Will you return to work for Harold?" asked Thena quietly.

Cassie fell back on the couch, covered her eyes, and groaned, "I need distance from that situation. Maybe it's time to try something new."

CHAPTER 28

Socrates & Harold Contemplate Now and Then

November 2015

A DAY HAD PASSED since Harold confessed—for the first time ever—intimate feelings to another human being. He slept a hard, dreamless sleep, putting in eight and a half hours, the likes he'd not experienced since childhood.

The next morning, as he prepared to leave for the Entwistles, Harold's brain was tossing around a new vegetarian dish he could surprise Persephone with at Thanksgiving. Every year, Harold crafted a delicious vegetarian dish that was often more popular than the traditional favorites. And every year, Persephone bestowed upon him a gaze of adoration that put a lightness in his step, as if, in this small thing, he had done some great service for the world. The shift back to his old self gave Harold a renewed sense of creativity.

Socrates had requested they meet up to discuss their plans to help Aeneas with his 'special talent' and Harold had put him off several times. This morning in a happier state of mind, he agreed and headed over to Freshy's.

Walking past the front window of the coffee shop, Harold came to an abrupt stop and leaned his face and hands against the window, staring at Socrates. Harold was oblivious to the barista's fiery stare as he smudged the window she'd spent twenty minutes cleaning a few hours before. The barista continued to stare at Harold as a passerby made a wide berth around the strange man pressing his face against the coffeeshop window. Socrates, engrossed in his book, paid him no notice until a few seconds later when the barista called out, "Hey, isn't that your friend? Tell him not to lean against the window."

Socrates jerked his head up and threw his arm forward, knocking over his coffee, and releasing some colorful swear words instead of his usual cultured, academic vocabulary. He waved Harold in.

"Hi, Harold," said Socrates flatly as Harold arrived at the table with some paper towels handed to him by the barista.

"We should leave a large gratuity," whispered Harold furtively.

"We?" replied Socrates, gesturing to Harold's imprint on the storefront window.

Harold slid into the booth, nodded to the book on the table, his face barely able to contain his questions.

"Oh, so, this is why you nearly collapsed the storefront window?" Socrates said, pointing to the paperback about physics and God.

"You once told me you were an agnostic leaning toward atheism, but willing to entertain the idea of intelligent evolution, Sox. This is a shock for me."

Socrates snorted. "Well, recently we've witnessed some unexplainable events, so at this point I'm open to avenues I've never previously considered."

"Have Archie and Miranda seen this book?" inquired Harold delicately as he carefully flipped to the section about the author.

Socrates glared at him. "No, and please don't mention it. It will only invite speculation and launch Persephone into sleuth mode."

Harold laughed loudly and received another cool glance from the barista. It was in everyone's best interest not to pique Persephone's curiosity.

Socrates lowered his voice. "Get some coffee and let's confer about our mutual interest." He now referred to his brother Aeneas in code.

"I might have you place my order and tell her to keep the change," said Harold sheepishly, sliding him a twenty.

A tiny grin crept across Socrates's face, and he grabbed the bill. It wasn't the first time he'd smoothed over a situation for Harold.

Five minutes later a frothy cappuccino and a carrot cake muffin settled Harold's concerns as he and Socrates got down to business.

"Aeneas is doing well in resisting the pull to enter the timestream. He knows how to identify the feeling he gets even before he sees the twinkling lights," offered Harold optimistically.

"But what about when he sleeps?" asked Socrates. "That's a big risk. A large earthquake opens the timestream at three in the morning... he's whisked away either into the past, or worse, the future. And for him, it feels like a dream. He doesn't know how to leave and head home."

Harold smiled. "I was thinking about something Cassie told me."

Socrates looked at him warily and tried to steady his voice.

"She's not come back again, has she?"

Harold wasn't aware that Socrates had forcibly sent Cassie back to her present two days before.

"No. It was something she told me about when adult Aeneas was swept into the timestream, and she followed him to attempt a rescue."

Socrates tried to keep a calm face. He didn't want an epic battle with a love-stricken programmer and a headstrong time traveler.

"Cassie was hypnotized and walked herself back through the events to find out some clues about where Aeneas had been thrown back into his past."

Socrates felt the panic release from his body, and he gave Harold an encouraging gesture. "Go on then."

"We could hypnotize Aeneas to wake up when the sensation hits—set some parameters in his subconscious so when the 'feeling' hits, he's alerted and puts the brakes on, so to speak."

Socrates was quiet. Harold turned his attention back to the muffin while Socrates mulled it over. Finally, Harold couldn't wait any longer, though to be fair it had only been about two minutes.

"Any objections to trying this out?"

"You know, Harold, it's totally possible that we could use this in the short term. In the long term, Aeneas needs to consciously decline. Kind of like someone knocking on his bedroom door in the middle of the night inviting him to go out. He'd wave them off and stay in bed."

"I still have a concern," said Harold, lowering his voice.

Socrates leaned in closer.

"We need someone we can trust, Sox. We can't leave loose ends. Aeneas will need to be protected from people who might use him for their own purposes."

~

April 2053

The sun peeked through the clouds as Socrates and Harold ambled along Alki Beach. Neither said much for a while. Harold knew they needed to talk about it, but where to start? They knew long ago that Cassie's presence in 2015 might have had unintended consequences. They just never assumed it would be for each of them.

"I don't remember not having Nia," said Socrates as they plodded along, gravel crunching under their feet. Harold grabbed a handkerchief and blew his nose. The cool sea air made his nose run. He raised his bushy eyebrows and looked at Socrates expectantly.

"What changed about your life that brought another baby into the picture?"

Socrates shrugged. "I kept thinking about when Keniah got pregnant with Nia. The circumstances around her conception. It seemed random, you know?"

"You weren't trying for another baby?"

"No, but we weren't very careful, either. We were having a great time. We'd gone to Iceland without the girls. We were carefree, driving the Golden Circle, loving Icelandic culture and the wild landscape."

"Who planned the vacation?"

Socrates stopped and thought back for a moment, giving Harold a sheepish grin. "Me."

Harold raised a bushy eyebrow. "And whose idea was it to go without the girls?"

"I don't recall it being a specific person." Socrates frowned, trying to recall the conversation. "We just decided. And off we went."

"Would the pre-Cassie, panic-prone version of you have left the girls behind or even gone so far afield when they were young?"

Socrates stopped. They sat on the seawall and stared out across Elliot Bay.

"It had to be because Aeneas was the man in the park that day and there was no kidnapping attempt," said Socrates. "That's what changed me. And that happened on Cassie's second return."

Harold tilted his head toward the beach. He liked to keep moving. It kept his neurons firing more efficiently.

"We don't have the benefit of the previous versions, except the details they've shared with us, so it's all speculation," said Harold.

"From what Aeneas says, you dated here and there, but never settled. Then after Cassie's second visit, you and Meg were married."

"It sounds creepy because I'm old now, but I was blown away by Cassie." A dreamy smile appeared on Harold's face. "She's like you and Miranda. She's magnetic."

"So, Cassie's second visit made you realize you had to move on or be stuck always pining away?"

"Well, that was Tabitha practicing her early therapy skills on me."

"Oh yeah. I remember. One of the few times I nearly punched you."

"Well, l was an idiot. You had every right."

Socrates laughed.

"Finding out Aeneas was the guy in the park was a huge relief, even though it was nearly nine years later."

"But that moderated you, Sox. It must've changed the choices that you made because one of those resulted in a baby!" exclaimed Harold.

CHAPTER 29

Nocturnal Invitation Consternation

Spring 2053

Nestled in her bed under soft cotton sheets, Cassie slept well for several hours. The discussion to decide the fate of Sadie drained everyone and when Cassie plopped into her bed early in the evening, she'd fallen instantly asleep. Around 2:40 a.m., a full bladder sent Cassie shuffling her way to the bathroom, doing what her mom used to call "sleep pee" where she was barely awake beyond the robotic motions of empty-ing the bladder, and then crawled back into bed. Cassie sighed and closed her eyes, resting her head on her pillow, her face turned to the right side, a favorite way to start her sleep. She was nearly there, just a few more seconds before her conscious mind shut down again when she heard an indistinct sound that caught her attention. Rolling over, Cassie sighed deeply, ready to fall off again when a twinkling drew her eyes up toward the ceiling. An ear-splitting scream alerted the virtual butler and immediately her bedroom room lights popped on.

"Madam! Do you require emergency services?"

Cassie leaped from her bed and was scanning the bedroom ceiling. The remnants of the timestream were open and she could have sworn someone had been watching her.

"Mr. House," cried Cassie breathlessly, "Is anyone else here?"

"No, Madam, you are alone," replied the virtual butler.

"House, check the PNSN (Pacific Northwest Seismic Network) for seismic activity," called Cassie, throwing on her robe.

"Madam, a five point two earthquake occurred offshore near the coast of Victoria Island two hours ago."

"Hmm. Glad I slept through that," mumbled Cassie trudging toward the kitchen. She was shaky and her heart was still slamming inside her chest when there was a knock on her door. Cassie leapt and let out another scream.

"Madam! We need to call emergency services," urged the virtual butler.

"Mr. House, who is at the door?"

"No one, Madam."

Cassie whispered, "Mr. House, someone knocked on the door."

"Yes, Madam, but no one is outside the door."

Cassie took a deep breath and focused. Maybe a neighbor heard her scream and knocked to check on her. She could hear Tabitha in her head, *the most likely explanation is usually correct, but always go with your gut.*

"Mr. House, check the video feed. Was anyone at the front door a few moments ago?"

"Madam the video feed shows no one outside the door; however there appears to be an envelope."

"This is getting stupid," grumped Cassie.

"SAIL, open the video feed for the door and play back the last five minutes."

A holographic screen opened, and Cassie reviewed playback of the video feed outside her front door. Nothing out of the ordinary appeared. She was about to close out of the screen and open the front door when an arm appeared out of nowhere, dropped an envelope, and rapped two quick knocks on her door.

"Wow. Could it get any weirder around here?"

"Madam, do you wish for me to call anyone?"

"No, Mr. House. I don't know anyone I could explain this to..." Cassie paused and rolled her eyes. "Except maybe Harold."

"Madam, I have sent a report to Harold via the SAIL."

"What?" squawked Cassie.

"Mr. House, it's three a.m. Harold is asleep!"

"Madam, that is not correct. Harold is awake according to the virtual butler program monitoring his home."

Cassie peered through the peephole. There was a small blue envelope outside her door.

"Mr. House, unlock the door while I grab the envelope then relock it immediately."

Locks clicked. Cassie turned the knob, leaned out, snatched the envelope as the door slammed and the locks clicked again. Handwritten in dark blue ink was her full name:

Cassiopeia Valentina Entwistle

The SAIL flashed. An incoming call from Harold.

"Damn it," huffed Cassie under her breath.

"SAIL, send message to Harold and ask him to meet me for coffee at seven a.m. sharp at our usual place in downtown Seattle."

"Madam, your SAIL is about to be overridden unless I can confirm you are safe."

"SAIL, send a picture to Harold." A barely perceptible flash passed before her eyes as Cassie's fake smile was sent to Harold.

Snuggled back in her bed, Cassie examined the dainty envelope. The handwriting on the front was a quick script slanted to the right.

The middle name was what threw Cassie. Valentina had been her middle name before Aeneas had altered Sadie's past. So, whoever sent the note was aware of the change, which meant it could be someone very close to her or someone she wasn't aware of who knew about her family. Cassie anxiously opened it.

Dear Cassie,

Please meet me tomorrow at the top of the Space Needle at 11:30 a.m. I would like to buy you lunch and discuss our mutual talents.

Sincerely,

Toshiro

~

A few blocks south of Pike Place Market, the coffee shop where Harold and Cassie were scheduled to meet was bustling at seven in the morning. A local couple had been searching for an investor and Harold had given them some start-up cash a few years back because he was completely sold on the name. Known as *The Rotator Cup*, the quirky cafe featured coffee cups stored in a giant rotating glass cabinet in the center of the shop. The ceramic cups were dispensed at random to customers who came to order coffee. Hand painted by local artists, inscribed with quirky or inspirational sayings, it was rare to get the same cup twice, but if you did, the coffee was free. It was a cheerful place where Cassie and Harold often met which was why she suggested it. Harold stood as she walked in. She gave him a half-hearted wave and waited for her coconut milk latte and breakfast burrito.

"How are you?" asked Harold quietly.

He'd been sleeping poorly. Things felt unresolved between him and Cassie, but he was hopeful her request to meet meant some forward progress could be made.

"It's been a weird couple of months, Harold."

"I agree. Your trip to the past shifted a lot of things. We'd always suspected that was possible, but it wasn't until you, me, and Socrates tried to save Aeneas that..." Harold stopped and stared into his green matcha tea.

Cassie picked up the conversation, "... that real changes occurred. But things filled in for non-travelers in ways that you might not have noticed if you weren't aware I'd gone back in time."

"What happens now?" Harold gestured to himself and Cassie. He thought he could wait for her to bring it up, but he suddenly felt the need to push things along.

Cassie swallowed. "I'm not sure if I want to keep working for you. A lot has happened with my family, and I really feel unsettled."

Harold started to say something, then changed his mind. It was best just to listen. He learned that from a lifetime with Meg.

"But I do need you in my life, Harold," said Cassie softly.

"I'm always here for you," replied Harold, reaching out to pat her hand but grabbed his coffee cup instead. He wasn't sure how to behave after sending the message from 2015. They sat in silence for a minute then Cassie pulled something from her bag.

"I have something to show you." She slid the blue envelope between them. "Can you read this while I eat my burrito?"

Harold's eyes widened as he examined the invitation.

"Mutual talents?" muttered Harold. He looked up at Cassie skeptically.

"Yes," replied Cassie between chews. "There are others in the timestream, Harold, besides the North Sky contingent. When I found the sapphire blue sphere-like anomaly on Mom's timeline and entered one of the pixelated realities, someone warned me to get out."

"Have you told Aeneas?" asked Harold as he stared at the outside of the envelope trying to figure out what was bugging him about it.

"Nope. There's already a huge mess to clean up. I didn't think I should toss anymore on the pile, as Dad likes to say."

Harold flipped the envelope to face Cassie. "Your middle name is Eleanor, not Valentina?"

"Depends on what version of the present we're in," replied Cassie dryly. "But let's skip that story for now. Wanna hear how this was delivered? Now that's an intriguing story." Cassie smiled jokingly at Harold, trying to find her footing in their unusual new relationship.

"I'll need more tea."

"And I'll need another burrito," chirped Cassie.

"Bulking up for a trip?" teased Harold.

Cassie glared at him. "We aren't there yet, Harold."

"Gotcha. I'll go place another order."

Three cups of matcha later, Harold wasn't convinced meeting Toshiro was a reasonable idea.

"If you're determined to meet this person, I think you should bring Aeneas along."

"I'm not bringing my dad with me to a lunch date," snorted Cassie. "I'm not a seven-year-old!"

"Lunch date?" repeated Harold.

"Meeting," clarified Cassie.

"Whatever you call it... you're meeting a stranger who is apparently more aware of you than you are of him. Reminds me of a scene in a movie where the audience looks back and says, 'she should have never gone to that lunch meeting alone.'" Harold crossed his arms and stared her down. He couldn't help being protective of Cassie.

Cassie rolled her eyes dramatically then stood up. "We'll be eating lunch in a public place, which reminds me, I need to get ready." Cassie backed away from the table, leaving Harold to contemplate his misgivings about her decision.

CHAPTER 30

Cloak and Dagger Meet Cute

Spring 2053

CASSIE TOUCHED THE LARGE white opal that rested halfway up her forearm. The iridescent gemstone was surrounded by smaller white opals set in an old-fashioned filigree, a gift from her grandmother, Miranda. Grandpa Archie had purchased the bracelet when he visited Australia back in the nineties. It was one of Cassie's most cherished possessions and had been gifted to her on her twenty-first birthday. She'd slid it on her arm at the last minute before she hurried to catch the bus.

Cassie wore two golden rings on her first and second finger of her right hand. The rings, gifts from her twin brothers on her eighteenth birthday, were inscribed with their names using the Greek alphabet and handcrafted from eighteen carat gold. Tor and Lux teased that they were the first men to ever give her rings then hooted in laughter until Tabitha threatened them with bed and no cake. The bracelet and rings along with her opal studs were the most jewelry Cassie had ever worn to any meeting or date and she was suddenly feeling a little silly about it.

The electric bus cruised downtown. Cassie felt her stomach lurch as each stop brought her closer to the Space Needle. She took a deep breath to offset the panic that wormed its way into her thoughts.

I've hardly had time to think about this.

What if this Toshiro guy is some kind of time-traveling mercenary who wants to kidnap me and use me for some evil purpose? I should've told Dad. I should've called Sheila and asked about other groups of travelers.

Harold's cautionary tale/horror movie scenario was playing pinball in her brain. Glancing at herself in the bus window, Cassie snorted.

I got all gussied up, as Grandma Freeman would say, for some guy I don't even know who might be a stalker or a kidnapper!

Cassie reached in her pocket. Her SAIL had vibrated several times and multiple colors flashed. Cassie slipped on her sunglasses and lightly tapped the left arm to initiate contact with the SAIL. A tiny holographic screen projected in her field of vision and the messages appeared in the order they arrived.

Two more warnings from a panicked Harold. One message from her mom about the imminent arrival of Lux, Tor, and the twits. And one from her dad asking to meet him as soon as possible.

Cassie tapped the left arm again, flipped the sunglasses back on top of her head and groaned, "I'm overdue for something fun."

A smartly dressed older lady seated across from her gave a quick wink as she stood to exit the bus and said, "Aren't we all, honey?"

Laughing, Cassie looked up and realized it was her stop, too. She grabbed her bag, made her way to the sidewalk, and stopped cold.

The back of her neck prickled. Cassie turned abruptly. People were milling about everywhere. She couldn't see anyone watching her, but her body definitely *sensed* someone. The Space Needle loomed above.

"Here goes," she whispered.

The new solar-powered elevator whisked her toward the top, doing nothing to curb the tension in her stomach. Cassie stepped off and steadied herself against a nearby wall while her inner monologue rattled off warnings, courtesy of her mother. *If my gut tells me it's a no-go, then I'm leaving.*

Wearing black slacks, a loose burgundy blouse that cinched at her waist, Cassie was effortlessly gorgeous as she walked into the restaurant. Her eyes scanned back and forth, searching for anyone who looked like he'd be called *Toshiro*.

"Late, I guess," muttered Cassie scrutinizing the occupants.

"Shall we find a table?"

Cassie whirled to her left to see the same dark eyes and a well-defined jaw from the day she escaped the sapphire sphere. A small gasp escaped her lips. Toshiro was the hottie!

"Apologies. I thought you noticed my arrival," said Toshiro, struggling to keep a modest grin.

"I did not," replied Cassie formally, trying to recover her poise having been caught off guard. Toshiro gestured toward a cozy table near some hanging plants.

"The table just a few feet to our left is open."

Cassie seated herself, making several movements, placing her napkin in her lap, and adjusting her chair. She wasn't quite ready for direct eye contact and busied herself to avoid it. Toshiro was taller than she'd imagined, his long black coat created a sleek line. His jet-black hair was swept sharply to one side, but his expression was just shy of a playful smile. The top two buttons of his white shirt opened to reveal a pendant necklace, but Cassie couldn't make out the symbol as she cut a quick glance at his chest. Deciding this was all too much to take in, Cassie dispensed with any niceties. She placed her hands delicately on the table and leaned slightly forward.

"So, you've been spying on me in the timestream?"

Toshiro raised an eyebrow. Cassie held his gaze without breaking eye contact. He stared back, then calmly answered, "I've been trying to find the right time to set up a meeting with you."

He wasn't easily rattled, and Cassie prodded further.

"So, how long have you been watching me?"

Toshiro hesitated as the server arrived, placed two glasses of water at their table and asked if they would like the lunch special. Cassie, still on the offensive and impatient for an answer, abruptly replied yes.

"I haven't even looked at the menu yet," he said, pointing to the digital screen on the tabletop.

"Are we really here to eat?" snapped Cassie.

"Well, not completely," replied Toshiro slowly.

"Here I am. What do you want from me?"

"I have important information to share with you."

"Well, go on then." Cassie was determined to keep their meeting all business.

Toshiro spoke in a hushed voice. "You really have no idea who you are, do you, Cassie Entwistle?"

Cassie rolled her eyes. She hoped this Toshiro guy wasn't some time-traveling cult leader trying to recruit her.

"I've been the same person for the last twenty-four years," countered Cassie. "Pretty confident I know who I am."

Toshiro started to speak when two cups of soup arrived with a flourish. The server was back. It hadn't been two minutes! Cassie's head jerked up.

"What's this?" she sputtered, as if the soup had somehow offended her with its presence.

"It's the starter," said the server irritably, looking at Cassie as if she should know what she'd ordered. "It's cream of artichoke soup. The next course will be out in about ten minutes."

The server turned quickly to deliver the same soup to a nearby table and vanished into the kitchen. Toshiro picked up a spoon and tasted the soup. He made a small noise of appreciation.

"Please continue," hissed Cassie impatiently.

"In my country, if someone orders food for you, it's considered the height of rudeness not to eat it," replied Toshiro, taking another spoonful. A mischievous smile crossed his face. "It's delicious. You should try it."

Cassie reluctantly picked up her spoon. The soup smelled wonderful. Toshiro continued to eat, then paused to wipe his mouth.

"In Japan, time travelers like you are born every few generations. Even among the Alaskan shamans who have held fast to their traditions and rarely let in outsiders, your strength and prowess in the timestream would be considered rare."

Cassie snorted. "Uh, I'm just an average time traveler, Toshiro." Three bites of the hot rich soup had relaxed her a bit. Plus, she wasn't buying this cloak and dagger business.

"You survived the multiple realities temporal anomaly created by your father's folly," said Toshiro, giving her a look of admiration.

"Hey, my dad's a romantic. It makes him illogical at times, but he's a good guy," replied Cassie. She knew Toshiro was right, but Aeneas was her father after all.

"I meant no offense. My wording was not tactful."

"And you're exaggerating my abilities. I've got a little more stamina than Aeneas in the timestream, but not much. I'm younger than he is and even though he wouldn't admit to it, I'm in better shape, too."

Toshiro quietly regarded Cassie. She was passionate and stubborn, but humble, too, which would be an asset if she accepted his offer.

"Here we are," said the server, placing plates in front of them. "Two chef's specials. Omelets topped with smoked fish, fresh herbs, and goat cheese."

Cassie looked bewildered and gestured to her plate. "This is lunch?"

"You ordered the special, miss," replied the server curtly. "And today's special is *brunch.*"

"Thank you very much," said Toshiro formally as he gazed at the plate, smiling.

"Do you like this sort of food?" asked Cassie, now embarrassed that she'd ordered his meal.

"Yes," replied Toshiro enthusiastically as he neatly cut a slice of the omelet.

Cassie took a bite and then another. Toshiro continued to eat until his plate was empty. Neither spoke as they ate.

The server dropped off a steaming latte for Toshiro and he sipped it while Cassie finished her last few bites.

"Your brother, Lux, knows more than he's telling you," said Toshiro evenly.

"This sounds like the plot of an old movie, and I think—" Cassie was interrupted by the return of the server to take the plates. He was annoyingly efficient.

"The geneticist," Toshiro continued, "has mapped your genome. He knows about you, or at least he suspects."

"Suspects what?"

"Ask him," urged Toshiro, taking a long drink of his latte and placing the cup on the table.

Cassie dropped her pushiness, and said softly, "Why don't *you* just tell me?"

"I think it would be best if you talk with your brother," replied Toshiro, tapping the table to pay their bill.

Cassie started to argue for more details, but Toshiro stood quickly. With a small smile, he bowed and said, "I'll meet you here for lunch again in two days and we can talk more. But next time, I'll order for us."

~

There wasn't much Harold could do but wait for Cassie's lunch to be over. He watched the exit carefully. He was lingering by Wright fountain when something caught his eye. A well-dressed young man walked into view and cut a glance at Harold. His long black coat and dark, spiky hair reminded Harold of a character in a movie. Harold watched as he was absorbed into the throng of people walking away from the Space Needle.

On impulse, he took off after him. *Why am I doing this?* thought Harold as he weaved around pedestrians. *It might not even be him.* He caught sight of the tall, dark-haired young man who slowed as he approached the Neototems Children's Garden, briefly surveying the area. The space was alive with giggles and squeals, parents, strollers, and dogs. Harold slowed, too. After a moment, the young man walked briskly toward some trees just beyond the whale fluke sculpture and Harold lost sight of him. He sped up, dodging around a cluster of kids playing, but when he reached the trees, there was no one. Not a soul.

Cassie Dishes, C.J. Comes Clean

Spring 2053

"So, what happened at this mysterious meeting?" asked Thena. Like Harold, she'd been waiting anxiously for Cassie to finish her meeting with the mysterious Toshiro, but unlike Harold, Thena was privy to the post-lunch debriefing.

"A lot happened, but first, Toshiro is the guy I saw in the timestream."

"Oh my gosh. I had a feeling it might the same guy!" cried Missi, nestled on her couch with a glass of wine. "Was he even better looking in person?"

"Does it matter?"

"Yes, it does!" exclaimed Missi with a cheeky smile. She eyed Cassie playfully. "Because if you're attracted to him then who better to date than another time traveler? Someone who could fully share your lifestyle." Missi had been chatting with Thena about how to supplant Cassie's feelings for Harold with a new distraction.

"Slow, down, sister," countered Thena, waving her hands emphatically. "Cassie needs to find out this guy's angle. So, go on. What did he say?"

"Toshiro indicated I was sort of... above average as time travelers go, and said that he'd wanted to meet me for a long time."

"Is he also above average?" asked Missi, barely able to contain her excitement.

"I'd guess yes. He was able to maneuver inside the timestream in a way I've never seen before."

"So, was what was this lunch about?" prodded Thena, wondering if this was less personal and more professional.

"I dunno. He was..." Cassie stopped. She was struggling to explain her impression of Toshiro. Thena knew if her cousin didn't divulge every single detail then she was withholding crucial bits.

"Go on," urged Thena. Missi smiled to herself. Thena would push Cassie until they got the full story.

"Well, I was leery at first, but after a while..." Cassie hesitated.

"What?" barked Thena, throwing Cassie a get-on-with-it glare.

"Well... intelligent, dry humored, cultured, polite... nothing weird that set off my gut alarms."

"Anything else?" pressed Missi who felt she'd been dragged through a conversation seriously lacking in detail and needed to determine if Toshiro could serve as a welcomed distraction.

"I already told you he was attractive, Missi."

"But that was in the timestream. What about up close and personal?"

Cassie slumped in her chair. There was no point in trying to cover it. "Tall, lean and muscular... stylish dresser. His hair was short and spiky, giving him a look of mystery. He wore an interesting pendant, too."

Missi grinned, rolling the last of her wine in the glass, gears turning.

Thena wasn't quite sold, though. "We've established he's easy on the eyes. What else did you talk about?"

"Toshiro said there was proof I was above average. He said I should talk to Lux. That Lux has some suspicions about my DNA that he isn't telling me."

"Do you believe him?"

Cassie shrugged. "I know Lux has been mucking around with my DNA for years. He's never said anything though."

"Well, he wouldn't, would he? Until he was sure," replied Thena. She considered Lux to be quieter and more reflective than Tor, at least when he was on his own. Putting the twins together was like egging on a chaos of silliness.

"But how did Toshiro know about this?" asked Missi. Thena nodded, giving her sister a satisfied look. Missi was a romantic and could get caught up in the fairy tale when there were real dangers lurking.

"That's where it gets weird for me, but we're meeting again at the Space Needle for lunch in two days, and this time I'll be ready."

"Well, don't let your guard down," warned Thena, exchanging a concerned look with Missi, who rolled her eyes, exasperated that her match-making plans had been stymied for now.

"Don't worry. I'll be vigilant. But first, I need to talk to my little brother."

~

C.J. closed his son's bedroom door. Aeneas, having eaten enough lunch for two, needed a nap. He wasn't looking well, but his appetite persisted. Frequent time travel, the implosion of his marriage, the shame of his mistake—combined with the lingering weakness from the time he spent in 2015 living as a homeless man—had worn him down. And C.J., self-appointed guardian of Aeneas, was fuming. He could easily blame Aeneas for all this, but Aeneas was doing a fine job of that without anyone else, save Socrates, adding to his guilt.

Lyla was tidying up the lunch leftovers in the kitchen when C.J. walked in looking for her.

"I'm going to see Tabitha," said C.J. placing a kiss on her cheek.

Lyla shook her head. "I would stay out of it. She's your cousin and he's your best friend, but it's *their* marriage." She hooked her arm through his and spoke quietly, "Do you absolutely need to butt in?"

C.J. had not confided to Lyla that the present had been changed and Sadie, whom she'd known for years, was never supposed to live past age sixteen. His hope was that things could be adjusted, and she would never know. C.J. yawned and ran his hands down his face.

"I know you're probably right, but Tabitha and I haven't talked since she threw Aeneas out. There are some things we need to clear up."

Lyla gave him the look she always did when they didn't see eye to eye and released his arm. C.J. wished he could tell her that what needed clearing up was Tabitha's persistent bossiness, but that was too long of a story.

Tabitha was busying herself for the arrival of her sons. Tor had sent a message asking if Lana and Lanna could be house guests and she didn't have the heart to decline. They'd not spoken to her since she told them that Aeneas was moving out and they were "giving each other some space."

C.J. called out as he entered the house; he was always welcome, but things felt strained since Aeneas's departure. Though no one had said it outright, a line had been drawn and C.J. was firmly on Aeneas's side.

"In here," called Tabitha.

C.J. found her in the living room stacking bath towels, hand towels, and washcloths on the sofa. Several small vases with fresh flowers were clustered on a table behind her. When Tabitha was young her parents were great hosts, ensuring each guest had their own fresh towels and their own space, no matter how humble. Thinking back, it seemed logical and hygienic. Plus, it helped Tabitha feel calm. That had become a challenge since she'd thrown out her husband, become estranged from Sadie, and watched her whole family pretend not to take sides.

"The boys are headed home today. I'm just sprucing things up for their guests."

C.J. nodded. "Lana and Lana?"

Tabitha rolled her eyes. "No, Lana and *Lanna*. Like lane change and lawn chair," replied Tabitha brightly.

"Huh," coughed C.J., suppressing a laugh. "Are you going to give them those nicknames, lane change and lawn chair? Because your daughter calls them the twits."

"She doesn't," gasped Tabitha.

"Well, I doubt to their faces, but you know how sharp Cassie can be."

Tabitha sighed. "Yes, we're all aware." Secretly she attributed her daughter's sharpness to Aeneas's gene pool, all evidence pointing to Persephone.

Tabitha eyed C.J. deliberately. "So, you've come on his behalf?"

"No. I've come on yours." Tabitha let her gaze settle on C.J. and he let his settle on her. The days when Tabitha could push him around with a glance were long gone. The staring contest lasted a full six seconds before Tabitha broke eye contact and muttered, "Well, get on with it."

"You've done this to yourself, Tab." The words hung in the air for a second. Tabitha flushed, ready to let loose on C.J., but he quickly dropped a hard blow, one he knew would set things off like a pack of firecrackers.

"And everyone knows but you," he gloated.

C.J. walked home pumped full of adrenaline. Tabitha had thrown him out. She'd yelled, "Get out, C.J."

But he'd had the last word, a minor triumph after forty plus years jockeying to feel at least her equal.

"Ask around. There are some terrible liars in your family," he called back as he exited the house.

Lyla was waiting for him in the kitchen when he got back.

"How'd it go?" she asked quietly, swiftly chopping vegetables. She paused and gestured toward the sunroom where Aeneas was watching an old Sounders game from 2019.

"He was rummaging through the pantry," she whispered, "so, I'm throwing together some stir fry so he can have something easy to reheat."

"Thank you." C.J. leaned in and gave his wife a long kiss. This bust-up between his best friends made him deeply appreciate his own marriage.

"What did Tabitha say?" whispered Lyla, playfully pushing him back.

"Not much."

"What did *you* say?"

C.J. glanced toward the sunroom. "I said what no one else would say to her, not even Aeneas."

"And what will that accomplish?"

"It'll force Tabitha to clean up her mess," said C.J. smugly.

Everyone Knows
But You...

Spring 2053

TABITHA PACED AROUND THE house trying to hold back tears. It had all happened so fast. Sadie had come to town to visit and talk about the next steps in her life. She'd been blindsided by her divorce and needed the company and advice of old friends. Aeneas had made the three of them dinner. Lux had gone out for the evening to listen to live music with friends. After dinner, Aeneas was prepping ingredients for some hot fudge sundaes and Tabitha left to get more ice cream. She'd walked back in from the garage, having forgotten to bring along her bags, and found them kissing. What followed was a screaming match that rivaled the old reality TV shows.

When Lux came home, Aeneas was packing some things to take to C.J.'s, Sadie had gone to a hotel, and Tabitha seemed done with everyone, even her son.

EVERYONE KNOWS BUT YOU...

Tabitha stopped pacing. C.J. seemed confident this situation was all her fault. And he wouldn't make that accusation unless he knew something she didn't. And then there was the crack about her family being terrible liars which meant all she had to do was ask and someone was bound to point the finger back at her. She stopped to look at her reflection in the glass paneled bookcase.

"I'm not ready to see Aeneas and I can't take anymore of C.J. right now," Tabitha said out loud. "Sox and Keniah are a no-go. Cassie's out of the question. That leaves Harold or Seph. And Harold would be uncomfortable if I asked him."

Tabitha hadn't moved a muscle, still gazing at her reflection. "I suppose the quickest way would be to ask Seph. Quick, but not painless."

Persephone and her wife, Caitlyn, lived in a spacious weathered cottage in the quiet community of Agate Point on the north end of Bainbridge Island. Tabitha decided to drop in unannounced and scrambled to catch the 5:40 afternoon ferry. Seph was always home from the lab by four p.m.

"Hi, Tabitha," said Caitlyn cheerfully, wrapping her in a hug. Caitlyn was a big hugger.

"Seph, honey, Tabitha is here!" Caitlyn ushered her past two leaping dogs of unknown breed. Tabitha smiled, giving each pup a hearty petting. Seph and Caitlyn had only been married a few years. Persephone had been a workaholic, but too many failed relationships had made her rethink her priorities. She'd met Caitlyn Wong at a charity function, and they'd been together ever since. Caitlyn's family was old Seattle tech money and she'd spent most of her life involved in charity work, but her real passion was criminal rehab through farming. She owned a farming rehabilitation center on Bainbridge Island and was opening another soon on Vashon Island. Tabitha slowed down as she approached the kitchen, wrinkling her nose. Persephone was stirring a pot of something that smelled hideous.

"I hope that's not dinner."

"I'm brewing some compost tea for testing microbes that can ingest older forms of non-recyclable plastic."

"In the kitchen?" Tabitha looked to Caitlyn for support, but she was still smiling, oblivious to the stench.

"This is just a practice batch using strains from my back-yard bin."

"Oh," said Tabitha, not sure what to say after that. She'd planned to dive right in, but the words got stuck.

"Something on your mind, Tab?"

Tabitha nodded, still unsure how to get the conversation going.

"I'll take the pups for a walk around the neighborhood, Seph." Caitlyn gave Tabitha a breezy wave and the two were left alone in the kitchen with the compost tea wafting around them.

"This thing that happened with Sadie..." Tabitha swallowed, trying to keep her composure. Persephone locked eyes with her. "Did I... was I...?" Tabitha heaved a huge sigh and closed her eyes tightly.

"Yes. It's definitely fifty percent your fault, perhaps more, depending how you view the situation," volunteered Persephone as if she were analyzing data from an experiment, which to be fair was kind of where her brain lived. Tabitha's eyes flew open. She expected Persephone to be blunt, but she hadn't prepared herself for a direct hit.

"Can you please explain this to me, Seph?"

Persephone shook her head, light brown curls bobbing back and forth as she gave another stir.

"Nope."

Tabitha was stunned. She was prepared to take a seat at the counter while a full dissertation spewed forth.

"Because?"

"Because when I need data, Tabitha, I go straight to the original study, not the sound bite."

The ferry ride back was a little choppy which did little to quell Tabitha's nausea. All she could think was how quickly Persephone had responded. And her certainty in Tabitha's culpability. If you'd asked her that morning if she were willing to talk with Aeneas, the answer would have easily been not a chance. But now she had no choice. She called and asked him to meet with her.

Aeneas met her at the ferry terminal, and they rode in silence to The Cookie Palace on the outskirts of Pike Place Market. It seemed a strange place for them to meet, but it wasn't too crowded, and Aeneas thought he might as well eat a cookie if things went badly.

The Cookie Palace was well-appointed with velvet armchairs, handsome ornate wooden tables, and beautiful rugs and tapestries. Aeneas walked back to their booth, which curved around an intricately carved table and handed Tabitha a small plate. She looked down and suppressed a smile. Dark chocolate peppermint. One of her favorites. Aeneas's plate had three cookies which all seemed to be variations of oatmeal.

"Hungry?" sneered Tabitha.

"Well, I'm not sure how this conversation's gonna go, so I thought I'd be prepared to be here a while," replied Aeneas. He waited for her to say something. She'd called him. Seconds ticked away and Aeneas felt uneasy. Finally, Tabitha spoke.

"You forgot the drinks."

"I'll go back to the counter," offered Aeneas.

But Tabitha had already walked toward the wooden bar where the barista was working. She came back with two milky coffees in silver-plated goblets, perfect for dunking cookies.

"Thanks," sighed Aeneas, taking his mug. Tabitha broke off a piece of cookie and dipped it in her coffee.

"So, why is this at least fifty percent my fault?" asked Tabitha, scowling. Aeneas sensed she didn't bring herself to this conclusion.

"Who told you that?"

Tabitha dropped her cookie. She looked even more incensed than she had that night in the kitchen with Sadie.

"C.J."

"Really?"

Tabitha's face bloomed red. "Yes, and later Persephone."

"Hold on, Tab," sputtered Aeneas, putting up his hands in mock surrender, "there's something I need to share with you."

"I'm waiting." Tabitha folded her arms. He could almost hear her grinding her teeth.

"It's a recording from my SAIL that I made recently about my life before I traveled back to Astoria to see Sadie in 2016."

Tabitha's left eyebrow popped up and she leaned in. "Why did you need to see sixteen-year-old Sadie?" Her eyes were cutting through him like lasers, and he felt terrible guilt about what he was about to divulge.

"I'll play the recording; then we can talk." Aeneas pulled out his SAIL.

"Do you have your glasses, by chance?"

Tabitha pulled them from her bag and Aeneas tapped the SAIL.

Tabitha focused on the bright blue button and the file opened. Small speakers on the arms of the glasses played the audio. Tabitha watched for several minutes without speaking. Aeneas munched on his peanut butter oatmeal cookie. There wasn't much else he could do but wait and eat.

"Sadie didn't die when we were kids, Aeneas," said Tabitha, removing the glasses and taking a quick drink of her coffee. "We all grew up together."

Aeneas stared at the two cookies left on his plate and shook his head. "No, Tab. She died in 2016."

"Aeneas, she's alive now," said Tabitha, gazing worriedly at him. She wondered if he was having a breakdown.

"Only because you asked me to go back and save her."

"Why would I do that? Bob North Sky has always told you that you can't raise the dead."

Aeneas couldn't look at his wife. He focused on the dainty crystal chandelier shaped like an orchid in the booth next to theirs.

"You were persuasive, Tabitha. I was feeling guilty. I thought maybe I could go back and see what happened and not get involved, but I couldn't watch her die. I don't have that in me."

Tabitha paled, squeezing her temples.

"This can't have happened."

Aeneas had been prepared for this reaction. He tapped his SAIL again and produced a copy of Sadie's death certificate.

A small hologram appeared before Tabitha. She glanced over the image and blinked. It took her several seconds to process what was written.

"Accidental death? Rogue wave?" she whispered, tearing up.

"I saw it," Aeneas said slowly. "She would've tumbled off the jetty and been washed out to sea. It was hard on everyone, Tab, because her body was never recovered." Aeneas's face was grim. Tabitha placed her hands in her lap to keep them from shaking. She'd counseled many patients about how to handle panic attacks and now she could finally empathize with the feelings of sheer terror engulfing them.

"But you didn't let that happen?" asked Tabitha, exhaling slowly. *Just breathe in and out. Slow and steady*, she said to herself.

Aeneas shook his head. "I saved her. I've got dual memories of her death, so I know what originally happened and what happened after I saved her. It's like two movies, but one's the remake."

"Aeneas, why didn't you share this with me before you decided to do something so risky? I would've told you not to do it!"

Tabitha's tone reminded him of how she spoke when chiding their children and Aeneas felt his blood pressure tick up a few notches.

"You begged me." Aeneas slid out of the booth and headed toward the exit. He'd been blaming himself this whole time, but now he realized C.J. was right. Tabitha was just as much to blame.

"Aeneas, wait! We need to talk. We need to figure this out!" called Tabitha desperately.

Before she could wiggle out of the booth, Aeneas had vanished into the street. She reached back to grab her bag and stopped cold. He'd left the two cookies behind on the plate.

CHAPTER 33

Cassie Wins the Genetic Jackpot

Spring 2053

IT WAS NEARLY MIDNIGHT. Lux was sitting on Cassie's couch. He shifted uncomfortably as his sister prepared a pot of jasmine tea. He'd been back home less than an hour when she sent a car to pick him up. She said it was urgent. She said come alone and he could tell by her tone she meant it.

Lux, like Aeneas, was tall and lean. It was also generally agreed he was the least headstrong of Aeneas and Tabitha's offspring. He had a quiet, thoughtful personality which endeared him to others, except his sister.

"Cass, I'm exhausted. Just tell me whatever's got you worked up. I'll sleep on it and help you in the morning."

Cassie plonked the pot of tea on the coffee table and handed him a small cup.

She took a breath—an annoyed breath it seemed to Lux.

"Is there something you've discovered about my DNA that you haven't shared with me?"

Cassie noted his surprise.

Lux hesitated.

"Well, as you know, Dad and I have been searching for unique genetic markers that time travelers might have in common."

Cassie motioned for him to continue. She'd squared herself directly across from him in such a way that he felt cornered.

"We've been comparing all DNA samples—yours with Dad, Great Uncle William, Sheila's two children, one of her nephews, and Bob North Sky."

"And?"

"I think I've isolated twenty-seven potential genes associated with time travel, but I don't have enough samples to be certain that twenty-seven is the max number."

"Meaning you need more DNA from other time travelers?"

Lux nodded.

"So, is there anything special about mine that I should know?"

Lux sipped his tea, buying a few seconds. He'd been meaning to talk with Cassie about what he'd suspected and finally verified, but life was just getting back to normal when his parents separated, throwing their family into chaos.

"You and Dad share twenty-two of the genes I've isolated," he said. "There are five others I've found among Bob and Sheila's family. You have those, too, but they are missing from Dad's genome."

Cassie leaned back against the couch and smiled thoughtfully. "That would mean they must've come from mom!"

"Yep," smiled Lux.

"So, how come you've been keeping quiet about this?" Cassie asked sharply. Lux tensed up. Just when he thought things were about to settle into an academic chat instead of an interrogation, Cassie-the-sharp-tongued came rolling back in.

"Cass, this is my life's work and I've been cautious to—"

Cassie cut him off before he could continue. "You aren't even twenty! How can this be your life's work?" squawked Cassie, rolling her eyes. The eye roll proved too much and flipped the switch Lux usually kept in the off position.

"I've been studying time travel DNA sequences since I was nine!" roared Lux, launching himself off the couch, clenching his jaw, trying to calm down. His sister had no idea how much of his life was spent staring at protein configurations from her genetic material. If he could ever publish his dissertation, it would be mind-blowing.

"Cassie, time travel is polygenic! The genes for this ability exist in the *Homo sapiens* gene pool. Every human has some of them."

He paused to make sure she was listening. Her eyes were glued to him now, so he decided to get it over with.

"Some of us have a few genes, others more. The more you have increases the likelihood you can access and withstand the timestream. Think about it. Seers, shamans, Druids, early astrologers, anyone who could peer into the future or glance back into the past had some of these genes. Even magicians and circus performers, people who can shift space and time to create illusions likely have some of these genetic markers. I also think extraordinary athletes might have a higher percentage of these genes, too."

Lux waited for Cassie to respond. Instead, she was perfectly still. Lux knelt, took her hands in his, and stared intently into her eyes. She was like a deer in the headlights as his dad would say.

"I've been able to determine from the samples tested that you hit the jackpot, Cass. You've got all twenty-seven I've identified. Four alone are found on your first X chromosome. And I know those are from Mom because Dad's X chromosome doesn't have those markers."

Cassie swallowed hard, willing herself not to cry. "So, I'm some kind of freak?"

Lux chuckled softly, "Yes and no."

He gently scooted onto the couch and placed his arm around Cassie.

"I was able to secure a copy of the genome from Ötzi, the five-thousand- year-old iceman. His DNA had eleven markers; he would've had some abilities, though marginal. I've also gotten tissue samples from three bog mummies. They all had the markers ranging from six to nineteen."

Cassie smiled for a second. She'd always treated Lux's research like a high school science project.

"So... the one with nineteen?"

"Yeah, that person would have been a traveler. My guess based on the tribal DNA data I've been allowed to access and the anecdotal information from Bob is that anyone who has sixteen or more markers can probably withstand the timestream."

"Then, where is everyone?" wailed Cassie.

"You mean travelers? Haven't you met others in Alaska?"

"I've only met any in Alaska. And they've all been related to Bob."

"Dad and I hypothesized that if you are in a seismically active region, the more likely those genes get activated, unless there's some other way to open the timestream."

"So, you could have all the genetic markers and if you weren't living near a major fault line or the ring of fire, then…"

"You might never experience the timestream. But then again, you might be able to shift yourself here and there. Dad's always said he can collapse space and time and move a little forward or backward with or without the timestream being open. I think he capitalized on this when he was playing soccer all those years." Cassie briefly flashed back to her father's description of how he collapsed the distance to evade the rogue wave when he saved Sadie.

"Lux, another time traveler, Toshiro, came to see me. He knew about your research, knew about my abilities."

Lux withdrew his arm and stood up. In the back of his mind, he'd always worried that his family could be in danger if their secret became known to people with what his mother called "nefarious intentions." Tabitha had explained this to him and Tor when they were very young.

"How could he know?" muttered Lux. "We keep a low profile. We use the latest encryption for all our data." He felt a pang of unease.

"I don't know about that, but I do know he's been watching me in the timestream. He said he's wanted to meet me for a while."

Lux shook his head. "This sounds dangerous, Cass. You need to tell Dad and Harold. And first thing tomorrow, we need to verify this Toshiro's identity."

Lux yawned, rubbed his eyes, and turned to leave. "I really need some sleep, Cass. Tomorrow we're taking Lana and Lanna on a tour of the city."

"Okay, Lux," said Cassie, returning the yawn. She couldn't bring herself to tell him the other things right now. Like if she went back and stopped Aeneas from saving Sadie, he and Tor would never meet Lana and Lanna.

CHAPTER 34

Slightly Estranged Breakfast

Spring 2053

CASSIE ARRIVED AT HER family home just after eight-thirty carrying a box full of fresh croissants. The house smelled of yeast, coffee, and cinnamon. Her mom was making cinnamon rolls for the boys and Cassie was supposed to help prepare the breakfast sandwiches. Tabitha was busy laying out silverware, napkins, cups, and plates on the counter for self-service.

"Anyone up yet?"

"No. I saw Tor sleepwalk to the bathroom earlier and I told him breakfast would be soon," Tabitha replied. "The flight got in pretty late."

Cassie leaned into her mother's right side and whispered in her ear, "Have you met them?"

"No. But, I expect you to be polite, Cass. Lux and Tor seem very happy with Lana and Lanna."

The front door opened and closed followed by brisk footfalls.

"Smells like cinnamon rolls," announced Aeneas walking into the kitchen carrying a duffle bag. Tabitha froze. Cassie gave her father a bewildered look. He smiled back at her challengingly.

"I'm moving back in! C.J. and Lyla have been very kind, but this is my house, too." Tabitha glared at her husband but said nothing.

"I'm going to be in the library, Tab. Cass, I need to talk with you."

"Cassie's helping me with breakfast. Lux and Tor are back, and they brought guests," remarked Tabitha coolly. Aeneas ignored her and headed toward the library which functioned as his office.

Cassie sighed. "Mom, I'll be right back." She followed Aeneas into the library.

"What in the hell are you doing here, Dad?" hissed Cassie. Aeneas was sitting in his favorite leather chair with his hands folded, looking fed up with the world. He yawned before answering.

"Your mom and I talked last night. So, there's no point in pretending anymore. She pressured me to save Sadie and like a complete fool, I broke the very rule Bob told me never to break and that's why we are in this mess."

"Does she know about the temporal anomaly?"

"Not yet. We didn't get that far."

Squealing sounds from the hallway caused them both to turn.

Cassie lowered her voice. "What was that?"

"My guess is it's time to meet Lana and Lanna," grinned Aeneas.

Cassie and Aeneas stopped as soon they were close enough to the kitchen to view the scene. Two tall, lissome females, clad in matching light blue pajamas, their bright red hair swirled into buns, were squealing and hugging Tabitha.

"Oooh, we love cinnamon buns, Mrs. Entwistle!" said the first twin, or maybe the second one. Aeneas wasn't sure. What he was sure of, though, was he felt a rib loosen as he struggled not to laugh like a barking hyena. He silently slid back into the hall to look for his sons, leaving Cassie without so much as a word. A second passed as Tabitha struggled to regain her composure. Then they saw Cassie.

"You must be Cassie!" cried one of the twins enthusiastically.

Cassie shook her head no, stunned into silence. She turned to her father for rescue, but he'd vanished.

"She's so pretty, Lana!"

"She looks like Mrs. Entwistle. Those green eyes!"

"Aren't those curls stunning, Lanna?" They moved toward Cassie like giant dolls in some crazy horror movie.

Tabitha gave her daughter a gesture of helplessness as the twins descended upon her, gleefully commenting on pieces and parts Cassie felt were off limits even in these open-minded times.

Twenty minutes later, they were all seated around the long wooden dining table. Everyone's plate but Tabitha's was loaded with cinnamon rolls, fruit, and breakfast croissants. The twins were cheerfully chatting as Tabitha sipped her tea and picked at some fruit. Aeneas and the boys were plowing through their plates. Cassie had eaten a croissant and was now eyeing the situation warily.

"I think it's so ironic that we had our hair in buns and Mrs. Entwistle made cinnamon buns. Don't you agree, Tor?" Lanna clapped him gently on the back and giggled.

"Just call me Tabitha," requested Tabitha, attempting to smile. Aeneas grinned as he took another bite of food. Watching his wife's discomfort amused him. Plus, C.J. and Lyla viewed breakfast as an optional meal, consisting mainly of coffee and toast, so he was feeling well fed and entertained.

"Of course," chirped Lanna with a big toothy smile.

Tor could tell something was up with his parents. His mom was edgy, and his dad was acting like he had something on her which had shifted the balance of power. He looked at Cassie who gave a slight shake of her head as if to say, "you have no idea how bad this really is." Lux caught it, too.

As breakfast concluded, Lana and Lanna insisted on doing the dishes. After a minute of canoodling with their new girlfriends, Tor and Lux headed out to the back deck with Cassie in tow, and Aeneas slipped back into the library. Tabitha lingered for a bit, showing Lana and Lanna where to store leftovers, then melted back toward the library as the chattering duo in the kitchen reached a crescendo.

"Good morning, Tab," cried Aeneas, as he thumbed through an old book.

"Don't 'good morning' me. Why did you leave last night?"

"Too mad to talk to you anymore. Angry at myself for letting you guilt me into something I knew was wrong."

"What guilt?" Tabitha snapped.

After getting a healthy start on his daily caloric intake, he was practically giddy which made him even more daring.

"You know, from the boys."

Tabitha did know. It was a memory, fuzzy and full of shame. The day she'd seen the sonogram of two babies, she had let loose an eruption of accusation and fury on Aeneas. They'd hashed it out years ago. But Aeneas's guilt persisted which made him malleable to her persuasion, something she was keenly aware of in times of need.

"How does that apply to Sadie?"

"It applies, Tab, because you know I can be shifted if you push hard enough after what happened when the boys were being born."

"You're saying I bullied you into this?"

Aeneas shrugged. "I don't use *that* term, but some people have."

Tabitha huffed. She knew exactly who used that term.

A peal of laughter caused them both to jump.

"What about them?" asked Tabitha wearily. Lana and Lanna were proving to be an unwelcome overload to her already taxed mental state.

"They're part of the remake, not the original."

"Oh no," groaned Tabitha, sliding into a leather chair, collapsing her head into her hands. Deciding what to do about Sadie was going to be brutal enough. But her boys were smitten with these chirpy redheads, though Tabitha had yet to work out the attraction.

"Is it just me or..." Tabitha broke off.

Aeneas caught on immediately and snorted. "Cassie may kill them, so we might not have to worry about them driving us insane."

Tabitha started to laugh. Aeneas set down the book and squeezed in next to her on the chair.

"Truce?" he whispered into her ear.

"Absolutely not," replied Tabitha primly.

"Well then... I guess... I must... take up...the challenge," rumbled Aeneas in a husky voice.

"Don't you dare!" hissed Tabitha.

Aeneas dove into her neck and smothered her with kisses causing Tabitha to release a wild scream that sent their children running into the house.

Tor pushed open the library door. Three heads leaned inside.

"Yes?" Aeneas was pawing hair from his face. Tabitha blushed.

Tor shook his head. "You two really need to make up your minds."

"Enjoy your day in the city," said Tabitha breathlessly.

"Dad, if you can disentangle yourself from Mom, I need to have another word with you both," announced Cassie, shaking her head disapprovingly.

"Righto, Cass."

Aeneas and Tabitha still had a lot to talk about. Cassie assumed that conversation was going to happen after she left, but for now they were seated together in the library like stone statues. The re-ignition of their thirty-year love affair cooled as Cassie told them about Toshiro.

Tabitha was deeply shaken. Her worst fears had been set loose and were now running around her psyche.

"We've worked so hard to keep this a secret. When you were little I was worried you'd be lost in the timestream. Then when you were older, I was worried someone from national security would show up at the door and take you away."

Aeneas slipped an arm discreetly around Tabitha's waist. This was one thing he and Tabitha had always been in sync about... protecting their daughter from anyone who might take advantage of her.

"Mom, maybe Toshiro knows about us because he's one of us."

"You've seen him in the timestream?" asked Aeneas, all business.

"Yes. He warned me when I entered the temporal anomaly."

"What anomaly?" interrupted Tabitha.

Aeneas hesitated. Cassie tilted her head toward her father. "You're up, old man."

Tabitha turned to Aeneas apprehensively.

Aeneas hesitated, then realized there was no reason to continue keeping this information a secret. "Tab, after I went back and saved Sadie, a branching sphere-like aberration appeared in your timeline, around the age you were when Sadie died in 2016."

"But Cass said temporal anomaly?"

"A section of your timeline has a multiple realities disturbance that looks like a sapphire-colored sphere-like structure," Cassie explained. "Toshiro mentioned it when we met up."

"What does he know about it?" asked Aeneas sharply.

"He knew you'd gone back in time and changed something. He was not very complimentary about it." Cassie was still angry. Her parents were supposed to be responsible, thoughtful people and the two of them had created a disaster.

"Cass, I think I need to meet Toshiro," said Aeneas, setting his jaw, "and this isn't a request."

CHAPTER 35

The Third Reality

Spring 2053

THE NEWS OF TABITHA and Aeneas's reconciliation rocketed through their family within minutes. Cassie sent a message to Thena and Missi who immediately informed Socrates and Keniah. Socrates alerted the clandestine group deliberating Sadie's fate, and it was decided they would all meet back at the gazebo that afternoon, this time including Tabitha. Lux and Tor were showing Lana and Lanna their favorite spots in Seattle and Tabitha felt that given the circumstances, their sons shouldn't be invited. Any changes made to the past could affect the present or as Aeneas was now describing it, the original versus the remake.

Aeneas took charge of the meeting. The last time they'd met, he'd been bogged down by shame and grief. Now he felt emboldened because he and Tabitha were a team again. No matter how insurmountable things might seem, they were in it together.

"Tabitha and I understand this is our mess."

No one corrected him. It was a somber mood. Everyone knew Sadie's fate was at stake.

Aeneas continued, "Bob feels that an important piece here is free will. I eliminated that when I forcibly rescued Sadie in 2016."

Persephone raised an eyebrow. "Is the plan for Cassie to intercept you before you save Sadie?"

Cassie nodded at her aunt.

Socrates looked around the table skeptically. "What if he refuses?"

"I won't," said Aeneas firmly.

Socrates sighed. "Brother, you don't know what you'll do. The person Cassie's going to confront isn't the person sitting at this table who's lived through the aftermath of your rash act."

Tabitha leaned forward and locked eyes with her daughter. "Take him a note."

Cassie glanced at her mother quizzically. Tabitha repeated her request. "Take him a note from me. A paper note. You can carry it into the timestream. When he reads it, Aeneas will listen."

"Hmm," mused Harold. "That might work, but Carl was there, too, right?"

"Carl never saw anything. Remember he went back for his hat?" No one acknowledged his comment and Aeneas suddenly realized he was now the only person with a recollection of Sadie's death since, for the rest of them, it never happened.

"I feel torn about the ethical dilemma this presents," sighed Socrates, glancing around the table worriedly.

"In her original life Sadie died at sixteen so I don't see the issue," interjected Persephone who'd never warmed to Sadie but felt that it had no bearing on her judgment of the situation.

"Sadie's alive, Seph. So, what we're looking at now is a third reality where she may live, or she may die depending on what interactions she has when Cassie intercepts Aeneas."

Harold tapped the holographic screen and started dashing off a list.

"Reality one... the original."

Aeneas pointed to the screen. "Add 'Sadie dies at age sixteen,' Harold."

Harold quickly made the edit, then continued his notes. "Reality two... Sadie is alive, our current reality. Reality three... Sadie has free will to live or die."

"This free will piece is the magic button to fix this?" asked C.J.

Aeneas shrugged. "It's the only solution Bob could come up with to correct the temporal anomaly."

"So, if Cassie intercepts you, and Sadie dies, what happens to all of this?" gestured C.J. apprehensively.

Socrates sighed again. "All of this never happened and the only two people who will remember are Cassie and Aeneas."

"As it should be," said Persephone. Everyone looked at her. Tabitha crumpled. Aeneas placed his arm around her. Persephone continued, "Sadie was destined to die. I'm not trying to be insensitive, Tabitha, but all the data Aeneas collected shows us that she died in 2016."

Harold decided to keep the discussion moving before things became too emotional to be effective.

"So, anything carried on your person within the timestream exists in a kind of time-free zone, so to speak?" He glanced at Cassie, who jumped in and answered first.

"I think of it as more of a neutral zone where the past, present, and future are temporarily suspended and the SAIL isn't affected."

"Cassie and I have dual memories," added Aeneas. "Basically, we have the original plus the remake, and soon, I guess, the reboot, too."

Harold spoke softly as he added his notes on the screen. "Time travelers retain memories of all possibilities they live through... everyone else is not cognizant of changes." Socrates scrutinized Harold's notes and pointed to the hologram.

"Wait a sec, Harold. We added new memories when Cassie interacted with us in 2015."

"Ah, yes," scribbled Harold. "So, affected individuals altered by time- traveler interactions may have new memories."

"Well, we didn't recall any of it, until Cassie came back to the present. The memories filtered in once she returned, and we were reminded of it. It was a strange sensation," said Socrates. Harold included the comment and waited.

"Then why won't we remember all this?" Tabitha circled her arm, gesturing to the group.

"We're not sure yet, Tab, but I think realities can shift based on the amount of interference," said Aeneas. "One would be a remake where there's a new reality overlaid, and only me and

Cass can recall the before. The other is like a slight revision... like Nia being born or Harold marrying Meg. Even then none of you knew any different the second time, but there wasn't any damage to anyone's timeline."

"That we know of," muttered Socrates. Aeneas shuddered. Sox was right. Their familial timelines needed to be closely scrutinized.

"So, when will Cassie leave?" asked C.J. No one responded. C.J. glanced at Aeneas, then over to Cassie. The quiet became awkward. Cassie leaving meant things would change again, and no one would remember except the time travelers. Aeneas turned to Harold. "This is being recorded right?"

Harold gave a brief nod.

Aeneas gestured with his chin, "All of that information will be lost once Cass leaves. You should transfer it to her SAIL."

C.J. pressed his hands against his cheeks. "None of this happens?"

"Depending on what Sadie chooses... I'm not really sure, bro." Aeneas reached over and squeezed C.J.'s shoulder.

"After Cassie comes back to her present, we all what?" C.J. glanced around the table. Everyone was clearly anxious.

"Aeneas will call another meeting, we'll review the new data and these meetings on the SAIL. It'll be a cautionary tale," offered Harold.

"Or Aeneas and Cassie say nothing and we all get on with our lives," suggested Persephone. Aeneas was secretly in favor of that option. He wanted to forget this whole mess ever happened.

"Has anyone had contact with Sadie recently?" asked Socrates. What they were contemplating was still hammering on his conscience.

Tabitha shook her head. "She sent me a long letter apologizing after she returned to Portland. I told her I needed some time, but now I feel awful about how we left things." Tabitha laid her head on the table to hide her tears.

Socrates turned to Aeneas.

"Nothing," replied Aeneas. "When she contacted me, I told her it was huge mistake and that I needed to make things right with Tab." The last few words choked him. Tabitha slid her hand on top of his and Cassie felt a flutter of happiness. She'd not let herself get upset like Lux and Tor, but she had dreaded the breakup of her parents' marriage.

"I don't want to cause anyone more pain, but it's best we limit our interactions with Sadie," advised Socrates.

CHAPTER 36

Lotus Blossom Corsage

Spring 2016

THE SPRING FORMAL WAS only a day away and Aeneas felt confident that he could dance in public. C.J. was pleased with himself as he sat in the bean bag while Aeneas tried on his new clothes.

"I wasn't sure how well these lessons would work out, but Jesús has definitely exceeded my expectations," remarked C.J. appreciatively.

"Man, I was so worried about all of this, but things really came together. I wonder if Jesús has a site where I can give him a good review?"

"He's strictly word-of-mouth. I thought that was strange, but someone told me one of his parents might be undocumented."

Aeneas frowned. He'd never want anything bad to happen to Jesús or his family. He was a great guy, the best, and he'd done Aeneas a solid for sure, especially with his kissing advice.

"Remind me that I owe him a favor, C.J. Listen out for trouble like you always do. I'll have his back if he needs any help."

C.J. nodded. His mind wandered to a worry he had. Aeneas told him that Sox and Harold were training him to lock into his present before he slept so he wouldn't get swept into the timestream.

"Do you ever worry that the timestream will open when you're in the shower or on the toilet and you'll get swept in with no clothes on or your pants around your ankles?"

Aeneas was speechless. Just when he was feeling calm, C.J. came out with a terrifying scenario that was more embarrassing than the last.

"No way that could ever happen. I mean, I'd... I'd stop myself. We've been talking about it. I'm working on cueing my body to hold back."

"Oh, that's a relief. I mean, imagine if you were having a bowel movement and bang! The timestream opened and there you went."

Aeneas shuddered, then groaned.

"Just say poop, bro."

"Never again. I'm elevating my language skills. I have no plans to say 'poop' all the time once my little sister starts talking."

Aeneas snorted. "I sure can't wait to hear a two-year-old say 'bowel movement' every time she's gotta go." Aeneas looked down at his pants. "Are these a little too long?"

C.J. shook his head. "No. They fit great."

Aeneas slipped out of his formal clothes.

"Any news on the baby name front?"

C.J. rolled off the bean bag and pushed himself up. He'd finally figured out how to get off Aeneas's annoying furniture.

"Yes. I've given my parents three options and they are deciding."

Aeneas suppressed the urge to laugh. C.J.'s parents had been so worried he'd be upset about a new sibling that they relented when he insisted on choosing the name. C.J. had bought a used book of baby names and carried it around for months, which had amused Tabitha and Aeneas, but they'd kept quiet to spare his feelings.

"So, hit me."

"Kamiko Misa, that's a first and a middle name," clarified C.J. "In Japan they don't use middle names, but we do here in America, so I chose a first and middle name for her that was Japanese. You know, I've always wanted a Japanese name," C.J. said wistfully.

Aeneas nodded sympathetically. C.J. didn't like his name and no one could blame him, least of all Aeneas and his siblings who'd also been given unusual monikers.

"Estelle Marie, a classic American name and Gwyneth Nyoko, a combo name."

"Wow! You've really thought about these. What've your parents said?"

"Not much. I left them on the fridge so they can see them regularly."

"What are you leaning toward?"

"Hmm. I think I want to name her Lotus Blossom."

Aeneas wrinkled his brow. "Then why in the heck did you pick all those other names?"

"Because who knows what crazy name my parents will pick once I let them at it. They need some realistic options."

C.J. lowered his voice. Persephone still didn't know what his initials stood for, and he rarely uttered his real name. "Colonel Johan, Aeneas. They named me after a chicken place and their favorite composer. These people have no business naming anyone."

Aeneas high-fived C.J. "Agreed. But what'll happen when your little sister is old enough to figure out you've named her lotus blossom?"

"She'll thank me, of course!" exclaimed C.J., smiling.

Aeneas's face became serious. "Will she?"

C.J. squared himself across from Aeneas, placed his hands up on his shoulders and spoke loudly, enunciating each word like he was addressing a contentious issue that could bring about the fall of humanity. "Aeneas, my mom loves to eat pears and my dad loves the smell of Pine-Sol. These people could name her Pearsol."

Aeneas laughed. "Lotus Blossom could work."

～

Tabitha tried on her dress and called Sadie for a video chat.

"I love it!" gushed Sadie. Tabitha smoothed her dress, turning from side to side in front of the screen on her laptop.

"It's better than I expected. The wrap is so soft. I love velvet. Oh, and I decided to wear flats. I want to dance, and my mom talked me out of heels. She said I'd end up on crutches."

"Of course she did." Sadie rolled her eyes then turned her head toward her bedroom door where her mom, Catherine, was within earshot.

"Also, my mom wants to know if you'll be wearing a corsage. She loved wearing them when she went to high school dances back a thousand years ago."

Tabitha blinked a couple times and shook her head.

"Uh... no? I don't think so. Aeneas never mentioned it."

"Hey, Tabitha," whispered Seth, popping his head in. Tabitha spun around abruptly.

"Seth, I'm talking to Sadie." Seth walked in and waved cheerfully to his cousin on the screen.

"Hi, Sadie."

"Hey, Seth. You've gotten taller."

Seth beamed. He was always excited when someone noticed he'd changed.

"Yeah. I've had to get new jeans for school." Seth backed up to the screen to show Sadie his jeans and Tabitha waved him out.

"Seth, scoot. I'm busy talking about my dress."

"That's why I'm here."

"Spill it, little man," called Sadie, smiling broadly at Seth.

"Persephone told me to tell you that your cosarge is tiny and will fit on your ribs." Tabitha and Sadie exchanged a look.

"Seth, do you mean *corsage* and *wrist*?" asked Tabitha.

"Pretty sure she said ribs," replied Seth confidently.

Tabitha gave Seth a pat on the shoulder and ushered him from her bedroom.

"Thanks, Seth. Appreciate the info," called Sadie. Seth gave Sadie one last wave and bounded from the room.

"Ribs?" laughed Sadie, holding her ribs.

"I should call C.J." sighed Tabitha. She was pretty sure Persephone said *wrist*, but since her dress was off the shoulder, it would be nice to know ahead of time.

"Text me when you find out!" cried Sadie, giggling.

~

C.J. was about to leave when he got a text from Tabitha.

"Hey, Aeneas, did you get Tabitha a corsage to wear with her dress?"

Aeneas had just said goodbye to C.J. and was headed to the kitchen to scrounge for an evening snack.

"Uh... if you tell me what a corsage is, I'll tell you if I got one. I'm pretty sure it's a no, though."

"A bunch of flowers made into a bracelet or a pendant. Girls wear them to dances."

Aeneas grabbed his phone and sent a text to his friend, Everett. A few seconds later his phone vibrated. Aeneas slapped his hand to his head, groaning.

"How come no one ever mentioned corsages?"

C.J. shrugged. He'd covered the dancing and the clothes.

"Does Everett have one for Bethany?"

"Yep," replied Aeneas glumly.

"You still have time."

"Time for what?" asked Persephone brightly.

C.J. let out a yelp and took a step back. Persephone had crept up behind him and waited a few seconds before speaking. She knew C.J. was easily startled, and even though there was an unspoken truce between them since the shopping trip, she couldn't resist.

"Seph, knock it off," barked Aeneas.

C.J. caught his breath and straightened up. "If you must know, Aeneas needs a corsage for Tabitha and we are working out the details."

Persephone smiled sweetly and C.J. took another step back. She was the most frightening when she was smiling.

"It's being delivered tomorrow morning around eleven."

C.J. tilted his head quizzically. "A corsage for Tabitha?"

"Yes," hissed Persephone softly, continuing her terrifying smile.

"Seph, you should've asked me first," grumbled Aeneas, folding his arms.

"I didn't order it," she replied tersely. Persephone gave her brother a haughty glare, turned toward her bedroom and called back over her shoulder smugly, "Mommy did!"

CHAPTER 37

Romance, First Dance & Painful Goodbyes

Spring 2016

GEORGE AND MARTHA WERE sharing a glass of their favorite cider at the kitchen table, reminiscing about how much Tabitha had grown up. They'd seen her off with Aeneas, Bethany, and Everett while Seth was conveniently invited to a sleepover with a friend. It was their first evening all to themselves in months.

"I can't believe she's going to a formal dance with a boy!" said George, taking a drink of cider, smiling wistfully.

"I can't believe she's going with Aeneas," snorted Martha.

"I can't believe you never saw that coming," chuckled George.

They sat in silence for a few minutes finishing the cider. Then George tapped on his phone. A trumpet played. George took Martha's hand, spun her close to him, and they danced to "La Vie En Rose."

Martha closed her eyes, enjoying the bliss of an evening alone with her husband. It was the last peaceful moment they would have for many months.

Tabitha admired the corsage as she ate her dinner. Three small orchids were bound together in cerulean blue ribbon. She leaned over and whispered to Aeneas, "The corsage is beautiful. Thank you."

They'd taken pictures with her parents, his parents, and Bethany's mom. Then Everett asked the server to take a picture of them at their table. They hadn't even gotten to the dance yet and Tabitha estimated at least forty pictures had been taken.

They'd opted for an Italian restaurant on Beach Drive. The table was cozy, and the server had been very kind to them. Tabitha had ordered a ravioli dish thinking it would be easier to eat than spaghetti. Aeneas was ploughing into a hearty lasagna in its own ceramic ramekin.

"I probably shouldn't say this," gushed Bethany, "but we all look fantastic." Everett beamed. It had been a great idea to double with Aeneas and Tabitha.

"Your tie is epic, Entwistle."

Aeneas gave Everett a thumbs-up since his mouth was full of lasagna.

"C.J. and Persephone found it for him," said Tabitha brightly, running her fingers along the edge of Aeneas's tie.

"Why squirrels?" asked Bethany.

"They inspire his soccer moves," answered Everett. Aeneas swallowed the rest of his lasagna and joined the conversation, acutely aware that Tabitha had made an intimate gesture caus-ing his heart to flutter.

"I respect their skill. Squirrels are super-fast. They shoot out in traffic and make it across the road without getting hit. Plus, they leap from tree to tree, and they tease all the dogs who can't ever catch them."

"He channels his inner squirrel on the pitch."

"That I do, bro," laughed Aeneas.

Everett surreptitiously rubbed his thumb against his chin, giving Aeneas a meaningful look. Aeneas blushed and wiped his mouth with the napkin. His mother Miranda had warned him about taking it easy on the food, keeping his face clean, and not staining his clothes before the dance. Luckily, Everett had his back.

The school gym was strung with fairy lights. Tall lamps and tiny tables with fresh-flower vases lined the walls. The area near the stage was packed with students and Aeneas decided he was all in. He took Tabitha's arm and escorted her to the dance floor straight away. He was surprised to see very few couples, but a lot of people dancing in small groups with friends.

The first song had a nice beat and Aeneas hung back for a bit before he tried the mixed dancing. Tabitha loved it. She laughed breathlessly as they moved around the dance floor.

"That was amazing! I didn't know you could dance like that."

Aeneas let out a breath, then whispered, "Can you keep a secret?"

Tabitha raised her eyebrows curiously. "Don't tell me you time traveled and found a dance instructor from the 1960s?"

"Nah. C.J. hired this high school guy who plays soccer in a division above me that has a side business as a dance instructor. His name is Jesús. He's top notch."

"Wow. I had no idea you'd gone to so much trouble." Tabitha was suddenly flushed with emotion. Everything about this night was stellar, better than she could have imagined.

"Hey, Entwistle. Nice moves!" called Everett walking over with Bethany on his arm. Bethany turned to Tabitha with an expression of surprise.

"I had no idea you were such an experienced dancer, Aeneas."

Aeneas shrugged. "I've been practicing a bit to get ready for tonight."

Everett high-fived Aeneas and clapped him on the shoulder. "Entwistle, you were sick out there."

Bethany glanced back toward the dance floor as another song started to play. "Hey, we're headed back for more dancing. Come with us!"

Bethany smiled excitedly at Everett as he guided her out to the dance floor. Aeneas took Tabitha's hand and they followed.

"I'm so glad she doesn't hate me anymore," whispered Tabitha.

"Why should she? Everett's cool and he's stunningly handsome."

Tabitha's bubbly laugh sent shivers up his arms. "You think so?"

"Well, I've never thought much about it, but I overheard a couple of ladies at our soccer game a few months ago describe him that way. So, it's gotta be true, right?"

Tabitha leaned into Aeneas's neck, giggling. "Yes it's true."

An hour later, the slow song Aeneas anticipated started to play. They were seated at their table drinking punch and eating tiny cakes called petit fours.

"Oooh, I love this song," Bethany cooed, strategically laying her hand on Everett's arm.

"Me too," smiled Tabitha.

Everett shot a glance at Aeneas, tilting his head toward the dance floor that was filling up with couples.

"I love this song," murmured Tabitha, as Aeneas took her hand and they started to dance.

Aeneas glanced down to check that his feet were the right distance away and felt Tabitha edge closer. Aeneas was relieved it was dark because he was blushing.

"Maybe it can be *our* song," suggested Aeneas, taking her arm and spinning her perfectly.

Tabitha looked up at Aeneas with such love that his legs wobbled beneath him. He leaned down and kissed her. For a second he felt like he was flying through the timestream. When the kiss ended, Aeneas and Tabitha clung together until the dance ended. *So much for my slow dance moves*, thought Aeneas.

When they got back to the table, Bethany and Everett were laughing and slapping each other playfully, but Aeneas and Tabitha had gone quiet.

~

George hurried toward the front door, then called back to Martha who stood stock still in the kitchen.

"Pack the kids some clothes for a couple days. I need to see Charlie."

Martha gave the slightest nod. She felt like she'd been punched in the stomach.

George started off briskly toward his brother's house but increased his pace to a sprint. He was breathless when C.J. answered the door.

"Hey, buddy," wheezed George, "I need to see your dad."

C.J. pulled the door open wide. "Come in, Uncle George."

George shook his head. "Send your dad out, buddy."

C.J. knew something was wrong but he'd no clue what, so he shot off to find his dad. Charlie walked toward George with strong purposeful strides. C.J. had told him something was wrong with Uncle George and that he'd refused to come inside the house. George was leaning against the door jamb with his eyes closed.

"What's wrong?" asked Charlie anxiously. George shook his head and lowered his voice.

"Close the door and come with me."

Charlie did as he asked. When they reached the sidewalk George stopped.

"We've got to leave for Astoria tonight. Sadie was washed out to sea a few hours ago. The Coast Guard is searching for her. Catherine and Carl are falling apart."

Charlie put his hand to his chest and started to heave. George quickly reached out and grabbed him. They hugged tightly for a few seconds then George pulled away and held Charlie squarely by his shoulders.

"We've got to be strong for our kids and our sister, Charlie."

"I know," he replied hoarsely.

"Go get packed. We leave in an hour. Martha's searching for a vacation rental nearby."

George picked up Seth from his friend's house, then drove to the school.

"I'm confused, Daddy. Why are we going to 'Storia right now?"

George frowned and turned to his son. There was no way to shield his children from what was about to unfold. If Sadie was still alive, the Coast Guard would find her before they reached Astoria. If she wasn't, then they would be there for the recovery. And the funeral. George's stomach felt like it was eating itself from the inside out.

"Sadie is missing, buddy. And we're going to help Aunt Catherine and Uncle Carl find her."

Seth nodded solemnly. "Okay, Daddy. I'll help." George fought back his tears and patted his son's arm. Seth was such a loving kid.

George stood in the doorway of the gym with Seth in hand. Tears poured down his face as he watched Tabitha dancing with Aeneas. She looked so happy. He'd asked a teacher to get Tabitha when the song ended. He didn't want to make this any worse by embarrassing her.

As soon as Tabitha got the news that there was a family emergency, she, Aeneas, Everett, and Bethany all headed to the exit. George tried to wipe his face clear before they arrived, but Tabitha spotted him and knew immediately something was wrong. Her first thought was Aunt Sakura's baby. Her second thought was her grandmother.

"Dad, what's wrong?" shouted Tabitha, rushing toward him. She flung her arms around him, and Seth squeezed in between them.

"Sadie's lost, Tabby. We're all worried and sad," said Seth softly.

Aeneas hovered just a few inches away unsure of how to support Tabitha or her family. He could sense the terror wafting from George.

"We have to leave for Astoria now, Tab."

"Okay, Dad." Tabitha looked back at Aeneas helplessly. Aeneas stepped in, hugged her tightly, and whispered in her ear, "Text me when you can."

Tabitha waved goodbye as the trio stood just outside the gym watching her leave.

Bethany was the first to speak. "Did her little brother say someone was missing?"

"Her cousin, Sadie," murmured Aeneas. He felt the lasagna curdling in his stomach. He needed to leave right now before he vomited. "I've gotta get home. Thanks for a great night."

Aeneas clapped Everett on the back. Bethany looped her arm through Everett's and called to Aeneas, "If Tabitha needs anything, just let me know, okay?"

Aeneas gave her a thumbs-up thinking he should call for a ride home, but he decided to run instead. His body was telling him he needed to move fast, to dash swiftly like a squirrel to keep that lasagna down. As he ran through his neighborhood a car drove past, hit the brakes then reversed. C.J. leaned out of the backseat window. His face was streaked with tears. "You've gotta take care of Sput, okay?"

"Yeah, bro. Whatever you need."

C.J. started to sob and Aeneas hugged him.

Sakura was in the driver's seat. She would take the first hour and Charlie would finish the drive.

"C.J., Aeneas, we have to go," said Sakura gently.

Aeneas let go of C.J. and waved goodbye. It would be nine days before he saw C.J. or Tabitha again.

CHAPTER 38

Cuddle Up to Both Versions

Spring 2053

"Remember our first dance?" Tabitha was leaning on one arm, admiring her husband. Aeneas was dozing next to her on their bed.

"Yep."

"I loved that song."

"Want to dance to it again sometime?" Aeneas mumbled sleepily.

Tabitha giggled, "Yes." Aeneas reached over and pulled her hand to him and kissed it. They laid together in the quiet for several more minutes. Cassie was at her condo and the boys were still out with Lana and Lanna. They were finally back together, in sync and in love. Tabitha sensed it was time for her to genuinely apologize.

"Aeneas?"

He opened one eye and smiled at her. Tabitha began her speech about their life together. She wanted Aeneas to know that she didn't blame him for the five terrifying minutes when she was giving birth to Tor and Lux.

"I remember an idyllic high school romance, then we broke up for a bit when I left for college and you dated Sadie a couple times, which did make me insanely jealous even though I was dating other people, too."

Tabitha planned to reminisce about their love-filled courtship, then finish with a detailed apology, but Aeneas shook his head sadly.

"That's the remake, Tab."

Aeneas sat up and rearranged the pillows so he could face her, leaning on one arm, too.

"The reality was much harsher. Sadie went missing the afternoon of the spring formal. You were whisked away that night along with C.J., and I didn't see either of you again until the funeral. It was gut wrenching. My whole family came to the funeral. Even Sput was there."

"I don't know if I want to remember that," whispered Tabitha. A sickening feeling crept into her belly. "My aunt and uncle must've been devastated."

"It was the most traumatic thing that happened in my childhood."

"So, those memories might be restored if you don't save her?"

"I wish I could say for certain. Whatever happens, Cassie will have recorded it all on the SAIL so at least we'll have documentation of the changes." Aeneas took Tabitha's hand again. "There's one more thing."

Tabitha sat up. Aeneas hesitated. She squeezed his hand.

"Go on. All cards on the table."

"We broke up after Sadie died."

"What?" squawked Tabitha, pulling her hand away.

"You broke up with me. I pushed too hard for you to be happy when I just needed to let you grieve." Tabitha covered her eyes, groaning.

"So, all the dates, the hikes, the concerts, the paddle boarding... none of that happened?"

"Well, yes it happened, because it's *happened*, but in the original version we didn't reconnect until I came back from Alaska. I think it was the beginning of your sophomore year at Western."

Tabitha swung her legs around and stood up, blown away by his revelation. She'd cherished those memories. Tears welled up in her eyes.

"We weren't even friends?"

Aeneas shook his head. "I was angry that you ended it and we kept our distance those first two years of high school. C.J. was hard hit by all of it. We became friendly again in our junior year but by then I was busy searching for other travelers and eventually met up with Bob North Sky and started spending summers in Alaska. My parents thought I was doing trail work and fishing."

"Aeneas, what I was trying to say earlier was that I was sorry about making you feel guilty about the boys," sobbed Tabitha.

Aeneas climbed out of bed, wrapped his arms around her, and tucked her head under his chin.

"Cassie's leaving in the morning. And things will shift... in whatever direction Sadie's free will takes us."

"And the only people who will ever understand what's happened are you and Cassie?"

"Mhm." Aeneas kissed the top of her head, still holding her close to him.

"So, this day we're having?"

"This day we're having right now will happen for me, but probably not for you. It all depends on how things end with Sadie."

Tabitha pulled away and sat back on the bed.

"I'm angry at her, but I can't imagine my life without her, Aeneas."

"But... in one reality, you already have, Tab, and that's the most prevalent memory for me."

"Why can't we just go on from this point and leave things as is... just let Sadie finish out her life?"

"Bob says the only way to restore the timelines is for Sadie to have free will and ultimately she must choose."

"Are you documenting this conversation?" Tabitha glared at him. "Even before when we were... ?"

"I can erase that," responded Aeneas. "Thing is, Tab, I need to track all versions and the SAIL backs up my brain, keeps it all straight for me."

"Won't today vanish from the SAIL once Cassie goes back to intercept you?"

The idea that events occurring in her life would be replaced with new ones was upsetting to Tabitha. She wondered how many times something like this had happened in the past and she was none the wiser. Aeneas gave her a reassuring smile.

"No worries. I made sure all my recordings are automatically copied to hers."

Tabitha smacked his arm. "Listen to what you just said, Aeneas."

"Oh no!" yelled Aeneas, catching on.

"I'll go in and delete that right now. It only sends Cassie's SAIL new data twice a day." Aeneas grabbed his SAIL, quickly opened a holographic screen, and located his daily recordings.

"We'd hear no end of that, Aeneas. And she'd tell the boys and the cousins! Then it would finally make its way back to Keniah and Sox."

"Yep. I can hear it now 'Mom and Dad accidentally uploaded themselves fooling around to my SAIL. Now I'm scarred for life,'" mimicked Aeneas.

Tabitha rolled her eyes at his spot-on impression of their daughter.

"It's deleted! Now let's order some pizza," cried Aeneas jubilantly, twirling Tabitha around then pulling her in close for a kiss, but even as Tabitha felt relief to be back in sync with her husband, she couldn't shake the desperate feeling that she was about to lose Sadie. She needed to make things right between them, especially since she was living in the 'remake' and might not have another chance to say goodbye.

CHAPTER 39

The Freewill
Scenario

Spring 2016

CASSIE AND LUX WERE reviewing seismic activity in the region.

"I don't want to fly to Alaska to find an opening in the timestream," groaned Cassie. "There's gotta be something happening nearby. I always see the timestream opening."

"You don't want to be waiting around, Cass. This needs to get done." Lux had arrived at her condo early. Tor was taking Lanna and Lana to Alki Beach for some paddle boarding. Lux knew once Cassie left to intercept their father, the day he was having might not be the day he started with, so he was recording everything on Cassie's SAIL. In fact, at Harold's insistence, everything had been moved to her SAIL, including all the details of Sadie's death, the meetings they'd recorded, and everything in the database that Lux kept on time travel anomalies.

The plan was for Cassie to give Aeneas a note from Tabitha, sending him immediately back to his present. Next, Cassie was to enact the free will scenario where she'd casually mention rogue waves and give Sadie the option to choose.

"I've got the SAIL prepped. Everything's on it and it's recording this, too," said Lux.

Cassie was feeling guilty. Really guilty. She was struggling with what to say to her brother about his new girlfriend.

"Looks like there was an earthquake about an hour ago near Edmonds—smaller, around one point four," he continued.

"There won't be much energy left when I get there. It's at least twenty-five minutes north of here. Just give it a minute," replied Cassie. "Some days it's like watching a popcorn popper, especially now that they can easily detect smaller ones."

Lux laughed. They chatted and drank green tea for a while, then Cassie decided that the best thing to do was to send him away.

"Lux, you should go. Meet up with Tor and the girls. Enjoy yourself." Cassie gave her brother a gentle shove.

Lux shook his head sadly. "I know, Cass. I've not said anything to Tor. But I know things will change."

"Then why in the hell are you still here? Go be with her!" urged Cassie.

"Because I can't face it. I can't see her and know that this day or all the days before when we were together will be erased for me."

Cassie sighed. "We don't know that for sure."

Lux eyed her. His green eyes, like hers, like Tabitha's, could bore a hole through your skull. "But you suspect."

"Yeah." Cassie reached over and took his hand. It was an unexpected gesture that was quickly interrupted by a flashing hologram that opened revealing a map.

"Look! Over near the east side of Lake Washington, one point eight."

"I have a car downstairs," said Cassie, grabbing her backpack, tucking the SAIL into a secure pocket.

"I'll come with you."

"I may not be coming back to the car. I might go straight to Mom and Dad's place. I've got to see what pans out."

Cassie dashed toward the door, calling over her shoulder, "Stop being a coward and go see her!" Lux shot her a look and Cassie knew she'd won the argument. Lux hated being accused of anything less than chivalrous behavior.

The car took Cassie across the 520 bridge and parked itself near the tennis courts adjacent to Fairweather Nature Preserve. Cassie glanced around as she exited the front seat. She saw someone entering a trail with their dog, but otherwise the preserve was quiet. She spun around slowly, activating her spidey senses.

Nothing. *Dammit,* thought Cassie. *This should be easier. Any other day when I'm out for a walk, I'd see it.*

Cassie paced around the parking lot, then decided to investigate a nearby neighborhood. She headed down a street that would take her closer to Lake Washington, passed by two enormous houses, nearly missing the sparkling lights of the timestream near a full-blooming rhododendron. She glanced furtively over her shoulder. A man on a bicycle passed by. She paused and waited. This was never the best situation, a neighborhood with so many door cameras, but she hoped it would appear she was taking a shortcut through the opening in the rhododendron hedge. She checked one last time and melted into a sea of bright pink flowers.

Cassie flew down her timeline. She felt joyous being back inside the stream surrounded by the golden pink atmosphere. She was bound toward a grim situation, but there was a strong chance stopping Aeneas could repair the timelines. Keeping that thought in her mind gave her a sensation of confidence and power. She wondered if she should ask Toshiro about this sensation. She'd passed through her birthing notch onto Tabitha's timeline then stopped cold. *I'm supposed to meet Toshiro for lunch today at the Space Needle! Oh well, I can be on time anytime, anywhere. Besides this shouldn't take more than twenty minutes and there's an offshore earthquake that should keep the timestream open for a couple hours at least.*

Cassie took a deep breath and centered herself with a single thought: *Sadie Willoughby, April 2016.* Cassie entered her grandfather George's timeline then launched onto Aunt Catherine's through her great grandmother, finally slowing her approach at spring of 2016. It seemed complex, but she'd taken this path before, developing a kind of time-travel muscle memory, which made it a hop, skip, and a jump to Sadie's timeline.

She looked at the life-sized pictures, searching the day near the polished orb, carefully avoiding the erupted branch gleaming like a strange appendage. Cassie shivered and refocused her attention on the scene. Sadie was leaving for Fort Stevens State Park with her father, Carl. Cassie pushed through the scene a little further and saw Sadie starting off on the sandy path that led to the jetty.

Cassie focused on a parked car in the C lot and landed behind it. Carl was ahead with Sadie, about to turn back for his hat. Aeneas was presumably ahead at the beach, waiting for Sadie.

Cassie skirted along the edge of the path, then decided to cut across Clatsop Spit. It was a little wet, but she'd worn her hiking boots. A tiny flash on the horizon told her something had shifted in the space-time continuum. Her father had arrived. She broke into a jog, mindfully sidestepping any standing water. Ahead she could see Aeneas scanning the afternoon sky with binoculars. *Clever*, thought Cassie, *pretending to be a bird watcher.* A glance back told her that Sadie was strolling toward the beach.

Then Cassie pulled out her SAIL and clipped it to the outside of her bag. "Initiate recording. All data."

"Hey, you, pretending to be a bird watcher." Aeneas whirled around so fast that he nearly lost his footing in the sand.

"Cass?"

"I have a note for you." Cassie held out a piece of paper for her father.

"What are you doing here? asked Aeneas, bewildered.

Ignoring his question, Cassie waved the paper forcibly in his face.

"Read the note."

"Cassie, I'm in the middle of something very—" Cassie cut him off by counting through a series of harsh adjectives on her left hand.

"Destructive? Life altering? Unethical? Inconceivably dumb?"

Aeneas was usually patient with his children, but Cassie could be very sharp at times. He took the note and opened it, surprised by the message.

I was wrong, Aeneas. Do nothing. Come back now.

Love, Tab

Aeneas was contemplating the note when Cassie walked on toward Sadie.

"Leave her alone," hissed Aeneas, reaching for her arm.

"Go back, old man. Bob North Sky has given me one way to fix this, and I've got to give it a shot."

"What's Bob got to do with this?" asked Aeneas. If Bob was involved, then it was worse than he could have ever imagined. Cassie was about to respond but felt it was best to say nothing. In one reality, this had already happened, and this version of Aeneas was part of the revised remake. Cassie noted that upon her return they would need to sift through all their memories and check the timelines to see what had become of the temporal anomalies.

Unbeknownst to the pair, they had caught Sadie's attention. She slowed her pace and turned ever so slightly to put them in her peripheral vision. She was a little concerned about the woman. There seemed an argument brewing. Cassie looked her way again and swore. "We've been spotted," she murmured.

"Pretend we're arguing over the binoculars." Aeneas waggled the binoculars making a stern face.

"Leave now, Dad," ordered Cassie through clenched teeth.

Cassie snatched the binoculars from him and stalked off closer to the shoreline so she could warn Sadie about rogue waves, but Aeneas was too intrigued to leave.

Once Sadie realized the disagreement was over a pair of binoculars, she continued to the jetty. Suddenly a large wave appeared about fifty feet out, rolling hard, and washed over the jetty. Sadie stopped. Cassie called to her.

"Looks like there might be rogue waves today."

Sadie nodded and resumed walking. She'd climbed out onto this jetty for years. It was the place she went to reset her creativity. The wave that had passed was quite big, big enough in fact to knock her off the jetty, but the ocean had instantly calmed, and Sadie eagerly climbed out onto the rocks.

Aeneas hurried over to Cassie who was surveying the ocean.

"That might've been the wave, Dad."

"I don't think so. It should've been a large, powerful rogue wave."

"That would've knocked her off, Dad. It was big enough and if she bumped her head on the rocks..." Aeneas winced, scrutinizing Sadie climbing along on the rocks.

"Besides, she was delayed. She was watching us argue. I wonder if that constitutes free will?"

"Why would that matter?" Aeneas's eyes were still glued to Sadie.

"It's what Bob said. She needs free will. You were about to violate her free will."

Aeneas blanched. "Oh. So that caused some issues then?"

"You've no idea," replied Cassie acerbically.

"But our presence here delayed her, Cass. If that *was* the rogue wave, Sadie should've already been washed out to sea." Sadie stopped and positioned herself on the jetty. Cassie turned abruptly to her left. She sensed it. Just a few feet down the deserted beach the timestream was open.

"It's open. Let's go."

"But..."

"No buts, Dad. She chose to stop. She could've ignored us and moved on, but she didn't."

"I don't think that counts, Cass. We disrupted the event."

"Well, she's alive, Dad. And the best thing you can do is never kiss her in the kitchen!" snapped Cassie.

"Why would I kiss her?" croaked Aeneas, shocked at the suggestion.

Cassie gave him a withering look. Aeneas stood up straighter and marched toward the timestream shaking his head in disgust. As if he would ever kiss Sadie. He held out his hand for Cassie, but she gently pushed it aside.

"Go on, old man. I need to check my timeline."

Aeneas planted a kiss on her forehead, stepped into the timestream and vanished. Cassie turned back for one last look at Sadie and felt like she'd been sucker punched. She gripped her stomach and squeezed her eyes tight, fighting back tears. A sickening feeling caused her to lose consciousness and she slipped into the timestream.

Carl was winded trying to catch up to his daughter. He saw Sadie ahead on the jetty, basking in the ocean breeze and smiled. Feeling light-headed, he stopped for a moment to rest and readjust his hat. When Carl looked up again, a large wave was rolling toward the jetty. Adrenaline shot through his body propelling him forward. He shouted her name, but the wind and surf silenced all other sounds. He screamed for help, but the beach was empty, and Sadie's eyes were closed. After the wave washed over the jetty, Sadie was gone. Carl screamed again searching for her blonde head to pop up, but the ocean was calm again and there was no sign of his daughter.

CHAPTER 40

Toshiro Tells All

Spring 2053

CASSIE SLOWLY OPENED HER eyes, feeling groggy and strug-gled to sit up. She'd been tucked tightly into a bed. The sheets were stark white and smelled different, clean, but not like her home. *Am I in a hospital?* she wondered.

She could hear rain and see daylight. Cassie pushed her-self up and swung her legs onto the cold floor. A large panel of windows revealed the Seattle skyline. In the distance she could see the port. There was a faint odor of something rotten. She sniffed, scrutinizing her surroundings. The bathroom was just off to her right. Still a little heady, Cassie gingerly made her way to the sink and checked herself in the mirror. *Is that vomit in my hair?* Cassie sniffed a lock of her hair and recoiled. *Yep. That smell is coming from my hair.* A fancy bar of soap sat in a dish, lightly used. Cassie lathered it up in her hands, leaned into the sink, and washed the affected strands.

"Would you like some broth or tea?" said a voice.

Cassie looked up and was surprised to see Toshiro standing politely just inside the bedroom door.

"Both," replied Cassie, hoping the request would give her additional time to figure out how she ended up back in Seattle.

Toshiro gave a brief nod and slipped from the room. Cassie quickly checked for her bag. Her SAIL was still recording. She snuggled back into the bed to keep herself warm.

"Pause and play back from second timestream entry." Cassie reached in her bag, grabbed her glasses, tapped the arms to initiate her SAIL. She watched the final few minutes from 2016.

After she entered the timestream, her body went slack. *I must've blacked out,* thought Cassie. *Seeing that wave barreling toward Sadie...* She shivered at the memory. Her body floated upward instead of zipping through the timestream, bouncing through and around other timelines she didn't realize she could access. A light appeared from the left of the scene and suddenly Toshiro, wearing goggle-like eyewear and his long black coat, secured one arm around her waist. *If he'd had a cape, he'd look like a superhero,* thought Cassie.

Toshiro leaped across timelines like a frog bouncing from lily pad to lily pad until they entered his own timeline and shot into his present. Toshiro set her gently down on his bed. *Was it his bed?* Cassie presumed so. He walked over to a small leather black case where he pulled out something that looked like a fancy thermometer. He pressed it on her neck briefly.

"You've had quite a shock, Cassie, but your vitals are strong."

Toshiro turned his head a little to the left, sniffing the air. "Something smells off in here, though." Toshiro tucked her tightly into the bed and stepped out of the room.

"Pause playback." Cassie cringed, pulling the dark blue velvet duvet in closer to her chin.

"Oh, could this be any more embarrassing?" she whispered. "I blacked out in the timestream and I smell like vomit." Cassie threw back the covers, still confused by what she'd seen.

He leaped across the timelines like a ballet dancer! Like he was taking shortcuts! Cassie bit her lip and smiled, intrigued.

Toshiro walked in with a tray from the cafe. The hotel where he was staying served modest meals.

"I can eat at a table," said Cassie, who felt self-conscious having Toshiro serve her in bed like an invalid. The living room had a small dining table with two chairs and an L-shaped red couch. A tiny kitchenette had bright red appliances and neatly stacked painted cups and plates. The table faced a wall of three windows that continued the amazing view of the Seattle skyline. Books lined the opposite walls and several small paintings hung around the room. Toshiro sat the tray down on the table and Cassie slid into the chair.

"Is this a condo?"

"No. It is a hotel suite."

Cassie glanced around the space. "It's nicer than my condo."

"I would not agree. The view is why I chose to stay here."

Cassie sipped her tea and tasted the soup.

"Chicken and dumplings," smiled Toshiro. "I tried this yesterday and found it to be very delicious."

Cassie took several heaping spoonfuls. She wanted to restore her energy before plunging in with questions.

"Can I speak while you eat your soup?" requested Toshiro politely.

Cassie swallowed. "Sure."

"I was recently assigned to monitor the situation your father created. Prior to that, in my spare time, I had been watching your progress as a time traveler."

Cassie's eyebrows shot up and she set her spoon down. Toshiro gestured toward her bowl. "Keep eating, please. You fainted. And I have more to share with you."

"My family has worked for centuries to identify and train superior time travelers like yourself. A few months ago, I deduced that the research facility your brother and father operate is a front for time-travel genetics research. I guessed that Lux was very close to discovering the time-travel gene sequence when he requested a sample of Ötzi. This was a public request. Their research database was not infiltrated, nor would we want it to be."

Cassie had stopped eating and fixed Toshiro with a hard stare. "What do you want from me?"

"I only want you to listen. And please, finish your soup. I know how much energy is expended moving through timelines."

Cassie tried to keep her face hardened but she softened at his last comment.

"I'm listening."

"For my family, I must document your abilities and request that you accompany me back to Japan for specialized instruction, a sort of time travel graduate school."

"What if I don't want to be *instructed*?" countered Cassie, peevishly, spoon in midair.

Toshiro bowed his head. "Then I will give you a way to contact me if you change your mind, and return home."

Cassie glared at Toshiro. "I still don't understand why you were monitoring my father?"

"I know as the daughter of Aeneas Entwistle you will have strong loyalties and love for him, but..."

"But what?" Cassie's spoon clanged against the bowl.

"Aeneas Entwistle is known in our community as a renegade, a powerful traveler who makes unpredictable choices. He has used time travel for social justice issues and even personal matters, such as the one you just worked to restore," said Toshiro evenly.

Earlier he had withheld any criticism of Aeneas in case it prejudiced Cassie against him, causing her to decline his offer, but now it seemed a good idea to reveal all. Cassie was silent as she considered this assessment of her father. She wasn't aware of all Aeneas did or had done, so before she unleashed her sharp tongue on Toshiro, a thought popped into her brain.

"Why wasn't my father trained by your organization?"

Toshiro frowned and held up a finger.

"The term we use is best translated as a fellowship of scholars."

Cassie sighed impatiently.

"He was known early on and been considered, but Aeneas aligned himself with the First Nation peoples of Alaska, specifically the renowned shaman Bob North Sky. We had no desire to infringe upon that, since we felt Bob would train Aeneas to respect certain ethical tenets of time travel we consider vital. Our relationship with the travelers of the North is based on an alliance of non-interference."

Cassie closed her eyes and let this all sink in, silently swearing that she'd turned off the SAIL.

"So, how long have you monitored my father?" She'd stopped eating and her eyes were intently boring into Toshiro's.

"I was recently employed by an association which monitors shifts and anomalies within the space-time continuum. When Aeneas saved Sadie Willoughby-Hoffsteder, a series of timelines was disrupted by an unusual sapphire blue multiple-reality interference, and I was sent to investigate."

Cassie raised an eyebrow. "So, you were already watching me when you were notified that my dad had violated some time traveler protocol?"

"More or less."

"What or who is this association?"

"The association is based in Iceland. It's relatively new," replied Toshiro haltingly. Cassie wasn't as gifted as her mother or Aunt Seph at spotting when someone was lying or concealing information, but the slight shift in Toshiro's calm demeanor was easily noticed. She took a guess.

"Your family doesn't know you work for them, do they?"

Toshiro swallowed, touched the unusual pendant he was wearing the last time they'd met, and tactfully changed the subject.

"Would you be interested in coming to Japan to meet with the fellowship of scholars?"

Cassie pushed her chair back and stood up from the small table. "Not at all," she smiled. Toshiro quickly stood, too.

"Would you at least like to visit and see the historical documents?"

Cassie shook her head firmly but realized this was just the sort of invitation Lux would dream of receiving and made a note to circle back to it at some point. Looking defeated, Toshiro turned toward the windows as the sun peeked through the heavy spring cloud cover.

"I do need a new job, though," offered Cassie, trying to appear charming, despite the faint odor of vomit still lingering about her. Toshiro turned abruptly, trying to contain his excitement.

"Any chance you can get me an interview with this association in Iceland?"

Toshiro kept his composure. No need for Cassie to know how fast his heart was beating.

"How soon can you leave for Reykjavik, Cassie?"

~

Harold paced around his office for a few minutes and decided he would make a cup of coffee, then head up to the rooftop to have a think. Cassie hadn't shown up for work today. Her butler, Mr. House, replied to his call and informed him Cassie was not available for the foreseeable future at her home address in Ballard. This had created a small panic. Harold had sent a message to her SAIL, but there was no immediate response. He was climbing the stairs to the rooftop gardens when his SAIL alerted him to a large series of incoming encrypted data along with a message from Cassie.

Dear Harold,

I'm on my way to Iceland. I've got a lead on a new job opportunity that seems like a great fit for me. Several things may have happened recently that you'll not recall, but Aeneas has dual memories so he can explain it, though it may be difficult for him because three possible realities of one event have now taken place. I have all the documentation of the changes that occurred when Aeneas went back and saved Sadie from the rogue wave—basically bringing her back from the dead. This caused significant upheaval within our present, and damaged familial timelines. I've securely transferred it all to your personal database.

The past has been restored, but things may have been altered; events didn't unfold exactly as they had the first time after I went back to stop him from saving her. You'll want to find out what's changed from the original version. I'm a little sad about Lana and Lanna... but I'm sure the boys will find love again. I'll be in touch once I'm settled.

Love to all,

Cassie

Harold plopped onto the alcove bench and stared into his coffee cup, too stunned to move. When he eventually heard voices, he wasn't sure how much time had passed. Lux and Aeneas appeared and were surprised to see Harold sitting on his own.

"Whoa, Harold. You okay?" Aeneas gave Harold his friendliest smile.

"You look like you just got bad news," said Lux sliding next to him on the bench, nudging his shoulder. Harold smiled briefly at Lux, then stood, squaring himself directly at Aeneas.

"Cassie has left the country. She's lined up a new job in Iceland. And apparently you've been taking things into your own hands again, even though you promised me you'd stopped for good after what happened with Jesús."

Aeneas froze. The color drained from his face. After all this time, he was still ashamed. He hadn't thought about Jesús or his father in years.

Lux was on his feet, scrutinizing Harold who seemed poised for a fight, something Lux had never seen before.

"What's he talking about, Dad?"

Aeneas stared off in the distance. The only other people who knew this story were C.J. and Tabitha and thankfully they never brought it up. He snapped out of it when Harold spoke again.

"I have all the data from Cassie. I haven't looked through it, yet, but if it was enough to drive your own daughter away, it must be worse than I thought," said Harold grimly.

About the Author

SHER STULTZ IS A science teacher and writer who lives in Western Washington. She loves to hike with her mini-Aussie, kayak, play ping pong and board games and attempt the occasional zipline. A non-singing music lover, a haphazard gardener, and a proud mother of an amazing daughter, Sher enjoys being out in nature. An ardent conversationalist, Sher enjoys listening to people's life stories and finds inspiration from her students. *The Sapphire Sphere* is the second novel in her Timestream Travelers series.

Acknowledgements

MANY THANKS TO MY editor, Michelle Krueger for her insights and feedback for the plot of *The Sapphire Sphere*. It's challenging to come on board for the second book in a time travel series and I am grateful for her collaboration. Vivien Reis created my vision for the cover and revised the cover for *The Rescue*, too, which energized me just when I needed it. And finally, behind every writer is their muse. And my current muse is Juniper, my mini-Aussie, who keeps me moving and to whom, along with her pack, this book is dedicated.

Made in the USA
Monee, IL
14 February 2024

53509637R00173